SHAME

They were on the bridge by now. Behind them was the magnificent view of the San Fernando Valley, reaching from Burbank right around to Northridge. The good weather was again allowing excellent visibility.

'I gotta go and work, lover,' Scott said.

Martyn nodded and cupped Scott's face in his hand, kissing him on the lips, but avoiding tongue work this time.

Scott pulled back from the kiss, grinning.

'I'm going to lose my job for sure, Marty. Thanks for that.'

Martyn shrugged. 'Come home with me. Leave all this behind. Forget all the trouble that Peter caused you, his drugs and everything.'

'You are joking? Aren't you?'

Martyn shook his head, realising how deeply he felt. 'No, sweetheart. No, come with me. My God, I can't believe I'm saying this, but I love you. I really, really love you.'

SHAME

Ray Pelham

First published in Great Britain in 1998 by
Idol
an imprint of Virgin Publishing Ltd
Thames Wharf Studios,
Rainville Road, London W6 9HT

ISBN 0 352 33302 2

Cover photograph by Colin Clarke Photography

Typeset by SetSystems Ltd, Saffron Walden, Essex
Printed and bound in Great Britain by
Mackays of Chatham PLC

This book is for Bex's mum
(as promised!)
and is dedicated to the memory of Tony De Vit, whom I
wouldn't be arrogant enough to call a mate, but who, along with
Simon, Greg, Mark, Quentin and Andy, made me feel so
welcome in Ibiza in '96

SAFER SEX GUIDELINES

These books are sexual fantasies – in real life, everyone needs to think about safe sex.

While there have been major advances in the drug treatments for people with HIV and AIDS, there is still no cure for AIDS or a vaccine against HIV. Safe sex is still the only way of being sure of avoiding HIV sexually.

HIV can only be transmitted through blood, come and vaginal fluids (but no other body fluids) passing from one person (with HIV) into another person's bloodstream. It cannot get through healthy, undamaged skin. The only real risk of HIV is through anal sex without a condom – this accounts for almost all HIV transmissions between men.

Being safe
Even if you don't come inside someone, there is still a risk to both partners from blood (tiny cuts in the arse) and pre-come. Using strong condoms and water-based lubricant greatly reduces the risk of HIV. However, condoms can break or slip off, so:
* Make sure that condoms are stored away from hot or damp places.
* Check the expiry date – condoms have a limited life.
* Gently squeeze the air out of the tip.
* Check the condom is put on the right way up and unroll it down the erect cock.
* Use plenty of water-based lubricant (lube), up the arse and on the condom.
* While fucking, check occasionally to see the condom is still in one piece (you could also add more lube).
* When you withdraw, hold the condom tight to your cock as you pull out.

* Never re-use a condom or use the same condom with more than one person.
* If you're not used to condoms you might practise putting them on.
* Sex toys like dildos and plugs are safe. But if you're sharing them use a new condom each time or wash the toys well.

For the safest sex, make sure you use the strongest condoms, such as Durex Ultra Strong, Mates Super Strong, HT Specials and Rubberstuffers packs. Condoms are free in many STD (Sexually Transmitted Disease) clinics (sometimes called GUM clinics) and from many gay bars. It's also essential to use lots of water-based lube such as KY, Wet Stuff, Slik or Liquid Silk. Never use come as a lubricant.

Oral sex
Compared with fucking, sucking someone's cock is far safer. Swallowing come does not necessarily mean that HIV gets absorbed into the bloodstream. While a tiny fraction of cases of HIV infection have been linked to sucking, we know the risk is minimal. But certain factors increase the risk:
* Letting someone come in your mouth
* Throat infections such as gonorrhoea
* If you have cuts, sores or infections in your mouth and throat

So what is safe?
There are so many things you can do which are absolutely safe: wanking each other; rubbing your cocks against one another; kissing, sucking and licking all over the body; rimming – to name but a few.

If you're finding safe sex difficult, call a helpline or speak to someone you feel you can trust for support. The Terrence Higgins Trust Helpline, which is open from noon to 10pm every day, can be reached on 0171 242 1010.

Or, if you're in the United States, you can ring the Center for Disease Control toll free on 1 800 458 5231.

One

Martyn Townsend was woken by a combination of bright light, heat and the impossibly close sound of an aircraft landing – a sound that shouldn't have been there.

OK, so Los Angeles in August was usually hot. And the sunlight had been exceptionally bright recently. But if an aeroplane was landing it was either an emergency or he wasn't in his own hotel room.

It was the latter (thankfully). Instant images of a hundred different disaster movies were banished from his head as he pushed himself upright.

From beside him came an unfamiliar moan and someone rolled away from Martyn and turned on to his back.

Dack Phillips. Yup, Martyn knew the guy's name – that made a change anyway. In this city, sex was as plentiful and available as it was anonymous.

Having eased himself out of the bed, Martyn tiptoed naked over to the pale drapes that were doing a very bad job of keeping out the morning light, and pulled them slightly apart, revealing a tiny airfield of the type used by small businesses and local traffic. A small Cessna was still trundling along the runway, heading perilously close to the freeway that bisected it. Nope: looking closer, Martyn could see that the traffic roaring past actually went into a tunnel under the runway.

Good. Still no likelihood of a disaster movie, then.

He looked back at Dack, sleeping soundlessly, covered only by a thin cotton sheet.

On the opposite wall, nearest the bathroom, Martyn saw his own reflection in a full-length mirror and ran a hand through his very ruffled, dark hair, trying to get rid of the horrible sticky-up clumps that refused his mental requests to flatten themselves.

He glanced at Dack, comparing their physiques. Dack was what Martyn could only assume was a standard Californian – he was well built, with good pecs, nice stomach and muscular limbs. All that surfing, swimming and clubbing they did. Martyn, of course, was equally typically English – pale with a slight red glow of sunburn, not too bad a body (but in need of a bit of trimming to lose the faint stomach bulge that threatened to grow larger) and nice legs, but his bum stuck out a bit.

Not that this had alarmed Dack last night, Martyn recalled. No problems there.

He looked back at Dack and noticed for the first time (this morning, anyway) his flaccid cock, outlined by the tight sheet, lying to the right but large enough to reveal that it was cut.

Martyn tiptoed back towards the bed and lifted the cotton sheet at the foot of the bed, trying not to awaken his apparently comatose partner/pick-up/shag/whatever.

He eased himself up under it, inhaling slowly the odour of incense that he'd already come to associate with Dack, which seemed to permanently surround the young American. He brought his head level with Dack's groin and slowly he let his mouth envelope the limp cock, gently easing it in with his tongue. He slowly ran his tongue around the shaft, stroking the flesh and trying not to smile as it began to harden. He sucked a bit, ran the tip of his tongue across the eye of the cock's head and then began moving up and down on it gently, causing the cock to harden even faster.

A slight moan of awakening from Dack made Martyn grin again and he continued the blow job, moving faster and faster. This was one of Martyn's favourite tricks in sex, bringing an unaroused cock to attention while its 'owner' was sleeping.

Dack was clearly wide awake now, his hand flapping around

under the sheet until it connected with Martyn's skull, slowing the frenetic pace and easing his head up and down at a more sedate tempo.

Martyn's own cock was rock-hard now, jammed rather painfully against the footboard. He eased his lower half further into the bed, keeping his lips firmly around Dack's solid flesh, and then felt the American move his own body, swivelling around, bringing his own head towards Martyn's groin and seeking, then finding, his own tumescence, until they formed the perfect 69, each man hungrily sucking at the other's pre-come. Dack's hand moved to Martyn's balls and he felt one of the American's thick fingers start to stroke their underside, tracing a line towards his arse.

Martyn shifted slightly, hoping this told Dack to forget that. Indeed, Dack's fingers edged back to the balls, stroking the hairy scrotum, and Martyn smiled again. Then Martyn pulled Dack over and above him, causing the American's cock to slip out of his mouth. But his tongue quickly found Dack's tightened balls, and he sucked first one, then the other, into his mouth, feeling them contract further.

He let his tongue play over them for a couple of moments and then let them go, pulling the cock back into his mouth. Dack's position meant he could get only the head in properly. This seemed to suit Dack – clearly the area where he'd been cut was sensitive, and Martyn nibbled on the slightly loose flesh before sucking harder.

Dack suddenly jerked, manoeuvring his own and Martyn's bodies so that Martyn was on top, his cock coming out of Dack's mouth. Martyn was again able to take in all of Dack's tool, sucking harder and harder until, with a gasp from Dack, he felt his mouth coated with hot come, shooting down his throat. Martyn kept sucking hard until he was sure that there was nothing more to come before Dack took Martyn in again.

Martyn fell on to his back, while Dack rolled back over and started using his bunched fist to wank Martyn harder and harder. Martyn came quickly, and tried not to snigger as most of his come hit Dack's ear and cheek.

Martyn then lay back, breathing deeply, feeling Dack crawl

3

across him, and their lips met and opened, and they kissed, both of them tasting of sex.

After a couple of minutes, Dack eased back, and Martyn stared up into his blue eyes, framed by his dark eyebrows and tanned skin.

'That's a hell of a way to say "Good morning",' he laughed.

Martyn shrugged. 'Better than a cup of coffee and a bagel, I thought.'

Dack nodded, using the sheet to wipe the side of his head. Then he glanced over at the LED clock and groaned. 'I have to be at work in thirty minutes. Which is not possible.'

'Why not?'

'Van Nuys to LAX in thirty minutes at eight in the morning? I can tell you don't live here.'

Martyn shrugged. 'Phone in. Tell them that you picked up an English customer as you showed him his hire car, took him to the other side of town and had rampant sex with him until four in the morning, then started all over again at eight in the morning. And he was so amazingly sexy you just couldn't pull yourself away.'

Dack shrugged. 'Trouble is that I use that excuse at least twice a week as it is. Except they're not always English!'

Martyn put on a look of mock hurt. 'You mean I'm not unique?'

Dack reached over to the phone and punched up some numbers. 'Carla? Hi. It's Dack. Can you cover for me for a couple of hours? Tell Heather I'm sick or something? Yeah, Van Nuys. Yeah, the cute English guy. Am I really that obvious? Oh, thanks. Love you, too. See ya later.'

As he hung up, he smiled back at Martyn. 'I need a shower. Fancy joining me?'

Martyn's cock was hard and ready again before they'd even got out of the bed.

Peter Dooken pushed his way past overlarge Californians and a couple of skinny Brits to finally flop in 28C, his favourite seat on any aeroplane. Being so close to the door meant no seats in front of him and he could stretch his legs easily. Being on the aisle meant he could turn well away from whoever sat in seat B and not find someone on the opposite side.

Normally, he knew, that row 28 tended to be reserved for unusually tall people who would be uncomfortable cramped into the usual economy-class seats to London. Peter didn't care. The young check-in clerk at LAX had wordlessly acknowledged that Peter was charming and cute and agreed to his request for this particular seat. Peter still had never grasped why exactly it seemed that 99 per cent of male airport staff and cabin crew were gay, but it nearly always paid dividends. A little smile here, a small flirtation there, and he could get what he wanted.

Peter watched as one of the stewards minced down the passage-way between seats, juggling someone's ridiculously overstuffed cabin luggage without thumping any of the seated passengers on the head and all but throwing it into an overhead locker behind Peter.

Peter stared at the steward – most likely in his late twenties, with closely cut mousy hair but without the crop and sideburns that so many Brits wore these days (despite the fact it made them all look simian), and blue eyes like Peter's own. His BA uniform fitted him perfectly, and a small series of national flags lined the top of his name badge – Derek. Peter noted that none of them were Dutch, but it didn't matter. English might as well be his own native tongue now, since he so rarely spoke Dutch these days.

As the steward stepped back, Peter knocked his book to the floor.

The steward instantly bent down to pick it up and, letting a split second go by, Peter did the same, ensuring their hands touched the book, and each other, perfectly.

'Sorry,' he muttered, deliberately thickening his accent.

'Not a problem, sir,' said Derek.

They both held the book – and each other's flesh – for a second or two longer than they needed to, but Peter wanted to see Derek's reaction.

Derek eased his hand away. 'Anything I can get you, sir?'

'Not yet, thank you,' said Peter. 'Maybe later?'

Derek nodded and smiled. 'I'm not actually on this part of the plane, sir, but I'll check up on you later, if that's OK.'

Peter nodded and watched Derek nimbly thread his way through the passengers, back towards the Business Class area.

At the last moment, Derek turned back to stare at Peter, who smiled mischievously.

Derek smiled back and, in his mind's eye, Peter could see him naked, his clothes just melting away, revealing a slender but trim body, long legs and an engorged, upright cock, spearheading a pair of large balls.

Peter's own cock swelled at the thought and, as he was wearing a pair of tight cut-off denims, he immediately decided to think of something else, especially as a suited man settled into seat B, next to a classy-looking, power-dressed woman. Both were talking animatedly and Peter focused his mind on what they might do for a living. Hollywood film moguls, perhaps? Representatives of a major sporting team? Perhaps they were software engineers, heading to Europe to sell their latest game to Sony or Nintendo.

Aware that his penis was relaxing again, Peter turned his attention back to his book. If Derek came by, well, he'd see what would happen. If he didn't, no big deal.

After twenty-five years of life, Peter Dooken was capable of going twelve hours without a fuck.

Just about.

Scott Taylor watched the plane take off over the sea, turn and head northward, away from Los Angeles and up towards Canada, which he knew it would pass over, taking in Greenland and Iceland before heading towards Heathrow.

Taking with it Peter, who Scott had thought loved him. But Peter had been like all the others, unwilling to help Scott when he needed it, unwilling to be loved as Scott desperately needed to love someone.

Sighing, Scott looked across the LAX car park and saw the red Subaru parked near the barrier. He swallowed hard, his throat suddenly very dry. This was irrational – it was a car. Like any other car.

Except that it had three people in it, unrecognisable from this distance. But three people.

Scott was wary of cars with three people. Scott was wary of buses with just three people. Or shopping malls with just three people.

He got into his own car, locking the doors to seal himself in, started it and drove towards the barrier. As he wound his window down to put four dollars into the machine, he heard the red Subaru start up.

The barrier seemed to take forever to rise and, by the time it did, the red Subaru was right up close behind him and he shot forward, seeing the barrier go down, briefly separating the two cars. He pulled forward, then at the last minute, instead of taking the exit route towards the 405, turned a sharp right, back into the flow of traffic that wove its way rather hectically around the terminals. He nipped in and out, between cabs, courtesy buses and private cars, moving sharply at odd moments, but never severely enough to receive the wrath of his fellow drivers. Unlike New York drivers, those in LA weren't all that quick to smack their horns in annoyance.

With adrenaline pumping through his body, the combination of tension and fear was almost erotic to Scott, as he felt himself breathing deeply to calm himself. He was aware that his cock had grown uncomfortably hard in his shorts. And he smiled – getting off on danger was one of the great joys in life. He kept concentrating on the traffic, determinedly thinking only of the possible consequences of the three in the red car catching him. He allowed himself a moment to take his right hand off the gear shift and rub his hardness, easing a small amount of wetness out of the end where it darkened a tiny patch on his pale shorts and, cruising in third around the corners, began gently stroking the head of his cock through the material, feeling the cotton against his favourite piece of flesh. With one eye on the traffic, and now passing Terminal Three for at least the third time, he speeded up a fraction but not enough to require a change in gear. The subtle extra growl from the engine heightened his tension and he squeezed his cock a bit tighter as he teased the end of it. Scott knew full well that jacking and driving were not a safe mixture – and that increased the

7

tension, thus increasing his pleasure. Finally he allowed his whole hand to cup his cock, which was pressing awkwardly against his shorts and threatening to push itself over the waistband. With the fluid movement of experience, he eased his shorts down a fraction and his swollen head, free of restraint, stabbed upward. But the movement caused him to jerk the steering wheel a fraction and he was greeted with the angry retort of a horn blast from a bus driver. 'Yes,' he grunted through gritted teeth, and came, shooting come all over the steering column, where it splashed back down on to his bare legs. Breathing more slowly, he let the car slow down and released the top of his shorts to snap back against his cock, causing a minor spasm that ejected a final bit of spunk upward. Putting his hand back on the gear shift, Scott looked in his mirror and relaxed – there was no sign of the red Subaru.

Smiling at his own daring, he breathed deeply and then turned away from the airport, picking up the Lincoln Boulevard and heading back towards Venice and home.

'So tell me,' said Martyn, gently massaging cheap, hotel-issue liquid soap on to Dack's shoulders, and letting the hot shower water splash into his own face, 'd'you do this often?'

'What?'

'Pick up customers, bring them to your favourite hotel and shag 'em?'

Dack shrugged. 'Shag?'

'Screw. Have sex. As in you and me last night?'

'Oh. Right. Cute expression. Over here, a shag is a kind of dance.'

'Well, I remember those old Walt Disney true-life films with the crabs, you know . . .'

Dack suddenly laughed. 'My God, this explains a lot.'

Martyn was now easing the liquid into the small of Dack's back. 'What does?'

'Shagging. You know Carla, right, who I spoke to just now at work?'

'No, but carry on.'

'Anyway, she and her boyfriend do shag dancing. A lot. It's a real hobby and quite popular in some districts of LA. So anyway,

8

she's telling these middle-aged Brits a few weeks back that she did this. They'd asked what there was to do in Woodland Hills, where they were staying, OK? And Carla, who lives further down Ventura, told them that she and her boyf go to the Hills a lot to shag. "Every Tuesday and Friday night, we get together with some friends and shag for a few hours."' Dack mimicked what Martyn could only guess was Carla. '"And loads of people come and watch. I've been doing it since I was ten." Jeez, no wonder the Brit couple looked shocked.' He laughed again. 'Carla even offered to give them "the phone number of the guys who got me into all this", but they said no and almost left without taking their car keys. Carla and I simply didn't have a clue what we'd done wrong.'

Martyn smiled at this. 'Well, now you can tell her. In Britain, this is shagging.' With some of the liquid soap on his finger, Martyn traced a line into Dack's arse cheeks and began massaging his hole.

'You can keep doing that,' Dack said, leaning foward, so his hands rested against the wall, water splashing off his back and spraying Martyn.

The young Brit dropped to his knees, parting the cheeks with his other hand, while his soapy finger entered Dack's arse and started exploring. A couple of grunts from Dack suggested this was the right thing to do, so Martyn experimented with a couple more fingers. Dack's hole opened easily, and, without waiting for an invitation, but knowing it wasn't necessary, Martyn removed his fingers and pushed his mouth right up close, dabbing at the hole with his tongue, lizard-like.

Dack's right hand reached back, gently stroking Martyn's head, and easing him further towards his arse, so Martyn began rimming him faster, forcing his tongue right into the arsehole.

'Uh-huh,' Dack muttered, but Martyn wasn't listening. He was too busy eating at his new friend's hole, and massaging his cock with his left hand.

Dack removed his hand from Martyn's head and Martyn was aware that he'd pushed the shower curtain aside and was blindly trying to find something on the sink outside.

After a few seconds, the scrabbling stopped and something splashed to the floor beside Martyn.

He rocked back away from Dack's arse and scooped up the rubber, tugging it from its wrapping and rolling it down his shaft in seconds.

Standing, he leant close to Dack's back. 'Ready?'

'Sure,' said Dack.

Martyn's shrouded cock slid into Dack's arse with very little difficulty at first – the fingers and tongue had loosened the muscles enough – but then it tightened and Martyn felt a rush of pleasure sweep through him at the sudden gripping of his tool. He shoved harder and Dack groaned, and then, with one final stab, Martyn went right in.

He began working Dack's arse slowly, easing his partner's legs apart slightly, to get a better posture. As he speeded up, he reached round and grabbed Dack's nipples hard. Dack gasped at this, so Martyn twisted them slightly.

Dack's affirmative grunts caused Martyn to pull harder and the American was clearly getting off on the two-pronged attack.

After a few moments, Dack raised his right leg back and up, making Martyn pause for a second in his fucking while he wondered what was going on. The change of stance increased the tightness around Martyn's cock, causing him to pump harder.

It also gave Dack a chance to start wanking his own cock, rhythmically in time with Martyn's movement, and within seconds they were completely in tune.

Martyn stared hard at Dack's swollen cock, the large balls slapping against the tanned thighs with each downward stroke, and he saw the sudden tautness in them that signified Dack was about to come – which he did, sending large amounts of spunk into the shower curtain. Even after that, Dack didn't stop wanking, ensuring that his tight arse was still rocking in motion with Martyn's fucking. About twenty seconds later, Martyn's cock exploded, gushing jets of come into the condom's teat, deep within Dack.

Together, they slowed their movement until Martyn stopped, and Dack let his leg ease back down to the ground as Martyn pulled out.

Ridding himself of the spent rubber, Martyn pulled Dack close and they kissed, letting the hot shower rain down on them.

Ten minutes later, showered, dressed and satisfied, Martyn was stuffing yesterday's clothes into his shoulder bag.

Dack came out of the bathroom looking immaculate. His hair was neat, his face shaved, and he had the aroma of very expensive and very attractive body spray.

If only he'd been wearing something – anything – Martyn could have resisted the urge to push him to the floor and fuck him rigid again. But Dack was completely naked, his cock swinging between his legs with each step, apparently oblivious to the effect he was having on Martyn.

'This your first time in LA, then?' he asked.

Martyn nodded. 'First time on the West Coast, actually. I spent five days in New York a couple of years back, though.'

'Why? I mean, why LA and why by yourself?'

Martyn sat on the bed, wishing his stiff cock would go down, and wishing his eyes would focus on something other than Dack's flaccid one.

'I don't know. New York looks too much like London in the TV shows, and LA has mountains. Plus the fact that I had the cash, so I thought, why not go as far across country as I can rather than stopping on the East Coast?'

Dack had finally buried his genitals inside a pair of very tight Calvins – so tight that Martyn could see the ridge between his cut skin and the head. He was buttoning up a crisp white shirt (Martyn had never mastered the art of keeping shirts immaculate inside overnight bags and, hating ironing, had long ago resigned himself to a life of T-shirts or sweaters), the emblem of the car-hire firm on the breast pocket.

He nodded sagely. 'I can see that. And, this time of year, LA is fun. But remember this – it's full of some weird people doing some weird shit. Keep that in mind, let nothing surprise you, and you'll have a ball! Know where you want to go?'

'Not really.' Martyn waved a *Time Out* guidebook indifferently at Dack. 'Thought I'd start on the page marked "Gay and Lesbian" and see what that suggested.'

Dack nodded. 'Take the car, use the 405, pick up the 101 and take a left on Santa Monica. Keep going for about fifteen minutes until you're in West Hollywood. Gay Mecca of the Western World.'

'Thought that was San Francisco.'

'Nah, that's what The City wants the world to believe. But West Hollywood is nicer. More welcoming. As a Brit, be cheerful and you'll get a hundred and one per cent service. In every sense. Shop till you drop, as they say, then hit Motherlode or Revolver.'

Martyn nodded. 'OK. Care to show a girl a good time tonight?'

Dack shook his head. 'Sorry, not tonight. Where are you staying?'

'I've rented a condo in somewhere alarmingly called Studio City. I'm already getting visions of all the houses having Mickey Mouse stencilled on them.'

Dack laughed. 'Nah, nice area though. Again, take the 405 and follow the signs. The freeway drops you near Magnolia, and your guidebook should help you find the way to wherever you're going.'

'Cheers,' said Martyn, then wished he hadn't.

'"Cheers",' mimicked Dack. '"Cheers" and "shag". Anything else I need to know?' He was finished dressing now and was checking himself in the mirror by the door.

'Only not to take the piss out of Brits – if it wasn't for us, you lot wouldn't be here!' Martyn stood up. 'Fancy another fuck?' He wasn't entirely joking.

Dack smiled, nicely, and Martyn was immediately taken again by his clear blue eyes and dark eyebrows. 'Not right now, but maybe tomorrow night? Call me.' He passed Martyn a card and then kissed him, gently, just on the lips. No pressure, no tongues, just a sweet but brief brushing of lips.

And he was gone.

After a few seconds, Martyn looked at the card – a standard business card from the car-hire firm, but with a (presumably) home number pencilled on the back, along with the words, 'Room's paid for. See ya.'

Martyn slung his bag over his shoulder, gave the room a last look and inhaled, breathing in the last traces of Dack's body spray, and, with a final glance at the shower, and a brief pang of pleasure and sadness, he left the room and walked down the plush hotel hallway.

He didn't need to pass reception to get to the car park – it was at the back, by the airfield. He found his compact Hyundai and threw his holdall in the boot, where the rest of his luggage had been safely stowed yesterday.

'Four oh five to Studio City,' he said to himself as he got into the driver's seat and (relieved he'd gone for an automatic transmission) prepared to embark on the most dangerous thing he could think of.

Driving on the streets of Los Angeles.

Two

Scott eased his car into the driveway of his apartment block in Valley Village and, as had become his habit over the last few months, selected a space that was not the one designated to his home.

Suite 109 was painted on the tarmac. Scott's was actually 101, but Mr Terrell didn't own a car since his accident and his occasional visitors usually parked on the roadway. Terrell wouldn't mind anyway. He and Scott got on reasonably well, and he would offer to get the older man something from the grocery store later. The store always stayed open until way after midnight, so if stuff was needed, he'd have plenty of time.

He looked over at the large garbage bins – collection was this morning, but still the garbage men hadn't taken away the huge slabs of yellow foam rubber stacked up beside them. No wonder: they smelt strongly of piss – probably Mr Terrell's cats. They'd been there a couple of weeks now and it made the parking zone stink. Oh well, someone would do something eventually. Peter always said they should call the –

Peter.

Shit, why did he have to think of him?

After seeing Peter off at LAX, Scott had gone to work, slipped in unnoticed so that his supervisor hadn't been aware of his tardiness, and quickly got into the routine.

14

By 6.30, he was ready to head home and stick a video on. Porn or *The Fifth Element*? Brian Madsen or Bruce Willis? Hmmm . . . difficult choice. Then he'd chill out for a few hours until he headed off to Revolver for a night out.

Thus, at 6.45, he walked through the wrought-iron gates that marked the start of the territory known as 1678 Lyon Drive, across the bricked pathways that led to a variety of different apartments until he reached his own.

It was a warm evening, almost sticky, and all Scott could think of was shedding his clothes, a quick shower while the microwave zapped his meal, and relaxation.

Except that the forced lock on the door and the note attached to the door by means of one of his own kitchen knives rather ruined the mood.

'Sorry we missed you,' said the note. 'Will call again soon.'

It didn't have a signature. It didn't really need one. Scott knew who it was from.

He felt around the lock – it wasn't broken. They had, of course, been experts. To cause damage to a door lock like this would has roused neighbours, so they'd slipped it. A credit card, probably. Great. And leaving it open was just another kind of message, which seemed to be saying, 'However, next time . . .'

Shutting the door to the outside world, Scott flicked the light on, and was surprised to see everything just as he and Peter had left it that morning.

It was just a warning, then.

He threw his jacket over the couch, wandered into the kitchen and opened the fridge.

Yazoo flavoured milk. Peter's. How many more things was he going to find? Scott lacked the energy to start throwing stuff out right now (although the distance between the fridge and the waste bin at least ensured the Yazoos were dumped immediately). 'But tomorrow night . . .' he muttered, used to speaking aloud and having someone answer. 'Ah, fuck you, Dutch boy.'

Scott hauled some Linda McCartney pies aside (not microwavable) and located a couple of cheese slices (microwavable, sort of). He threw them into the microwave slightly more violently than he intended, set it to three minutes and pressed start.

15

He was stripping off as he went back through the living room and towards the bathroom, where he ran the shower. He looked at himself in the mirror. What was wrong with Peter? OK, Scott wasn't perfect, and he might not have come off one of those Euroboy calendars. But, shit, he could still hold his own in a club of California's boldest and most beautiful. Five foot ten, mousy brown hair, dark eyes, a nice cleft chin, which most people found attractive. He worked out three times a week, so while he wasn't a Schwarzenegger, he looked good: he had definition and a flat stomach.

A ping from the microwave told him his food was done, so Scott stepped into the shower and washed the day off.

Five minutes later, dressed in only a pair of white Lycra briefs, he fished the cheese slices (sagging but eatable) from the microwave and grabbed a fork from the drawer.

They'd bought the cutlery together from a cheap store in Burbank. The stuff that came with the apartment was wrapped up in a bin liner in the bedroom, along with all the other items on the inventory that they hated. Most of the apartment's movable objects in other words.

'Never get another boyfriend, Scotty,' he said to himself. 'Fuck strangers, chuck 'em out in the morning and forget 'em.'

He switched the TV and video on and pressed play. God knew what was in the machine, but right now he didn't care.

Last night's *Spin City*. Oh well, at least with Peter gone, Scott wouldn't have to suffer any more shit comedy. Even so, Michael J. Fox still looked a babe. If you squinted hard enough.

After fifteen minutes of finding nothing amusing about the show, Scott stopped the tape and replaced it with some hardcore porn. Two guys, a redhead and a blond, getting butt-fucked by a postman three times their age and weight. A Muscle Mary versus the Brady Bunch.

Still, it gave him an instant hard-on. Hell, the blond guy sucking his buddy's astonishingly large cock was getting him quite horny.

Scott relaxed and let his cock stretch against his Lycra briefs. He glanced up – good, the curtains were open, his lights were on. Anyone passing by would almost certainly see in. Good. Now he had to make sure he could come before anyone did so.

He eased his cock out and then knelt on the couch and slowly started jacking in time to the muscle guy fucking the young redhead.

Mesmerised by the sight of the enormous cock slamming against the young butt cheeks, the huge balls swinging in their sac, Scott felt himself beginning to come. He slowed his jacking – not too much just yet, pace yourself.

Just as he started to go faster again as the muscle queen started fucking the cute blond, the doorbell went.

'Fuck.'

Letting the briefs slap against him, his hot cock straining to get back out, Scott tiptoed to the door and opened it.

'Hello, Mr Terrell,' he said cheerfully, ignoring the fact that the old man's eyes were instantly drawn to Scott's erection. 'What can I do for you?'

Terrell was resting heavily on his walking stick – possibly more than usual.

'Sorry to . . . uh, interrupt . . . Scotty . . . I just wondered if you were going . . . you know, to the . . . uh . . . store later. Yeah, the store.'

Scott casually rubbed his cock, causing it to push out further, but never took his eyes of Terrell. 'Sure, in about an hour or so. What do you want?'

Terrell swallowed, and finally managed to drag his eyes to Scott's face. 'Uh, cat food.' He produced a five-dollar bill. 'Keep the . . . uh . . . change.'

'OK, I'll drop it by before I go clubbing tonight, all right?'

Terrell nodded and, with a last (feeble) furtive look at Scott's crotch, hobbled back to his apartment.

Scott watched him go and then went back into his own apartment.

On the television, the two guys had obviously accepted the mail from the burly postman and were now washing a car, making sure that they got each other soaked in the process, complete with close-ups on the tight, wet shorts, through which everything was clearly visible.

17

Scott decided to close the curtains and then forwarded the tape a bit so he could watch the blond fucking his redhead friend over the hood of the car.

The open air, the danger of being seen. That was Scott's kind of fun.

He went back to the front door and opened it again, leant against the door jamb and got his cock out, jacking himself hard, feeling the heat from outside mixing with the air-conditioned atmosphere of his room.

He glanced over to 109, Terrell's place, and suddenly thought he saw a twitch in the curtains.

Terrell was watching. Possibly.

Good.

Scott jacked himself harder, turning his attention back to the video image, as the blond held his friend face down and naked on the car and wanked, sending come all over the other guy's back.

Scott climaxed at the same time, shooting his come on the ground outside his apartment. Finished, he replaced his tool inside his briefs, sighed and then closed the door again, as if he'd done nothing more unusual than taking the garbage out, or arriving home.

But he knew Terrell had watched him. And he smiled.

An hour later, the people who had attached the note to Scott's door earlier sat in their red Subaru, watching the gates that led to the apartments.

There were three of them – one driving, two in the back. All three were dressed in black T-shirts and grey sweatpants and Reeboks. The two in the back seat wore dark glasses, the driver, a large black guy, was resting his chin on his steering wheel, eyes darting around at every slight movement.

His two white accomplices were bored and irritable. They lacked his professionalism. His experience. He knew that ninety per cent of their job was waiting around.

The two guys in the back were getting on each other's nerves, as well as his. Tough shit. If they couldn't hack it, they'd soon be out. One word in the right ear from him, and the two of them wouldn't even be in LA any more, let alone in his car.

'It's only a fag,' one was saying. 'At college we used to crush their balls, just to make sure they couldn't fuck with no one. Ever.'

His associate laughed. 'Yeah? Great, let's do it to this guy. He's just trash.'

The driver ignored them. He doubted that the first one ever went *near* queers at college. He lacked the brains to do much more than walk and talk – and had difficulty doing both together. Working out who was gay and who was straight was a bit beyond his capabilities. His friend wasn't much better – he was only employed because he was an expert at breaking and entering.

The gate opened and the driver sucked in his breath. 'There's our boy,' he said quietly.

'Let's fuckin' squash him,' one of the guys in the back said.

Without turning around, the driver told them to shut up. 'We need him alive and kicking, OK? At least until tonight.'

The driver watched Scott Taylor walk across the road to the drugstore and return five minutes later with three cans of cat food (they hadn't seen any evidence of a cat in his apartment), some candy and some other things too small to see.

'Condoms,' said a voice from the back. 'Fags always carry condoms. That's how you can spot 'em. No one normal needs 'em 'cos it's a tart's job to take precautions, right?'

The driver didn't bother replying. He'd already decided that, after tonight, these two would be unemployed if he had anything to do with it.

Scott pushed open the gate, and wandered over to his apartment, unlocked the door and went in.

He opened the bag and took out his chocolate, some toilet paper, a bottle of water and a packet of condoms, which he slipped into the back pocket of his jeans.

He then picked up the bag containing the cat food and went out and across the path to Terrell's apartment. A breeze was getting up, which was good. A break from the humidity was welcome.

He knocked on the door and realised it was open.

'Come in, Scotty,' called Terrell from inside.

'I've got your cat –' Scott started to say as he went in, but stopped.

Mr Terrell was sitting in the middle of the room, stark naked apart from a huge baby's nappy around his midriff, a baby's bonnet on his head and a large tin potty beside the television.

Scott wasn't sure which was more ridiculous. The sight of a man in his mid-fifties, sagging gut and tits everywhere, or the fact that he had a huge rattle in one hand and a lollipop in the other.

'If you can jack off in public, I can do this in private,' he said simply.

Scott couldn't argue with that.

'Where d'you want this?' asked Scott, holding up the bag of cans.

Terrell pointed to the kitchen. 'Can you do something for me, Scotty?'

Scott smiled and wondered what. 'I've not had much experience at changing nappies, Mr T,' he said.

He looked over at Terrell and realised he'd taken off his nappy, revealing a hardened cock, quite short but very, very thick. It reminded Scott of the head of a mallet.

His own cock was stirring slightly and, for once, he sent a mental signal begging it not to go any further. Jacking off over porn boys was one thing – this was kinky.

And well weird – the last thing he'd have expected from Mr Terrell.

'My wife never understood,' he said.

'Really? I am surprised. I'm not sure I do, but it's your life. What can I do?'

'Make me . . . come? I haven't had sex of any kind with anyone but myself in three years.'

Scott backed away. 'I'm not really sure that I . . . I mean . . .'

'I know, Scotty. I'm a bit older than what you're used to.'

'A bit? Jesus, I've never touched a prick older than twenty . . . seven. Ish.'

'I promise I won't ever ask it of you again. But tonight, watching you, I realised how much I just need the touch of another hand on my penis. Just to have that sensation again.'

Terrell put the lollipop and rattle to one side and patted the floor beside him.

Scott realised he was sitting on a large square of foam rubber, like a baby would play on to protect itself from a hard floor.

Scott shrugged. 'Well, I'll try anything once,' he said, and stripped off to his briefs, finally letting his cock swell.

Terrell reached up and took Scott's hand and immediately Scott relaxed and knelt beside the older man. Terrell was being very gentle, almost tender. If Scott expected him to act like some kind of desperate old man, he was wrong. Terrell stroked his chest, tracing around his pronounced nipples, then down to where his pubic hair was almost visible above his shorts.

Scott felt a slight chill go down his back – but not one of fear or panic. No, more of something strange, unique. Excitement.

This was going to be a very new experience and Terrell seemed suddenly very vulnerable. Very sad, without being pathetic.

He slipped his briefs off and slowly moved Terrell's hand to his cock, letting the older man explore its contours, its veins and its texture. The fingers moved to the balls, stroking gently, then back up to the head, where they passed over his cock's eye, taking with them a trace of pre-come.

Scott breathed out deeply and let his own hand take Terrell's smaller but thick tool, feeling it swell further in his hand. It still didn't get longer, but, as he squeezed harder, he felt it get even thicker. Terrell had closed his eyes and was smiling.

'God, that is wonderful. I'd forgotten how much just touching could do,' he said.

His eyes were still closed as Scott took his hand away and bent down, opening his lips so that he could fit the cock into his mouth.

Terrell tensed immediately, but Scott stroked his legs gently, assuring him everything was all right.

Scott began to work the cock with his mouth, feeling it against the back of his throat. He could get the whole tool in with no trouble, and no threat of gagging, so he speeded up.

He was aware that Terrell's hand was again on his cock but, each time Scott moved, Terrell lost contact so he slid his body down and around, so he was lying on his side, his cock jammed into Terrell's closed fist. Terrell wasn't trying to jack him, just squeezing gently every so often, but Scott found this equally exciting.

After a couple more minutes, Terrell let go of Scott's prick and pulled his own slowly from the young man's mouth.

Scott looked up into his brown eyes and said quietly, 'Mister Terrell, have you ever fucked another man's arse?'

Terrell shook his head.

'You want to?'

Terrell didn't reply, so Scott smiled. 'Let me put it this way, I really want you to fuck me, Mr Terrell.'

He reached back and took the new condoms from his jeans and slipped one out, removed the wrapping and stretched it.

'Ever worn one of these?'

Again Terrell didn't answer, but just picked up his rattle and shook it gently. 'Dada,' he said quietly.

'OK,' said Scott, realising that a degree of role-playing was going on here. 'Dada wants you to fuck him hard, OK?'

Scott rolled the condom on to Terrell's prick – with some difficulty, as condoms weren't often asked to stretch to this particular width. He then eased Terrell on to his back, sat astride him and gently lowered himself on to the chunky cock.

He winced slightly – his arse was used to having cocks up it, of varying lengths, but never one with a girth like this. He forced himself down, noting the very un-baby-like gasp of pleasure from Terrell, and then it was in.

A wave of fire shot through Scott's body – this hurt like fuck, but was also wonderful. All the sensations he normally associated with fucking were magnified, but it was fantastic. After the initial shock, he found he loved this and began easing himself up and down, feeling every inch of cock inside him.

Terrell's hand again started squeezing Scott's own cock, and, with the sensations from both ends, Scott was in heaven. Forget the initial fear that this was a man old enough to be his father – this was great, novel sex.

He shot his load into Terrell's face and hair as he rode the old man hard, pumping his ass up and down until he could feel the cock inside explode with pent-up come.

Terrell's eyes were wide open, a huge grin on his face.

'Thank you, Scotty, thank you,' he kept repeating.

Scott eased himself off Terrell's dick, wincing slightly as his asshole again adjusted to the incredible width as it popped out.

He reached down and used Terrell's oversized nappy to wrap around the condom as he removed it. Then he leant over and kissed Terrell, forcefully on the lips. The older man's mouth opened in surprise, and Scott shoved his tongue in, hungrily exploring the new mouth.

He pressed his naked body against Terrell's and they lay side by side, kissing hard, erect cocks twitching and squashing against each other, remnants of juice squeezed out against their stomachs.

Finally, Scott eased back and rolled off the foam rubber and on to the carpet. 'Fucking hell, I enjoyed that.'

'So did I,' said Terrell, his voice betraying the surprise and delight he felt. 'I really did. Thank you, Scotty.'

'Tell, you what, Mr T – Dada here liked it so much, he wants to do it again. Tomorrow night.'

Terrell nodded and watched silently as Scott dressed, reaching out for one final stroke of Scott's now shrunken cock.

'G'night, baby,' said Scott coyly.

'One last thing, Scott . . . Dada,' Terrell said quietly. Scott raised his eyebrows questioningly. 'Will you piss on me?'

Suddenly Scott remembered the smelly foam mattresses by the garbage. And shivered.

'That's something Dada doesn't do, baby, sorry.'

Before he could turn away, he saw Terrell nod, lie back down and instantly wet himself, sending sprays of golden water all over his stomach and legs and on to the foam.

Deciding not to say a thing, but smiling at the whole new image he'd have of Mr Terrell from this day on, Scott pulled the door closed behind him, crossed the path and went back into his own apartment, ready to go out clubbing.

He took another shower, trying not to think of what had just happened (even so, thinking about trying *not* to think of it gave him a hard-on), and then towelled himself dry.

He went into the bedroom and began sorting through his

23

clothes. Dark-grey chinos, a blue-and-white-striped top and some baseball boots.

He reached down for his lucky pendant – he'd last worn it eight months ago when he'd met Peter Dooken at Revolver. Beside it was a small photo of him and Peter on Malibu beach. He turned it face down and put the pendant around his neck.

Tonight he would try again – although, he had promised himself earlier that he was not going after a boyfriend, just a fuck. Peter was a ghost to be exorcised.

He took a look around the bedroom, smoothed out the duvet and pillows, opened the window just a fraction (but not enough to let unwelcome visitors in again) and then turned off the light.

He went back into the living room and set the VCR to record *Homicide* – not that he'd actually watched the last three episodes he'd taped, but, without Peter, he might have a chance to catch up on a lot of unwatched tapes.

With a last check on his hair in the mirror – and a wettened finger to smooth down a disarrayed eyebrow – he smiled to himself and headed for the door, patting his pockets for cash, keys and other essentials. All present and correct.

Today was going to be the first day of his new life and, despite the unwelcome attentions of note-stabbing-to-the-door types, he was going to start enjoying himself.

An hour later, the black driver started his vehicle's engine and eased away from the kerb, following – at an expertly judged distance – Scott Taylor's car as it headed for Mulholland Drive and eventually West Hollywood's gay nightclubs.

Three

Born and brought up in southeast London, Martyn Townsend thought he knew a lot about big cities. Negotiating the tubes and night buses of central London, knowing how to get from GAY to Paradise, or from Popstarz to the Hoist, in the quickest and shortest ways possible was an art he'd long ago mastered.

Foolishly, he'd expected Los Angeles to be the same, just larger. Like New York. OK, he knew there weren't tubes (at least, not yet – LA seemed to be going through some kind of building programme to create a subway network, but the collapsed and uneven roads he'd seen on Sunset that afternoon were a testament to the unsuitability of the city's foundations for such a venture), but he thought the roads would be easy to negotiate as a result. Not so. The sheer volume of possible routes to everywhere, added to the general aggression in LA drivers, alarmed him. On the freeways, no one treated the three lanes with the regimentation he was used to back home. People moved fast (well, as fast as they could, bearing in mind the volume of traffic), weaving in and out of lanes, narrowly avoiding each other's front and rear ends with a practised expertise he doubted he could ever relax around. Tiny Japanese cars jostled for pointless inches of advancement against a multitude of four-by-fours. There weren't the long, slick Cadillacs of the movies – LA was a far less grandiose than New York – and that increased Martyn's sense of claustrophobia as he drove. It was bad enough to be a foreigner, who could so easily make a slip regarding some local law, but driving abroad was by far the most frightening experience. All it would take was one slight slip and he could be wrapped around another car, trying to explain to some no-nonsense cop that he hadn't quite grasped the intricacies of the freeways, he was terribly sorry and could he go home now please? And he imagined that same cop would stare at him from behind mirrored shades, draw a gun (everyone in LA had a gun, it seemed, and would use it with little provocation) and drag him off to some seedy prison to share a cell with drug pushers, pimps and downtown gang members.

With a sigh, Martyn forced these ridiculous clichés out of his mind and concentrated on getting towards Santa Monica Boulevard and finding somewhere to park in West Hollywood.

After a few minutes of going up and down side streets, he pulled up behind a small red tow truck parked under a street lamp. There was nothing to say he couldn't park there, so, with fingers crossed, he locked the hire car up and wandered on to the main road.

West Hollywood was certainly very glitzy at night, beautifully lit up and nowhere near as seedy or rundown as London's Soho. The walkways were swollen with (mostly) young men, many with arms around the waists of their lovers, pick-ups or friends as they milled in and out of bars and shops. It was 9 p.m. and still everything was open, clothes shops, bookshops and a couple of tacky disco-specialist CD stores all doing a roaring business. Within moments, Martyn was swept up with the general feel-good atmosphere of the area. There were no bad vibes, no hostility, no worries that, any second now, someone was going to pull a knife on you, or heckle you for being a fag – again, quite different from Soho.

Tentatively, Martyn wandered into a coffee bar and ordered a hot chocolate (with extra cream, naturally), sat down and began thumbing through some of the free papers and guides. A few eyes flicked in his direction, probably more out of curiosity that he was alone than anything else. Certainly, the place didn't have the feel of a meat rack that so many pubs and bars in Old Compton Street possessed.

Martyn felt quite relaxed, almost at home here. Not-too-loud music was playing (Madonna mixed in with a bit of Sheryl Crow and Alannis Morisette); a couple nearby were having a good bitch about some friends; and the young black waiter kept mincing around, topping up people's coffee cups (a great tradition that – unlimited coffee).

As the minutes passed, Martyn decided to think about clubbing – he was no great dancer, but he enjoyed the atmosphere of clubs and he had promised himself that this would be the night he explored new territories.

Back home, he was a bit of a loner at clubs. His last boyfriend had been into camp and kitsch – Saturday night was GAY night, Sunday was the Limelight and the occasional Friday was spent at Camp Attack. Martyn preferred the music of Popstarz or Marvellous, so they had rarely been spotted together. Needless to say, while their diverse interests had seemed refreshing at first, a couple of months down the line, they'd parted.

Since then, Martyn had been skirting away from boyfriends, commitment and all they entailed. Instead, he'd been making the most of an uncomplicated lifestyle, lots of sex, lots of free time and lots of fun.

Work had been nagging him to take some overdue leave, so he'd saved the cash for a cheapo flight and headed to Los Angeles because . . . well, why not?

As these thoughts were swirling around in his head, a young guy hovered beside his table, making an enquiring look as to the availability of the seat. Martyn nodded, and the guy sat.

'Gets quite crowded soon,' he said, 'so I thought I'd get a seat now.'

'Coffee?' asked the waiter, placing a cup down in anticipation. The newcomer nodded and he and Martyn sat in silence as the coffee was poured.

'Another chocolate?' The waiter smiled at Martyn, who nodded, and asked for a piece of banana cake as well.

'Me, too,' said the newcomer, and the waiter wandered back to the counter.

'Chad Lesterson.' The newcomer proffered his hand, which Martyn took and gave his name. 'English?'

'Yup. On holiday.'

'How long for?'

Martyn shrugged. 'A couple of weeks or until I get bored.' He smiled at Chad. He was in his early twenties perhaps, but had an air of greater maturity about him, which Martyn found rather compelling. He had dark-brown hair and even darker eyes – almost black – with an unusually pale complexion for a Californian. Especially in the 'body beautiful' area of West Hollywood. And, when he smiled, something responded in Martyn's head and he grinned back. Considering they were just exchanging greetings and pleasantries, Martyn was quite amazed at how permanent the grin felt on his face.

'What are you doing exactly?' Chad was looking down at Martyn's array of papers. 'Planning some nights out?'

'Something like that. I'm just taking it as it comes really. What d'you recommend?'

Chad shrugged. 'First time here?'

Martyn said it was and so Chad began counting things off on his fingers.

'You have to go to the Observatory – on a clear day you can see right down to Long Beach. It's a great way to see the whole of LA in one scoop. Venice Beach is nice during the day, not so good at night. Good shopping nearby, as well.' Chad thought some more. 'Oh, and of course you've got to head out to Disneyland and also the Universal Studios lot and do the tour. It's real cool. And, if you can afford it, the new Getty Museum. You'll even be able to spot the place where Bill Cosby's son was shot.'

'I'm not that ghoulish, I'm afraid.'

'You'd be surprised how many people are, though. You can find people who'll take you to where Rodney King was beaten or to O.J. Simpson's house.'

Martyn decided to change the subject a bit. 'How about shopping?'

Chad held his hands wide. 'Hey, you're in the city of shopping. You name it, you can buy it. What are you looking for? Clothes, CDs, books, sex toys? Or what?'

Martyn paused. 'Not really the latter, I have to say. I guess clothes, because they're so much cheaper. And CDs. Anything. I like shopping. I'm a shopoholic!'

'Well, forget central LA – Sunset's a bit dreary. You need to head out toward Burbank or one of the huge malls such as Pasadena or Westlake or Glendale. You got a car and maps, Brit boy?'

Martyn said he had, and Chad explained that made life a lot easier. They discussed shopping, movies, American cars and how they both hated football (and only realised after ten minutes that Chad meant American football while Martyn was slagging off soccer), how cheap the food was in America and how much better the architecture was in Britain.

Martyn found himself warming to the younger guy – he seemed remarkably friendly and charming, and (although he hated the word) cute.

After about thirty minutes' discussion about life, the universe and everything you could buy in Hollywood's huge variety of stores, Chad stopped talking suddenly and leant forward, bringing his face closer to Martyn's. Martyn hoped he wasn't going to kiss him – that would rather cheapen the mood – but instead Chad just spoke, but much more quietly, more confessionally. And Martyn warmed to the tone of his voice immediately.

Chad glanced around before speaking, to check no one could hear him clearly. 'I went to England once. To Wales.'

Martyn couldn't be bothered to correct him. 'Where exactly?'

'Swansea. I had a cousin there.'

'When?'

Chad shrugged. 'Couple of years ago. Just after my eighteenth birthday. It was great.'

'I like Wales,' agreed Martyn. 'Full of hills and mountains and –'

'Sheep. It was full of sheep. You don't see many sheep in Los Angeles. At least, if you do, you don't go to the right places.'

'Yeah. Right. Sheep. Everywhere.'

Chad was nodding. 'My cousin, Alun –' he pronounced it in the Welsh way, so it sounded more like 'Alin' '– took me everywhere. He was nearly a year older than me but looked far more.'

The waiter came back with their drinks and cakes, then went away again when Chad put a five-dollar bill in his hand.

'He was the first guy I ever had sex with.'

Martyn wasn't sure who was more surprised – he because a complete stranger had just told him about one of the most important parts of his life, or Chad, who seemed genuinely astonished that he'd opened his mouth and those particular words had come out.

There was an embarrassed pause so, feeling rather voyeuristic but not giving a toss, Martyn smiled again. 'Go on, this sounds interesting. Does it involve any sheep?'

Chad laughed, a slight red glow in his cheeks now. He looked down and stirred his coffee, despite the fact that it didn't have sugar in it. He spoke again, but still at the coffee cup rather than Martyn. 'Only as witnesses. He lived near a small pub and opposite it was a huge field, surrounded by woods and hills. His parents, my aunt and uncle, they worked in the pub, so Alun and I headed off exploring. We went into this huge field the morning after it had rained heavily, but that hadn't occurred to us. We set off, walking along, with Alun telling me all these Welsh names for the hills. Of course, I couldn't even begin to try to pronounce them – hell, I don't know if Alun was even speaking real Welsh 'cause everybody there spoke English. Mind you, the road signs were bilingual . . .'

Martyn just nodded, sipping at his chocolate and forking off a chunk of banana cake, intrigued.

'Anyway, I told him he was lying, making it all up, you know? And he suddenly shoved at me, playfully, I guess, but I went over on to my ass. Alun thought it was really funny, but I have to say I couldn't quite see the funny side. Anyway Alun's a bit . . . chunkier than me. Not fat, but broader. He reached down to help me up so I just pulled him over as well. Trouble was, he rolled and landed in some mud. I could see he was cross about this, but was just laughing. Then Alun tried to get up and couldn't – he was stuck in the mud. Or so I thought. In fact, he was sinking – very slightly, but he was sinking. It was already up to the top of his boots, this muddy water slopping inside, pulling his foot further down. Then it started to rain and I was frantically trying to haul him out.

'All I could think of, though, was how large his hands were. Huge, and gripping me very tight. I don't really know what it was, but this made me feel really hot, really burning up, yet it was freezing cold. I could see the veins on the back of his hand and also on his neck, really jutting up as he strained to get out. But, the more he struggled, the further he seemed to sink.

'Anyway, I began to panic, although he didn't. He told me to go and find a piece of wood and, when I came back with one, it was up to here.'

Chad drew an imaginary line across his upper leg, about four inches above his knee.

'I was really worried and said I'd go for help but he pointed out that, by the time I got back, he'd most likely have gone under, especially as it was raining so hard. So anyway, he grabbed this tree branch I'd gotten, ripped off his shirt and tied one of its arms to the middle of the stump and wrapped the other around his wrist. I picked up the stump by both ends and pulled, and eventually Alun was eased out.

'And you know what? All I could think of was his chest – it was fantastic. Like something out of a Batman comic. I mean, really muscular. And his arms and his stomach – everything was like you see in those "So you want to be a real man" ads.

'Well, I was really upset, shaking and everything, and he was fine. Dead calm. He sat me down in the wood for shelter and threw his arms around me, telling me I'd saved his life. I was just leaning against his bare chest when I realised I had a hard-on. I mean, God, why then? And in front of my cousin. I don't think he noticed at first, but, when he stood up, he started stripping his wet trousers off and stood there wearing nothing but a pair of boxers. I couldn't take my eyes off him – he was using his shirt to towel himself dry and I just stared at his body. Every time he moved or bent over, or brought a foot off the ground, I found I was staring at his boxers, trying to see inside the fly, to see if his cock was as perfect and large as the rest of him.

'After a couple of minutes, I think he realised because he stopped drying himself and stretched, reaching right up, so his crotch was pushed forward. He pointed out that it had stopped raining and he needed to wait a while for his shirt to dry out a little. I just nodded and he waved me over and pointed upward. I thought he was going to show me a bird or a leaf or something, but instead he took my face and kissed me, really softly on he lips, and told me that it was a thank-you for saving him. I couldn't speak and then I felt his hand touch my cock. I mean, I didn't know whether to run and hide or cheer or what. He asked me if I was gay and I told him I guessed I was – that I probably had been since I was about thirteen – and he said he was too. And that Swansea wasn't the greatest place to be gay in the world and asked me about California.

'So we talked for a while but, every so often, his finger would start to trace the outline of my cock in my pants. And then I saw his, poking right out of his boxers. It was huge, I mean fucking huge! But it was also beautiful, and I touched the end of it. I'd never seen anyone with foreskin before – I mean, here everyone is cut automatically, I think. And he showed me how to roll it back over the head, and slowly I began jerking him off. As I did so, he stripped me until we were both standing in our boxers, cocks hard, and then he dropped down and began sucking me off. I'd never had a mouth on my cock before but it was the most fantastic sensation. Each time he moved up and down it, I felt, like, these explosions in my head going off – I just wanted to shout and yell. It was fantastic. He was so gentle and yet so perfect and, even when he stopped, I felt as if his mouth was still there.

'I remember we made a sort of sheet of my clothes and lay on them, totally naked by now. He guided my head down to his cock and showed me how to give head, and I loved it. The taste of it was so . . . so new, so invigorating. I mean, God, skin is so wonderful to touch and I ran my tongue over the veins, and around that foreskin and over the head and everything. He put my hands on his balls and they felt so different from mine – heavier, I guess. Bigger perhaps.

'Then he asked me if I'd ever fucked anyone. I just said I'd never seen another cock outside of a magazine, let alone had any kind of sex. He went to his wet pants and brought out a rubber, took it out of the packet and put it on my cock. That was a weird feeling – not just that feel of the rubber but a man's hands, big hands, smoothing something over my cock.

'He then turned around, leaned against a tree and spread his legs. He reached back and gently pulled me toward him, by my cock, until it was resting by his asshole. He told me to push and I tried pushing, but obviously not hard enough. I thought it'd hurt – both of us, not just me. But he told me to push really hard and I did. God, I can't believe the fantastic feeling that went through me as I entered him – those explosions went off all over again inside me and I just wanted to hold him, never let go. He showed me how to fuck him and after a couple of seconds I got into the rhythm of it. D'you remember your first fuck? I mean, Jeez, it's just an amazing feeling. I kept going and then I came. I came inside another man's ass, for God's sake. This was sex! I couldn't believe how marvellous it felt. When I'd come I just hugged him from behind and he let me, telling me how good I was and how I'd been really great. Of course, looking back, I was probably shit with a capital S, but Alun was really kind to me.

'He then eased me off him, threw away the condom and asked me to suck him off again. I didn't need persuading, you know? I took that fantastic cock back in my mouth and sucked as hard as I could while he fucked my mouth, really gently. I remember him warning me that he was coming, but I didn't care by then – I really wanted everything, I wanted to eat come, and, Christ, he shot it right down my throat.

'It seemed to be never-ending – just stream after stream of it, hitting my guts, that fantastic taste on my throat, my tongue and my teeth. I could taste it for hours afterwards. Then we just stopped. He was smiling, I was smiling, and we hugged and kissed for ages.'

Chad stopped. He looked at Martyn. 'And why the fuck am I telling you this?'

Martyn was grinning too much to give an answer any more coherent than 'Why not?'

He just stared at Chad's dark eyes, imagining the younger guy's virginal cock spearing his own arse, previously untasted semen in his throat, and drank the last of his chocolate. 'Lucky bloody Alun is all I can say.'

Chad laughed. 'Yeah. He lives in LA now – came over last year with his boyfriend.'

'How did that make you feel?'

'Jealous as fuck, I can tell you – especially when he started telling the boyfriend all about it.'

'Good way to get into a threesome, I'd have thought,' muttered Martyn.

Chad smiled knowingly. 'Oh, it did. And I brought my current boyf round as well after a while, and we have a group session maybe once a month or so.'

Martyn tried to picture this, and found it rather pleasant.

'You got a boyfriend?' asked Chad.

'Nah, can't be arsed with all that. A few casual flings, that's all I'm here for.'

Chad nodded. 'Look, Martyn, I've got to go – we're going to Revolver later. Are you?'

'Don't know yet.'

'Well, if you do, it'd be great to see you inside. If not, call me if you feel like, you know, a really good time.'

Martyn watched as Chad placed a piece of paper on the table and wrote a number on it plus his name. Before he passed it to him, the American boy looked hard at Martyn. 'Fuck, I'm sorry. I've shocked you, haven't I? It's just, you looked a bit . . . well, kind of nice and a bit lost and now it looks like I'm trying to entice you into some sordid fuck-buddie club. Hey, forget it, OK? If you just fancy a drink sometime, just the two of us, that'd be cool, too.' He started to move towards the door, then turned back. 'In fact, that'd be nicer, OK? Call me, Brit boy.'

And Chad was gone, back out into the warm late-night air.

Martyn shrugged and remembered Dack's warning about weird people and not letting anything surprise him.

Chad's 'confession' had been weird, to say the least. Not so much the story but the suddenness with which it was told. Was this a routine Chad did? Or did Martyn have some kind of agony aunt aura surrounding him and caused people to open up?

Either way, he rather liked Chad, and his story.

He pocketed the number, deciding that he'd wait a couple of days, then call and go and have a drink.

Just the two of them.

Four

It was 11.48 by Martyn's watch and the Latino guy was getting a bit too leery – and a bit too drunk.

'I just wanna fuck you,' he said into Martyn's ear. Which was just as well because, had he been a quarter of an inch further away, he wouldn't have been heard over the music.

'Very nice of you,' Martyn shouted back, 'but no thanks.'

The Latino guy tried to stand and look affronted. Instead, the mixture of too much drink and too little food made him stagger backwards and knock into another group of lads, who looked angrily over at Martyn.

He shook his head, as if to say the clumsy one was nothing to do with him, but his apparent innocence was exposed as a fraud when the Latino grabbed at one the party he'd knocked into and pointed at Martyn. 'Stuck up English cunt,' he yelled and staggered off.

Just as Martyn thought he was free of him, the Latino screeched from further away, but loud enough to be heard over the music, 'I offered him nine fuckin' inches and he's just a tight-assed –' Whatever came next was finally lost under the techno-induced throbbing from the dance floor below.

Martyn wandered to the edge of the balcony and looked down to where a huge number of guys and a few girls were dancing to the music.

He hadn't intended to come to this club, La Diva, but he'd simply sort of fallen in as the drag queen on the door had yelled at him.

'Hiya, hon,' he'd said. 'Looking for some nice guys?'

Martyn hadn't intended to reply but he must have said something enticing, because the drag queen had then grabbed his hand and pulled him inside. 'No charge to you, gorgeous,' the queen cooed, and this seemed to be some kind of signal to the bouncer to almost drag Martyn past the ticket booth and straight into the dance hall.

Not being the greatest dancer in the world, Martyn wound up in the bar on the next level up, watching the men, sipping a Coke and suddenly being chatted up by the drunken Latino.

And it wasn't even midnight.

The music started to change, veering away from some of the more chart-based stuff he recognised into the heavier sounds of handbag and hardbag. Martyn actually preferred it, even though he couldn't name a single record or artist. Most of the music was European house or British techno, rather than American R 'n' B or rap or hip-hop. He liked that – it was what had persuaded him to stay. He needed to like the music in a club, otherwise he could never relax.

The annoyed crowd beside him started to move away and Martyn opted to head to the loo before getting a stronger drink.

He saw a queue for one toilet and then noticed another right around the other side of the balcony, so he headed there, where there wasn't a queue.

As he went in, he could see why more people wanted to use the other toilet, but he again told himself to follow Dack's advice and not be surprised. After all, it might not be every day you saw a stark-naked man with a hard-on lying in the urinal trough, but there was nothing to say it was wrong. Weird maybe. Wrong, no.

Martyn actually lost any urge to pee, but nevertheless he was fascinated to take in the picture that greeted him.

The toilet was well lit, with white-tiled walls and a black-tiled floor. To the left was the urinal, taking up the whole wall. At the back were five or six cubicles and along the right wall were two single urinals and a set of basins and a large mirror.

Two guys were at the hand basins, but not washing their hands. Instead, they were watching the guy in the trough via the mirror – both were wanking hard. The two single urinals were being used by two guys who looked most uncomfortable and apparently couldn't wait to finish their business and flee.

Should've gone to the other toilet.

All the cubicles were occupied, but Martyn had no idea by how many people, but it wasn't hard to imagine.

But it was the large urinal that kept drawing his attention.

The naked guy was lying on his back, his long hair matted with urine, his skin soaking and glistening in the lights. His eyes were closed but he was grinning, his right hand holding the bottom of his hard shaft, his left pressed against the wall.

Five other guys were standing over him. Four of them were pissing on him, two on the chest, one aiming at his extended arm and the last one straight on to his balls.

The fifth man was wanking, very slowly and carefully, standing at his feet. His eyes were closed and he was smiling as he very gently and deliberately massaged his cock, squeezing without crushing. His trousers were around his ankles, revealing a pert arse, his legs slightly parted, and a massive pair of shaved balls, which hung really low down so that they swung in time with each movement of his hand.

Martyn noted that the guy pissing on the naked man's hand had zipped up and gone over to wash his hands, as if he'd just been peeing in any old urinal – not a flicker of emotion or surprise.

'How are your balls, Frankie?' asked the man pissing on the naked guy's bollocks.

'Great, man,' replied the prone Frankie.

As the man finished what he was doing, one of the guys pissing on his chest moved to resume spraying Frankie's bollocks.

Martyn could feel his cock stirring at this bizarre scene. The two guys by the basin were now wanking each other ferociously. The guy with the slow wank was still smiling and Frankie's last two pissers finished and moved away.

Frankie opened his eyes and looked over to Martyn. 'Hi, use me or use the ones by the basin. I don't mind.'

Martyn didn't know what to say, so Frankie smiled.

'Piss or come – I don't mind either. Or both, even.'

Martyn actually wanted to leave, but there was something mesmeric about the scene – as though it was in a strange art-house movie rather than a real toilet in a gay club in Los Angeles.

The two guys by the basins both came simultaneously, splattering the basin and mirror with their come before zipping themselves up and leaving, neither saying a word to the other.

This was too much for Martyn, who quickly pulled his own cock out and stood over Frankie and, swallowing slightly, began a slow wank.

He'd never really looked at his own cock before, but standing upright in front of a urinal with one guy doing the same beside him and somebody lying in draining piss below, waiting to be come over, was not that normal either.

Lying on his back, staring at the ceiling if he was alone, or looking at some guy beside him, sure – he'd wanked himself off loads of times. But he realised that he never actually looked at his own cock when he did so.

As a boy, Martyn had noticed other boys' cocks in the showers after sports at school. He'd mentally kept a record of who had the largest, the smallest, the circumcised and the not-cut. He'd observed people's pubic hair sprouting, their balls getting larger and, occasionally, he and some others would catch one of the newly pubescent friends wanking in the toilet, hoping they wouldn't be caught.

The other boys at school of course had always made those they caught feel really bad, but Martyn had always just been fascinated, watching erect cocks at different stages of development shoot their seeds into toilet bowls, or waiting tissues. He knew right then that he was gay – he loved seeing cocks too much to think otherwise. While some boys had been beating themselves off thinking or talking dirty about some of the girls from their class (or a couple of classes older), Martyn had quietly fantasised about those boys, and what it would be like to hold their cocks and see how different from his own each one felt.

As he stood in the toilet over Frankie, doing something that he never thought he would, he realised that, although he could picture every cock he'd ever sucked on, every pair of balls he'd ever rubbed, he actually couldn't picture his own cock. He'd never had to describe it, even mentally to himself.

So as he stood there, looking at it, swollen in front of him, it felt like he was wanking someone else, and that really turned him on – the warmth of his own flesh in his hand, the feel of the skin moving up and down in his palm and the slight churning in his balls as he got closer to coming.

He looked over to where the other guy's hand was still wanking himself, incredibly slowly but clearly satisfyingly, and Martyn ached to reach over and help him, but sensed that was not what the guy wanted. He was happy with himself.

Martyn tried to focus on the wall ahead, but kept letting his gaze wander to Frankie beneath him and therefore his own cock. He saw a tiny ooze of his own pre-come moisten the eye of his cock and he began beating himself a bit faster.

He enjoyed feeling the tenseness in his hand, and loved the sudden rush he was sensing between his legs as his balls, still trapped inside his trousers, started pumping.

Knowing he was coming, sensing that fantastic feeling of release and warmth and incredible pleasure wash over him, Martyn wanked that bit faster, feeling it coming, getting nearer and nearer, causing him to gasp breathlessly out loud and then, with a final surge of excitement and prickly heat, his cock sent white spray forward.

As this happened, Martyn leant over slightly, pushing his cock down, trying to make sure as much come as possible hit Frankie's drenched bollocks.

Frankie for his part quivered happily as the come splashed on to his inner thigh and balls, his own cock twitching pleasurably.

Martyn slowed his breathing and waited for a few seconds before relaxing, leaving his cock erect and outside his jeans.

Beside him, the slow-wanking man suddenly turned to his left and Martyn took a step back as he too came, sending a lengthy stream of come straight forward, going well over four feet and hitting the end of the trough, before leaving a long line of spunk trailing down and along Frankie's entire body, settling in his hair, his face, chest, stomach, and finally just by his knees.

'Thanks, Jerry,' Frankie said, wiping a bit of spunk from around his eye. 'That was worth the wait.'

Jerry grinned broadly, his cock red with pumped-up veins and still proudly erect. 'My pleasure as always, Frankie. See you tomorrow?'

'Sure.'

Jerry pulled his trousers up and over his swollen cock, adjusted himself through the denim slightly and then walked out.

By now only Frankie and Martyn were in the urinal area, and Martyn became aware that at least one of the cubicles was occupied by two or more men, going by the increased noise levels and slight thudding against the door.

'Steve and whoever he's picked up tonight,' Frankie said matter-of-factly. 'He's one of my regulars. Pisses on my neck, always gets the Adam's apple right on target, then drags some black or Chinese guy who he's left watching into a cubicle and fucks them for about half an hour. Coupled with the size of his cock and that length of time, they're going to be goddamn uncomfortable for a few days, I can tell you.'

Martyn just shrugged, unsure of what to say. His cock was shrinking now, but he didn't put it away.

'You do this every night?'

'Oh no,' said Frankie. 'Never on Sunday. That's God's day. I'm at my mother's for evening meal and mass on a Sunday night.' He smiled again, his eyes twinkling under the bright light. 'She'd die if I said I was going clubbing on a Sunday.'

'Does she know you do this?'

Frankie shook his head, as well as he could without actually getting up. All this did was spray the floor with pee that had collected near his hair. 'No, she thinks I'm at home with Marsha and the kids.'

'Kids . . .'

'Yeah, kids. I'm married – and Marsha doesn't mind. Or care. She gets a huge wad of cash from me every week to do whatever she wants, and on weekends we take the kids everywhere together. I'm a lawyer – I can afford it, you know?'

Martyn just said 'Right' and looked towards the urinals on the other side.

'How long you in LA for, then? Or d'you live here now?' Frankie asked.

'Just a week, ten days or so. Got in last night.'

Frankie pointed at the empty urinals. 'If you're going to have a piss, Mr Englishman, don't waste it over there. Wash this spunk off of me with it.'

The door behind them opened and two young guys came in, took one look at the scene that greeted them and went out again.

'No guts to try anything new. I'm impressed that you did it. None of that English resolve and pomposity we hear about, then.'

'Well,' said Martyn with a shrug, 'I guess I'll try anything once.'

One of the cubicles opened and a tall, bronzed guy emerged wearing a very tight white T-shirt that picked out his muscles and nipples perfectly.

'Hi, Craig,' said Frankie.

'Yo, Frankie,' said Craig, washing his hands.

The running water made Martyn remember he needed to pee and so he sighed and let it all out, splashing over Frankie's genitals, shifting some of his own and some of Jerry's come.

Frankie closed his eyes again and muttered, 'It reminds me of being born again,' just as Martyn finished, zipped himself up and went to wash his hands in one of the basins not used by the wankers earlier. He looked back at Frankie in the mirror and smiled.

'Thanks, Frankie. That was fun.'

Frankie gave him a thumbs up. 'What's your name?'

'Martyn. Call me Marty.'

'See you again, Marty, yeah?'

'Maybe, Frankie, maybe. Take care now.'

And Martyn walked back out into the balcony bar area, realising how well soundproofed the toilet was as a wall of techno assaulted his senses.

He glanced around, trying to regain his sense of direction – and located the bar. He ordered a bottle of Becks and sauntered over to the railing that stopped those on the balcony plummeting on to the dance floor.

Opposite, some jerk was tipping a bottle of Coke over the

edge, raining it down on the dancers below, who seemed oblivious in the sweaty heat of it all.

Indeed, the club seemed to have filled up enormously during Martyn's toilet adventure – there seemed to be three times the number of people in the place, most of them crammed on to the dance floor.

Breaking through the general noise, Martyn recognised the strains of the Prodigy from below, meaning even more people shoved their way on to the less than spacious dance floor, making Martyn even more glad that he'd stayed up top.

He watched the dancers for a while – a young guy with his friend, moving with practised ease to the sound; a girl and a youth – she was having a ball while he seemed rather self-conscious, so Martyn assumed they were straight; a few guys near the edge, stripped to the waist, unbelievably huge pecs and washboard stomachs twitching along with the beats; a couple of lithe black guys, every muscle perfect – skin so dark and sleek that the light seemed to be absorbed by it, giving them an air of total physical perfection – wearing cut-off denims, their oft-quoted-by-jealous-white-guys endowments clearly visible and lending further credence to the rumours. The DJ was in his mid-forties and had the air of a man who knew his stuff. Hanging around beside him, helping select records, was a skinny, bespotted lad, probably just out of school, who probably got his arse fucked good and hard by the DJ every night in return for 'being seen' with a 'star DJ'.

Martyn relaxed – all memories of the toilet washed away by the music, the smoke and the ambiance of the club.

A couple of times people brushed past him, rather obviously groin first, in case he reacted. He didn't. He was spent, frankly, and just wanted to relax for a couple of hours, listening to the chemical beats and wallowing in the freedom of being able to do as he chose, without being answerable to anybody.

A tall, thin Latino with pebble glasses and a goatee sidled up and asked him if he needed anything, but Martyn shook his head and ignored him.

'You sure, man? I can get whatever you need. You just ask.' The man kept looking around, as if he was frightened of being seen. Stupid really: all he was doing was drawing attention to himself. Probably uncomfortable being in a room packed with fags.

'No, I'm fine really. But thanks. Good luck elsewhere.'

The dealer shrugged and wandered off. After a few moments, Martyn felt another hand on his back and, assuming it was the dealer, he let himself get slightly annoyed.

Turning to give him a piece of his mind, Martyn found himself face to face with Chad, from the coffee house.

'Hi,' Martyn said.

Chad smiled and kissed him, deeply and passionately on the lips.

Martyn let his mouth open, taking in the tongue that licked and poked rather savagely.

They snogged for a good two minutes before Chad came up for air, grinning that grin again.

'Hiya, gorgeous, good to see you.'

Martyn just nodded, smiling himself. Damn Chad! He was horny again, and, if they'd been alone, he would have shagged his brains out on the spot.

Mentally ordering his swelling cock to simmer down, Martyn noticed someone else behind Chad – slim, freckled, with a hooded top and an earring.

'This is Mickey, my beloved. I told him we might see you here.'

Martyn shook hands politely. 'You always let your boyfriend greet friends like that?'

Mickey laughed. 'You want to argue with him? Besides, how often do you get kissed that fantastically?'

Chad had the decency to at least fake a look of coyness as his boyfriend sang his praises. He then reached forward before Martyn could stop him and grabbed at his cock through his jeans. 'I dunno,' he said to Mickey, 'I just come within two yards of him, and wham bam, up it goes, ready for action.'

Deeply embarrassed, Martyn tried to pull Chad's hand away, but he just gripped tighter and smiled again. 'Admit it, Brit boy, you love it!'

Chad took Martyn's hand and placed it on his own cock, which was both rock-hard and, Martyn could feel easily, decidedly large.

'My offer still stands, you know,' he said. 'Either a drink or a full-on fuckfest. You up for that, Mickey?'

The slimmer guy nodded. 'Sex is sex and sex is fun,' he said.

Chad released his hold on Martyn, who did likewise with Chad. 'Call me, Brit boy,' he said, walking away.

Mickey stayed behind just for a few seconds and leant close to Martyn.

'Sorry – he's a bit pissed and gets a little carried away sometimes.'

Martyn shrugged. 'That's OK. But thanks for telling me.'

'Oh,' Mickey added, 'and, for what it's worth, he was right. You are very attractive and it would be nice to hang out sometime, when he's sober and not quite so testosterone-inspired, yeah?'

Martyn found Mickey's candidness attractive and refreshing. And it never hurt his ego to be told he was attractive rather than just have his cock grabbed. 'I appreciate it, Mickey. See you soon, 'kay?'

Mickey nodded and followed his boyfriend into the crowd, where Chad was already hugging, almost crushing, some other friend.

Smiling and turning back to his inspection of the dance floor, Martyn was aware that his cock was just a little tender where Chad had grabbed it. Dack last night and this morning, the strange thing in the toilet here, plus countless erections while his cock was shrouded in his jeans – they were all taking their toll.

'No more action tonight, Martyn Townsend,' he muttered to himself. 'Time to call it a night.'

The music was Daft Punk slowly segueing into Air when he caught sight of someone who made him forget everything.

It was like a moment in a bad third-rate movie. It could have gone deadly quiet for all Martyn knew, with no one else there and a harsh spotlight beaming straight down to the right of the DJ booth.

And Martyn felt a strange twist in his insides as someone he could only think of as his idea of sheer physical perfection started pushing through the crowds.

He was slender, blond, nicely dressed, with broad, thin

shoulders. He was looking over his shoulder, anxiously, as if he was lost. Or frightened.

Vulnerable-looking. Needing to be mothered. Little boy lost.

Everything Martyn was searching for, without realising he had been looking for it.

Something inside Martyn said he wanted to know this young man. Discover who he was, why he was here, why he looked so . . . so in need of a hug.

He could only be a couple of years younger than Martyn, but Martyn felt an overwhelmingly protective feeling towards him.

All this went through Martyn's head in less than one second, as he immediately saw what the young man was worried about. Three older men, one black, two white, all looking out of place, were following him. All three were separated by the milling throng of dancers and hangers-on, but the methodical way they eased themselves through the crowd, forcibly but without once causing antagonism, reminded Martyn of bouncers at a concert. Or policemen.

Maybe the cute guy was a criminal or a drug dealer, or was carrying a knife or the takings from the ticket booth.

Then again, one of the white guys had a grin on his face that told Martyn a totally different story. These guys were enjoying the chase too much to be police. Or bouncers.

Air segued into Chemical Brothers

The fugitive was at one of the spiral metal staircases that would bring him up to the balcony bar – to go up it meant he would be seen by all three pursuers.

To stay down there, in the confined dance space, meant they'd soon get him.

He started up the staircase.

And Martyn realised he was easing through the crowd to intercept him.

The cute guy reached the top of the stairs first and glanced back. His quick pace as he surged into the bar crowd told Martyn that his three pursuers had already started up behind him, and, sure enough, the black guy was already there, rapidly followed by his two cohorts.

All three were dressed in black T-shirts and grey sweatpants and Reeboks, dark glasses clipped over the necks of their shirts. One of the white guys was holding his left hand to his hip, as if holding something in place beneath the top of the sweatpants.

Martyn allowed them to pass him before he ducked back the way he had come, keeping level with them, with a good twelve or fifteen people between him and them at all times.

He was sure the guy was holding a knife against his hip – just an intuition, but he was positive.

And that wasn't good news for the cute young man.

This was insane – what the fuck was he doing? Getting involved in something, putting himself in potential trouble just because some twenty-one-year-old stirred his cock?

This was stupid. Really stupid.

Like a dream. As if this was actually happening to somebody else and he was just watching it from afar.

Except it wasn't. He, Martyn Townsend, was being stupid enough to become involved.

Oh, fuck.

The younger man was standing about three inches to Martyn's left, just behind a pillar, where they couldn't see him. Yet. He was simply terrified – an expression of total vulnerability and helplessness carved into his blue eyes, perfect cheekbones and narrow, slightly angular mouth, with its thin but red lips. As he pressed himself against the pillar, trying not to disturb the typically immobile crowd already there – some of whom gave him filthy looks – Martyn felt a sudden and completely unexpected urge to defend him. As the three guys in the sweatpants got closer, Martyn reached out and tugged the young man towards him. The blond's eyes transformed from surprise to panic to quizzicality in a split second. Martyn couldn't see what happened next, but he could imagine the reaction of the three pursuers as he swung their quarry round so now his own back was to them and kissed the blond long and hard, sheltering and protecting him.

He counted to twenty, before letting the guy's mouth slowly peel away from his own. 'Have they gone?' he said quietly, hoping his new friend could hear him over the music.

The Chems had segued into David Holmes.

The newcomer's eyes held a confusion of emotions. Fear? Astonishment? Gratitude?

Lust?

Either way, he slowly nodded. 'I don't think they saw what happened. They must think I went back down via the other steps.'

Gently, Martyn relaxed his grip on the guy's shoulders and they both straightened up. Carefully, Martyn turned and did a 360-degree pan of the balcony. No one seemed to have noticed. Or, if they did, no one cared.

And the three pursuers were certainly gone.

Easing the young man aside, Martyn took a tentative look over the balcony.

Sure enough, they were back on the dance floor and Martyn watched for a couple of moments as the two white guys argued with the black one, presumably their leader, about who had lost their victim.

Suddenly the black guy swung around and looked straight up.

Staring directly into Martyn's eyes.

But he couldn't have seen what Martyn had done. It had to be a coincidence. Because, if he suspected that Martyn, one of a hundred or so faces peering down on to the dance floor, was in any way responsible for disrupting their chase, Martyn somehow knew they wouldn't forget him.

What the hell had he got involved with?

The black man suddenly raised his finger and pointed directly at Martyn. It was a gesture that seemed to say that Martyn's was a face that betrayed that it knew something.

The black man wagged his finger, as if working something out, then placed his shades over his eyes, still staring up at Martyn.

'You're marked,' the body language seemed to be saying.

And, by the time Martyn had stopped shaking, the black guy was following his two cohorts out of the club.

Still he couldn't take his eyes off where he had been standing. The threat was unmistakable. And Martyn just wanted to cry in terror.

No wonder the guy he had rescued had looked so frightened.

Whoever the three men were, they weren't used to being pissed around. And they certainly weren't used to losing a battle.

Martyn was barely aware of the arm that tightly wrapped around his waist, almost ignorant of the thin wrist and slender arm that was hugging him, short thin fingers digging into his hip.

David Holmes segued into the Propellerheads.

And Martyn looked around and straight into the face of the man he realised he wanted to spend the rest of the night with.

If not the rest of his life.

'Thank you,' said the young blond guy. 'I'm Scott Taylor. Thank you so much.'

And they kissed again. This time not out of desperation, not out of fear or protectiveness. This time they kissed gently but thoroughly. Deeply. And for a long time.

This time they kissed because they really, really wanted to. And nothing in the world was going to stop them.

Five

___

They didn't fuck that night.

But that was all right, because neither of them wanted to. Neither of them had the energy, or the desire, to go that far – not because they didn't want to eventually, but simply because it did not feel appropriate. There was a spark between them that Martyn was sure he'd never felt before – that little something that meant every time Scott spoke, or laughed or looked anxious or . . . anything, Martyn just wanted to hold him. Tightly.

And never let go.

They had left La Diva very soon after the kiss – each of them rather too politely checking with the other that he didn't mind abandoning the music, the sweat, the cigarette smoke and the drunken queens littering the stairwell, all searching for a fellow desperado to get a shag with.

Martyn had been drinking Coke and beer – but Scott hadn't touched a drop. Nevertheless, he was the shakier of the two, so Martyn drove, heading for the UCLA, then picking up the 405.

'Turn left here,' Scott had said abruptly after a few moments of silence.

Without querying a thing, Martyn took the turn on to Mulholland Drive, going straight up through the Santa Monica mountains.

After a few moments, they reached the apex and Scott silently pointed to a pullover point. After Martyn stopped the car, Scott got out, wandered around and opened Martyn's door, then turned and sat on the bonnet, staring forward, over the drop of the mountain.

Martyn hovered beside him, unsure what to do. Scott was still nervous, that much was obvious, so he didn't want to push his luck, freak him out or come over like some kind of pervert.

The kiss had signified an attraction, sure, but had it been out of gratitude? Desperation? relief? Was this going to turn into a 'Sorry, I might have led you on back there, but I think I'd like to go home now' conversation.

'Ever see *North by Northwest*?' Scott asked quietly.

Martyn said that he had – a special National Film Theatre showing some years back for some Hitchcock anniversary.

Scott pointed at some houses opposite. 'Those places always remind me of James Mason's house at the end. Weird. I couldn't live in one.'

He was indicating a series of rather flat-looking houses, probably erected in the fifties or early sixties, which were built into the side of the mountain, a majority of the floor space supported simply by huge pillars reaching far down into its side. They didn't look remotely safe.

'I had a friend who lived in a place like that. Every time I went there, I expected the house to give way and tumble off the mountain. I mean, those two stupid-looking supports – how can they keep it up there? And yet they do. They are all that's stopping the people inside falling to their deaths.' Scott pulled a packet of cigarettes out from his jeans and lit one, offering another to Martyn.

'I don't, I'm afraid.'

'Don't be. I gave up six months ago. Tonight has made me start again.' Scott took a long drag, then blew a perfect smoke ring. Illuminated by the lights from the distant houses, it floated up and dissipated. 'My head's giving me weird shit, Marty. I think what I want to say is, right now you're like those pillars there. Tonight, you supported me. I would have fallen if not for you. Thank you.' Scott said all this without taking his eyes off the houses. Without even glancing at Martyn.

The young Englishman still didn't know what to do. 'Thanks,' he said, wanting to kick himself for sounding so lame. 'It was nothing.'

Like fuck it was nothing – that black bastard knew who he was now. Maybe he'd come looking for him next.

'Who were they, Scott?'

'I don't know, and that's God's honest truth. They followed me from home – they were there earlier today as well. They broke in and attached a warning note to my apartment door. I have no idea what it's about.'

'Wrong person?'

Scott shrugged, still not catching Martyn's eye. 'Could be. Or maybe they were after Peter.'

Martyn went cold. 'Peter?'

'Yeah, my boy – my *ex*-boyfriend. He did some weird shit recently and went off his head. I had to get rid of him.'

'So maybe they wanted you, thinking you were Peter?'

'Maybe. Either way, I thought I was going to die until you kissed me.' Finally he turned to look at Martyn, took a final drag on the cigarette and blew all the smoke out of his lungs. Tossing the butt away, he lunged forward and threw his arms around Martyn's shoulders and burst into tears.

Astonished, Martyn held him tightly, stroking the back of his head, letting his fingers run through the short, fine hair.

Smelling it. Breathing in the aroma . . .

'I'm so . . . sorry,' Scott was trying to say, but Martyn told him not to worry.

After a couple of minutes, Scott cleared his throat and pulled back, tossing his head as if to clear it. 'Christ, you must think I'm really fucked up.'

Martyn shrugged. 'Sure. I mean three guys do your apartment over then later try to kill you in a crowded club. Yeah, I've *no* sympathy for you.'

Scott laughed, rather hollowly, though. 'Thanks, Marty.' He sighed. 'So, what d'you think of our wonderful mountains?'

'The first clean air I've had since I got here. It's a fab view.'

'"Fab"? Jeez . . .'

'I could always take you back to the club, you know . . .'

Scott suddenly squeezed Martyn's hand. 'If I had the money, I'd buy you one of these places.'

'How much?'

'Couple of million, at a guess. Maybe less now. Since the earthquake, and the mudslides, they've probably lost a bit of their appeal. But there's always some rich MF to buy one, to impress their society friends. LA is the ultimate in social climbing, you see. Without money in LA, you're nothing.'

'You have money?'

Scott laughed. 'Nah. I'm really nothing, believe me. On my salary, I'm lucky if I can feed myself seven days a week.'

Martyn sat on the car bonnet beside Scott and risked sliding an arm around him from behind. For his trouble, he was rewarded by Scott leaning back into him, and then hugging his arm even tighter to him.

And all Martyn could smell was his hair.

He leant his chin on Scott's shoulder. 'What do you do, then?'

'I work for Universal. At the Tour. Sometimes on the *Back to the Future* ride, sometimes on *Jurassic Park*. At the moment, my job is to give out fake passports to three-year-olds taking the *ET* ride. Coping with smug adults who think it's really amusing to give fake names like Hugh Jass and Mike Rotch, like we haven't *ever* seen *The Simpsons*!'

'Sounds fun.'

'I'll show you round one day, yeah? Get you in for nothing. I've got a day off this week. We could do it then.'

'You want to spend your downtime at work? You *are* weird.'

'That's me, Scott Weirdo Taylor.'

Martyn smiled and lifted his head off the American guy's shoulder. Scott was implying at least that this wasn't a thank-you-and-sod-off kind of thing. That Scott wanted to see him again.

A breeze waved some of the shrubbery that lined the pullover point and Scott shivered. Martyn held him tighter, and Scott leant his head back on Martyn's shoulder, looking straight into the starry sky.

Then he slowly turned so that his lips were a fraction away from Martyn's chin. Instinctively, Martyn turned and their lips met, parted and then kissed. Gently. Warmly.

Lovingly.

None of the aggressive rush that usually accompanied a first date. None of the snatching tongues and brief passion of a one-night stand.

They simply kissed firmly but softly.

After a minute or so, they parted. 'I ought to go home, Marty. I need to get up for work tomorrow. And, annoyingly enough, my car's back on Santa Monica.'

'Is that a request for a ride home?'

'Could be.'

'Then I'm your chauffeur, m'lord.' Martyn detached himself from Scott and stretched. 'Hey, Scott, I like it up here. Thanks for showing me. I'd not have done this on my own. As a tourist, you tend to stick to the freeways in case you get lost.'

'Then I'll make it my duty to show you the nicer routes over the next ten days.' Scott paused as he reached the car door. 'I'm hoping that you want to meet up again.'

Martyn couldn't stop himself grinning. 'God, you *are* unique. Yes, Mr Taylor, I do want to see you again. And yes, I'd like you to show me the city, the tourist bits and the others. So yeah, I guess I am saying I'd like to see more of you.'

'Cool,' said Scott, dropping into the passenger seat.

As Martyn reversed the car and then resumed their journey over Mulholland and down into the Valley, Scott asked if he'd met anyone else he intended to see again.

Martyn told him about Chad and Mickey – although he didn't go into too much detail, and definitely missed out the cock-grabbing moment – and said he'd made a provisional arrangement with Dack, again not saying how he'd met him.

Scott directed him down Mulholland, through the back of Encino (pointing out some of the more tasteless houses of the rich and wanna be famous) and on to Ventura.

As they drove through the never-ending shops and mini-malls, Scott rested his hand on Martyn's right thigh, casually letting his little finger stroke his crotch, while pointing out various restaurants.

Martyn felt a tiny thrill run through his balls at the soft, relaxed contact. Within a few moments he knew his cock was getting erect and, while Scott was looking out of the passenger window, he allowed himself a quick glance down at Scott's groin. Sure enough, his cock was hard and pushed against his jeans. There was something really nice about knowing that and, although he guessed that they wouldn't have sex that night, he was flattered by Scott's attentions. And probable *in*tentions.

Scott removed his hand to point out a couple of turns that took them into Valley Village and directed him towards a set of wrought-iron gates on the right. 'That's my place, Marty. Thanks.'

Martyn nodded. He wanted to go in with Scott and shag him senseless. Another part of him desperately hoped that Scott wouldn't suggest it so that they could save themselves for a time when they were more prepared, less exhausted.

As he pulled up to the kerb, both men sat back in their seats and sighed, each waiting for the other to speak first.

'Where do we go from here?' Scott broke the silence, a slight tremor in his voice.

'I go home,' Martyn heard himself say. 'Tonight. But I would love to see you again. As soon as possible, if that doesn't sound too desperate.'

'No,' said Scott. 'No, it doesn't sound any more desperate than it would if I'd said it. And you beat me to it by seconds.' He paused. 'I have to say this now, Marty, because I'm tired and slightly emotional and, if I don't say it now, I never will because, come tomorrow, it'll sound bloody stupid . . .'

'I know the feeling,' Martyn said quietly.

'OK.' Scott turned and took both of Martyn's hands in his, looking him straight in the eye. 'There is something special about you, Marty. It's more than just a euphoria brought on by gratitude. What you did for me tonight was enough in itself. But there's . . . there's something more. Something better for us, I think. I felt it in the mountains, just looking at the stars. Meet me here tomorrow evening at seven, yeah?'

Martyn gripped Scott's hands tightly. 'Yeah. You bet, beautiful. I'll be here.'

Scott reached over, released his grip on Martyn, and kissed him on the side of the neck. 'Thank you again,' he breathed. 'For everything.'

Then, silently, he got out of the car and walked towards the gates, turning at the last minute to call back.

'Oh, Marty, you're "fab"!' And he went inside.

Martyn waited half a minute, then turned the car in the road and drove back the way he'd come, heading towards Colfax Avenue and his rented condo.

After a few moments, he swung into the short drive, got out and unlocked his door.

He didn't bother turning the lights on – he just headed straight for the bathroom, shedding clothes as he walked. By the time he flicked the bathroom light on, he was stark-naked. He turned the shower on. Letting it run for a couple of moments, he regarded himself in the mirror before it steamed over.

Scott was not what he had wanted. Or what he had been looking for. This holiday was already a bit weird, but Scott was tipping the scales. Martyn had so not intended to get a partner, even for the duration of his visit. Hell, holiday romances were worse than long-term ones!

But there was something about the guy that Martyn couldn't resist.

He got into the shower, scrubbed himself down, and got back out, and headed straight for the bedroom, where he set the alarm clock for 8.30 – just seven hours away.

He lay on the bed in the dark, a spread-out towel absorbing the wetness from the shower, just the red LED stating it was 1.35 a.m. for company.

Despite the open window, the Valley was warm tonight and, almost instantly, Martyn fell asleep, thinking about beautiful blue eyes, sweet-smelling hair and cheekbones you could rest coffee cups on.

As Martyn Townsend settled into an emotionally charged sleep, Peter Dooken was starting to think about his first day of job hunting.

He'd got in at five in the morning, UK time, after a gruelling eleven-hour flight from Los Angles (without setting eyes on Derek the steward again). He'd had to get a black cab into southeast London, because the tube ride was just too dreadful to contemplate (as was the haul from Terminal 4 to Terminal 3, as the Terminal 4 Piccadilly Line station wasn't even open yet!), and getting to New Cross, where Lisa lived, at that time in the morning would have been hell.

And so Peter had arrived on Lisa's doorstep at 7.45 a.m. — jet-lagged but quite bright and cheerful.

Lisa had been less so — until he told her his news.

'Sis, I got shot of the little jerk.'

'Well, thank God for that,' she said, preparing some tea and toast. 'Dad'll be pleased as well.'

'You told him?'

'He asked!'

'You didn't have to tell him, though! Oh God, oh God, oh God . . .'

Lisa came out of her tiny kitchen area and put some tea in front of her brother, and a reassuring hand on his shoulder. 'Peter, Dad knew. Dad's always known.'

'Oh, great . . .'

'It's Mum you have to worry about.'

'You didn't tell *her*?'

Lisa sat beside him, spreading strawberry jam on brown toast. 'No.'

'Oh, thank God for that.'

'Dad did.'

Peter wanted to curl up and die. 'Great. They don't talk for six years. Then what? He decides to phone Rotterdam just to say "Hello, Anna, your son is a faggot. Just thought I'd add to your woes"? Great.'

'That's just about it, actually.' Lisa began munching on her toast. Peter politely refused, because the British Airways breakfast — 'scone and real English clotted cream' — was sitting far to heavily on his digestive system. Lisa continued her explanation. 'Mum's been trying to screw more cash out of him since her company went belly up. He refused, naturally.'

'Naturally.'

'And so they argued.'

'Naturally.'

'As you say, brother, dear, "naturally". It all came out in one thing, apparently. I was shacked up here with Phil – mum, by the way, managed to turn "interior design consultant" into "beatnik hippie painter" . . .'

'And your point is?' joked Peter, and regretted it immediately as Phil walked in, waving lazily and rubbing sleep from his eyes. He was wearing just a towelling robe. Peter guessed that he'd woken them both up, but, while Lisa had got up immediately, Phil would no doubt have moved his arse in his own sweet time.

Lisa continued, slightly more menacingly this time. 'Dad then added that you were "shagging your way around America with some fifteen-year-old arse bandit".'

'"Shirt-lifter",' corrected Phil from the kitchen. 'Your dad wouldn't know a phrase like "arse bandit".' He returned to the living room, tea in hand, suddenly looking wide awake at the thought of inter-family (in-law variety) problems. As he sat he smiled at Peter, making sure he held his legs together. 'Nice to see you, by the way, "arse bandit".'

'Charmed,' lied Peter.

Lisa got up and went back to the kitchen. 'More tea, anyone?'

'Hey, he wasn't fifteen. He was nearly twenty-two.' Peter was determined to put that right, at least. 'You think I should call him?'

'Who? Your jailbait?'

'No. Dad.'

Lisa came out, her mug refilled, and she sipped at it, then blew on it in a pointless attempt to cool it down. 'Could do. Wouldn't suggest you call Mum, though. I don't think you're favoured son any more.'

'Wasn't aware that he ever was,' added Phil good-humouredly.

'Yeah. Well . . . don't think *you're* going to get that "honour", Philip.' Peter finished his tea, with a grimace. 'Not until you put a band of gold on my sister's finger.'

Lisa's hand suddenly swung in front of Peter's face – the requisite ring glinting. 'Knew there was something I forget to tell you. I'm Lisa Anderson now.'

Peter didn't know what to say. He looked over to Phil, who smiled at him.

'It's all right,' said Phil, 'I'll let you kiss the bride.'

Peter stood up and Lisa hugged him. He kissed her cheek. 'I'm . . . over the moon,' said Peter. 'After, what, six years of waiting? Congratulations.'

Over Lisa's shoulder, Peter stared hard at Phil, who just nodded, and gave two thumbs up.

Lisa extracted herself, brushed down her clothes and said she had to head off to work. 'I'll just clean my teeth.'

'Do either of them know?' Peter called after her.

'Not yet,' answered Phil. 'I thought it best to wait a while. We only got married on Wednesday.'

Now that Lisa was out of earshot, Peter turned to Phil, anger all over his face. 'Why?'

'Because your sister is beautiful? I mean, what do you mean "why"?'

Peter rested his head in his hands. 'You know what I mean. Why didn't you wait, so they could come? So I could be there?'

Phil shrugged. 'Our lives. Our wedding. Our decision.'

'Yeah. Right. *Your* decision, more like.'

Phil stood up, pulling his robe tightly around him. Lisa popped back in then, glancing at both of them in turn.

'You,' she said to Peter, 'find a job and a flat. You can stay here for one week, OK?' She then looked at Phil. 'And you . . . You can get dressed and get into the office. There are some designs that lady from Hither Green wants you to look at.' She moved closer and kissed her new husband goodbye, waved to Peter and was gone.

Peter went to the window and watched her walk down the hill, past the school and on to the road that New Cross Gate station was on. He watched even after she had become a tiny blob among other tiny blobs.

He only stopped watching when he felt a hand on his shoulder.

He didn't need to look to know it was Phil.

'You don't like me, do you "brother"?' Phil said quietly.

'Not really. I wonder why.'

Phil was smiling. Peter knew that, without even turning around.

Phil's other hand draped over Peter's other shoulder. In it was a brown envelope. 'Present for you,' he said and then moved away, dropping it to the window sill.

Peter waited for Phil to leave the room before opening the package.

Inside were some photographs, about twenty of them. On the back of one was written, 'Don't think Lisa would want to see these, do you?'

Peter dropped them back into the envelope, crossed the room and stuffed it deep inside his bag.

Silently, he walked out of the room, past the bathroom and the spare room and up the four steps to the major bedroom.

He was going to knock on the door but changed his mind and just marched in.

'What do you want from me, you little –' Peter started, but then stopped.

He knew the answer.

Phil was lying on his back on the bed, naked, a nine-inch erection stabbing straight towards the ceiling.

'You know the answer to that, "arse bandit",' Phil said sharply.

Peter found it hard to breathe. 'But what if Lisa comes back?'

'I've double-locked the front door. It can only be opened from the inside. Now suck my cock!'

'Go fuck yourself!' As soon as he'd said it, Peter knew that was a mistake. Phil was up and across the room in an instant, slamming Peter's face with the back of his hand. It would bruise, but Phil knew how not to draw blood. He'd become an expert at that. For nearly six years, Phil had been practising on Lisa's little brother.

'Strip.'

Peter started to shake his head, so Phil raised his hand again.

'Come on, Peter, let's be honest. You enjoy it deep down.'

'For Christ's sake, Phil. I've just got off a plane. I'm tired. And no: you know what, I don't enjoy it. I never have, not with you. And I never will. So you can thump me as much as you like. If there's one thing that I learnt in America, it's that I'm not going

59

to be fucked around with any more. You want to play happy couples with my sister – that's fine. But I'm out of here. And don't worry: I won't tell her why. With any luck, she'll find out one day for herself and see you for the sick psycho you really are.'

Shaking, both with fear and anger, Peter turned and marched out of the room, back to the living room, and grabbed his bags, all the while expecting Phil to be behind him, either ready to hit him, or push him to the ground and assault him. Or both, as had happened last time.

But there was nothing.

Pausing to listen for any sign of trickery, Peter edged back towards the hall, placing his bag right beside the front door, and undid the double lock.

Telling himself not to, knowing it was dangerous, but intrigued by the change from the normal pattern of verbal abuse, assault, fuck and assault that he'd suffered for years, Peter sneaked a look back into the bedroom through the crack in the doorway.

Phil was lying on his back, pumping his huge cock until great wads of come shot across his broad chest. The whole thing was mechanical in nature. There wasn't even a sigh of satisfaction when he'd come.

Peter, relieved that his own cock wasn't even slightly aroused by the sight, turned and walked out of the flat.

He had nowhere to go, no money and no idea how to get some. He couldn't go to either of his parents – his dad simply wouldn't understand, and his mum over in Holland would refuse to talk to him.

And, to top it all, he had the photographs. No amount of suffering abuse, or running away to America or finding comfort, however briefly, with Scott, could alter the fact that the photos existed.

And he knew that Phil would have given the negatives and probably another set to one of his contacts, for safekeeping.

He was in just as much trouble in London as he had been in Los Angeles.

What the hell was he going to do now?

Six

The sun was bright enough to break through even the heavy sleep that Martyn was in. Dimly aware of the light on his eyes, he stirred, rolled over and pushed his face into his pillow.

Aware that this was likely to begin suffocating him in minutes, he moved again and forced open one eye to look at the clock.

It was 1.32 a.m.

He shut his eye.

No. That had to be wrong. It was 1.32 last time he looked and it had been pitch-black then.

He rolled on to his back and pushed himself into a sitting position, rubbing the sleep from his eyes. He'd slept on top of the duvet, and beneath him was a scrunched-up rather damp towel. Gingerly he shoved it on to the floor and leant over to find his watch.

No clothes.

Ah. On the floor of the living room. Of course.

Scott!

And everything came back, bringing with it a warm, happy feeling inside and a fair degree of excitement.

Tonight – he was meeting Scott tonight, but at what time? He knew Scott had said a time, but when?

He moved off the bed, cursing his memory, the damp towel and the hard-on he'd gained just by thinking about Scott. As his cock bounced in rhythm with his steps, he began focusing on the rest of the day – Scott wasn't until tonight. There was stuff to do today.

He found his watch where he'd dropped it by the bathroom door. It was 10.20-ish.

A shower. A cool shower. Calm himself – or bits of himself – down.

Moments later, he was standing in his bedroom again, rubbing himself with last night's damp towel. Still, he thought, he'd soon dry off anyway in the LA heat. Even through the blinds, the heat was quite oppressive.

Wrapping the towel around his middle, he crossed back into the living room and collected his discarded clothes and watch and chucked them on the couch – not exactly neat and tidy, but neater and tidier than before.

He opened the front door to let some air in and saw that something was leaning against the screen door.

He opened that and picked up the object – wrapped in red paper were a dozen red roses. A tiny card was taped to the side and, as he took them in, Martyn read it.

Thanx. I owe you. Dinner. Dive! 8pm. See U there. S xxx

A crude smiley face had been drawn beside the message.

Martyn sat on the couch and stared at the flowers as he laid them beside him. He didn't know whether to laugh or cry. A wave of . . . something washed over him, making his stomach tremble, and he found he was clenching his fists.

'Yes,' he said quietly. 'Yes, yes, *yes*!' The last one was very loud.

He wanted to hug someone (preferably Scott) but all that was handy was an oversized cushion, which got a squeeze to end all squeezes.

He needed to tell someone, but who? He didn't know anyone here and there was no one back in England he felt that he particularly wanted to gabble incoherently at. His mother would just say she'd heard it all before; his friend Miles would get grumpy because no one liked him enough to buy flowers; and

Gary would just say 'That's nice' and launch into a long explanation of how *his* life was really great and no doubt end the conversation with 'Oh, sorry, what did you call for again?'

Then he remembered, and began hunting through the back pocket of his jeans (Christ, they stank of cigarette smoke and poppers) until he found Chad's number.

Without thinking, he punched the number into the phone and waited. After a few rings (the single long ring of the States took some getting used to), it was picked up.

' 'Lo?'

'Chad? Mickey?'

'Uh-huh. Which?'

'Either. No, Chad. Is that Mickey?'

'Yeah.'

'Sorry, didn't mean to be rude, but is Chad there?'

'Sure. Who is it?'

'Marty. From England.'

There was a thud, which Martyn took to be the phone being dropped rather heavily, and he could hear voices in the background but was unable to make them out.

Then a crisp American voice that was clearly a hundred times more awake than Mickey had been could be heard nearing the receiver.

'. . . and for God's sake clear that up, it looks disgusting.' Clunk, as the phone was picked up. 'Yeah? Brit boy, that you?'

'Hi, Chad, yeah. What are you doing today? Can you get away from work at lunchtime to meet up?'

'Work? Bless you, gorgeous, but Chad J. Lesterson Three don't work for no one, no way, no how. Now, where are you based?'

'I'm in Studio City. Colfax.'

'God, the Brits know how to slum it. Car?'

'Yeah.'

'Good. Lunchtime, right? OK, meet me on the corner of Melrose and Larchmont. I'll be in the cool record store buying old, beautiful vinyl. We'll go Italian, if that's OK?'

'Fab.'

' "Fab", right. Do I bring the wife or are we going to fuck in private?'

'Bring the wife.'

'He wants you to come for lunch as well,' Chad suddenly bellowed. 'For fuck's sake remember to have a bath this morning!' Chad turned his attention back to Martyn. 'Sorry, sweetie, but if I don't sort it out now, it'll never happen. One thirty, yeah?'

Martyn confirmed that, got off the line and decided to get dressed. As he did so, he fumbled through his *Time Out* guide to Los Angeles, looking for Melrose.

He found it and traced the lengthy road until he found the junction.

Martyn pushed himself up and away from the couch and wandered into the bathroom, catching sight of his own naked body in the full-length mirror as he hung the towel over the top of the door to air.

He started to look at himself from all angles, wondering what Scott would make of it if they got that far tonight.

He pushed his chest out a bit, trying to give himself larger pecs, sucked in his stomach (no escaping the dreaded love handles, though, although they weren't *that* bad) and clenched his buttocks.

Walk like that all day, he decided, and you'll do yourself a mischief. He let it all go and opted to believe (hope?) that Scott would want him as he was.

Slowly but surely he began freshening himself up for the day – underarm deodorant (quick squirt under the balls, just to stop him sweating), body spray, added some nice CK2 (passé, he knew, but Martyn was never much of a fashion victim and, anyway, *he* liked the smell) around his neck and applied some moisturising cream to his face, hands and cock.

Well, better to have all angles covered.

Ready for the day, he threw some clothes on (new olive-green T-shirt, tan jeans, CATs) and hung a tiny blue crystal on a leather thong around his neck.

Satisfied, he secured the apartment and prepared to leave when he saw the roses.

Quickly he found a vase under the sink, rinsed it and half filled it with water. He used a rather blunt knife to trim the stems and put the flowers in the vase, placing it on the coffee table so that anyone walking in would see them before anything else.

Perfecto!

Eventually, he locked the door, fastened the screen door, too, and drove off.

He was thinking of trying to find his way over to Mulholland, but instead opted for the safer freeway – at least then he couldn't get lost.

Taking the 101, just as it veered off towards the city, he realised he was passing Universal Studios Tours, where Scott probably was right now. There was a temptation to stop and go and surprise him, but no. Scott hadn't offered that option – he'd been very definite twice now about meeting only that evening. Better to accept that.

Besides, if he stopped too long, he'd be late for Chad and Mickey.

Hitting the city meant he could get off the freeway and drive up Sunset, past the Beverly Hills Hotel and towards Melrose. He hit West Hollywood and started to slow.

As the day was hot, a majority of the guys walking around West Hollywood were in shorts and sandals and bugger all else. Tanned, well-sculpted bodies littered the streets, open-top cars and cafés and shops. Men (and women) of every size and shape were there, not all – Martyn was relieved to see – in the 'body beautiful' range.

He slowed the car down and stopped outside a small bookshop that had a coffee house attached. He was in the mood for something to drink and had an hour before needing to get to Melrose.

He got out of the car, throwing his shirt on to the back seat – his T-shirt fitted sightly tighter than he'd have liked and as far as he was concerned exposed the promise of the slightly sagging belly and lumpy hips that were inevitable if he didn't start doing something about it now.

Across the road a rather swish-looking clothing store, which people were going into and out of like ants – and all those leaving were carrying a bag of something. Clearly a popular haunt for the local fags.

He sat at a table and a stocky guy with a leather queen's moustache minced out and took his order – iced coffee.

While he waited, Martyn flicked through the morning's *LA Times*, which someone had draped over the back of a now vacated seat.

Nothing much – more allegations of corruption in the Governor's circle, a couple of hold-ups, two or three murders in downtown LA (the usual photos of trainers hanging over telephone wires, suggesting they were gang-related) and a mention that NBC were cordoning off the road outside the studios today to film an 'exciting chase scene for a top TV show', which he took to mean it was an action-packed moment being created to boost some ailing soap. God, how cynical he'd become.

His eye was caught by mention of an exhibition by Annie Lebowitz in one of the small rooms at the Getty Museum. Martyn wondered if Scott was interested in such things – he'd missed her exhibition at the Portrait Gallery in London and wanted to go.

His coffee arrived, brought out by a different guy, this one twenty years younger, much slimmer and with a huge grin on his freckled face. He had a thin, angular face, bright blue eyes and a short cut of ginger hair – which made him look like one of the guys from *Happy Days*. When the waiter spoke, however, it was with an English accent, albeit broad Geordie.

'Anything else?'

Martyn shook his head and smiled. 'No, thanks. You been out here long?'

Obviously pleased to find a fellow Brit, the waiter shrugged. 'A few months. Just a long holiday really. Came out here with my boyfriend. We split, he went home, I stayed to avoid him. I'm going back in a couple of weeks.'

Martyn offered his hand. 'Martyn Townsend. On holiday.'

'Brian Lawrence. Working his arse off.' He picked up some discarded cups and plates from another table. 'Anything else, Martyn?'

Martyn threw his hands wide. 'Dunno. I've got an hour to kill before meeting someone in a record store.'

'Which one?'

'Not sure. It's on Melrose and Larchmont. Meantime, what can I do but sit here and watch the world go by for a bit?'

Brian laughed. 'What everyone else does in West Hollywood. Spend money!'

Martyn returned the paper to the chair and sipped his iced drink. 'Hmmm. That's nice. How d'you rate the store over there?'

With his head, he indicated the busy clothing store.

'Not bad actually. Nice T-shirts, good lightweight suits as well. Bit glam, and pretentious, but the staff are friendly and you can try anything on. Except briefs.'

They both smiled at this. 'Guess I'll go and take a look. Thanks, Brian.'

Martyn finished off his drink, slipped Brian a five and wandered across the road, dodging a couple of cars (no one drove half as fast or as recklessly as they did in London) and nipped into the store.

It was a white, one-level building, with a smoked-glass frontage and sliding doors. To the right was a small area of briefs, vests and T-shirts. To the right, a second room of trousers, fashionable tops and jackets and the curtained-off changing rooms down a short corridor. Further on and bending around into an L shape was a third room of smart suits and evening wear.

Martyn casually flicked a couple of price tags as he walked in. Not cheap, actually. Certainly not for the States. Jeans here were about $55 whereas in some of the out-of-town malls he had seen he could pick up Levi's or Wranglers for $35 or $40. But the fashion clothes were nice, bright colours. Nothing too lurid or campy – a proper clothes shop for the local clientele rather than the usual outrageous show-offy clothes that marked out a 'gay' store as opposed to any other.

He grabbed a couple of tight tops and a pair of black Levi's, nodded at an assistant, who pointed to the changing rooms.

These were accessible behind a curtain, which led to a thin white corridor, blunted at the far end. There were three tiny changing rooms, cordoned off by small wooden saloon doors. In each cubicle were two opposite full-length mirrors, but the doors didn't really offer much privacy.

Martyn could see a well-muscled black guy in one of the other rooms trying on a variety of linen shirts, each one hugging his well-developed chest and stomach perfectly. The guy was clearly built to wear smart clothes well, and Martyn was jealous.

He slipped his own jeans off and started to try on the new pair, but they were fractionally small, and rather tight around the crotch (let alone the waist, meaning he couldn't quite do up the button fly or top without sucking in and holding his breath). Flattering maybe, but bloody uncomfortable to walk in, definitely. Before taking them off, he relaxed and tugged off his T-shirt, and was about to pick up a red one he'd taken a fancy to when a voice came from behind.

'Nice cut of jeans.'

Martyn found Brian leaning on the swing saloon doors, smiling at him, a blue sweatshirt slung over his shoulder.

The black guy opposite had finished and left the changing room, throwing the two Brits a quick smile before disappearing back on to the shop floor.

'Nice sweatshirt,' said Martyn.

'Yeah, I thought so.' Brian entered the changing room and threw the sweatshirt at a peg, but it missed and dropped to the carpet. Ignoring it, Brian pulled off his white shirt, revealing a slim but taut frame, with two tiny erect nipples – one of which was pierced with a gold ring – and a small plume of ginger fur surrounding his belly button, burrowing down beneath his waist-line. Brian obviously worked out to some extent, because, as he reached down for the sweatshirt, Martyn could see each muscle in his arms and shoulders moving perfectly.

Brian suddenly straightened up with a curse. 'I pulled a muscle this morning in the coffee shop,' he explained. 'My fault. I nobly decided to carry more dirty plates than I should, and when I bent over to put them in the kitchen, my shoulder complained. Painfully.'

Martyn dropped to the floor and picked up the sweatshirt, and, turning slightly, he realised he was facing Brian's crotch. The younger man's hard-on was etched into the fabric of his dark work trousers, pushing as far as it could.

Instinctively, Martyn reached out and tapped the end of it. 'And where did that come from?'

Brian actually looked embarrassed. 'Sorry. Suppose that's my fault for coming in here.'

Martyn frowned. 'I don't understand.'

Brian took the sweatshirt and covered his chest with it. 'Oh God, my mistake. I thought you were . . . oh, shit . . .'

'What?' Martyn was more intrigued than annoyed.

Brian sighed loudly. 'This place is known as a bit of a pick-up joint. When you asked me about it in the coffee shop, I thought it was a . . . er . . .'

'A "come on"?' prompted Martyn.

Brian, going as red as his hair, nodded.

Martyn looked around. 'The changing rooms? Bit obvious, isn't it?'

Brian shook his head. 'Ralphie, the guy in charge, he saw me come in. I'm a bit of a . . . er . . . well, I come here a lot and he keeps other customers out for about ten minutes and . . .'

Martyn smiled widely. 'You mean he lets you use this as your own personal knocking shop?'

Brian nodded dumbly. 'By the way, Martyn, right now, I just want to die. I'll go now and, well, sorry.'

Brian turned to go but Martyn reached out and held his shoulder, pulling him back towards him, so his chin was level with Brian's right ear. 'Seems a shame to waste it, though.'

He reached down and squeezed Brian's prick, feeling it surge and swell in his grip.

Brian tried to turn to face Martyn, but the older man held him fast, undoing his trousers and letting the engorged cock into the open air, feeling his own pushing against Brian's arse. With his other hand, he traced a line around Brian's nipples, one, then the other, twisting the piercing ring a few times. He felt Brian relax against him with a deep sigh. 'Oh God . . .'

Then Martyn eased him around, took his face in his hands and kissed him powerfully on the lips. Brian's mouth opened greedily, and he forced his tongue into Martyn's equally receptive mouth. Their tongues fought for supremacy, each one pushing the other aside in an attempt to explore the new mouth first.

Brian's hands were grabbing at Martyn's trousers, loosening the tight, new jeans. They didn't drop easily and Martyn eased the redhead away so he could tug them off himself, letting his briefs go with them. Within seconds, both of them were in nothing but socks, rock-hard cocks tapping at each other, a long strand of pre-come linking the two heads.

Martyn realised he'd never had sex with someone whose pubic hair was bright orange before – and all those schoolboy thoughts about how no one ever wanted ginger pubes between the teeth swam into his mind. But he didn't care – the boy's cock was up and ready and Martyn dropped to his knees, taking it in his mouth in an easy swallow, sucking really hard and letting it reach into his throat as the whole shaft went in.

Brian gasped from above him, and Martyn sucked harder, imagining the blood pumping into the shaft, swelling it more. His own cock was desperate for some action, so he moved slightly, making it touch Brian's leg, leaving stickiness up the side.

Brian started pumping Martyn's mouth, slowly.

'Bite me,' he hissed. 'I mean really use your teeth.'

Without waiting for confirmation, Martyn let his teeth add pressure on the base of Brian's shaft and the redhead moaned louder. He also increased his rhythm, making Martyn bite harder.

Then he touched Martyn's cheek – a message to let go, and Martyn did. Brian then let himself drop right down, easing Martyn into the corner of the changing room, making him sit on the carpet. Brian was on Martyn's cock in seconds, not giving him a blow job, but finding looser skin and nibbling gently on it. Never hard enough to draw blood, but fierce enough to make Martyn suddenly aware of a new sensation he'd never experienced before. Brian used his teeth on the end of the foreskin, ever so gently, then down the shaft. He started licking Martyn's pubic hair, then took first one ball, then both balls, into his mouth, running his tongue around them, using one hand to pump Martyn's cock, the other massaging the line leading to Martyn's arsehole. A finger found its way to the start of his arse, pushing its way into the hole. Martyn let himself relax, moving slightly so that Brian's finger could enter easily, the extra sensation bringing him closer to climax.

'Stop,' he hissed to Brian, pleadingly. 'Not yet.'

Brian did as ordered and stopped everything and came up for air, grinning.

'I want to fuck you, Brian. I want to fuck you within the next ten seconds.'

Brian feigned looking at his watch and shrugged. 'Make it thirty, and you're on,' he said, reaching for his trousers, tugging out a rubber and rolling it on to Martyn's twitching cock.

Then he turned and lay on the floor. His pert buttocks reminded Martyn of peaches, a slight haze of fine down on the flesh.

He eased the cheeks aside a little, but Brian wasn't giving too much aid, and Martyn thrust in, tunnelling his way inside Brian, who barely breathed as the older man entered him.

As he pushed, Martyn realised that Brian wasn't used to this – hell, maybe this was his first time. He lacked the pliancy of someone used to being fucked, and so Martyn reached down and eased him into a slightly raised position.

'You OK?' he asked quietly.

'Just fuck me, OK?' was Brian's only reply.

Martyn squeezed the boy tighter, staring at his smooth, unmarked back, powerful shoulders moving in time with Martyn's urgent stabs.

He could imagine Brian's own balls and cock, slapping against the stomach and thighs with the movement, and felt the boy sweat under his palms.

Martyn also hoped that this wasn't the moment Ralphie outside would decide they'd had long enough and bring a couple of real punters to the changing rooms!

Well, they'd get a shock if he did!

Smiling at the thought of discovery, he squeezed Brian's sides comfortingly, feeling himself preparing to climax.

As if sensing this, Brian tightened his arse, giving Martyn an incredible feeling of power and pleasure as he went deeper and deeper into the redhead's guts and finally exploded inside him, letting it all come out, wad after wad. Slowly he started easing off the pumping and soon he had stopped, breathless. He started to come out, but Brian told him not to, instead guiding Martyn's hand round him until he found his cock and started wanking him, slowly, with careful measured movements. With each stroke, Brian pushed backwards, clenching his arse tighter on the still hardened cock inside him.

Martyn also reached around and found the nipple ring, gently easing it around.

'Hard,' Brian almost spat. 'Real hard!'

Martyn suddenly twisted the ring, hoping he wasn't doing any damage. Hell, hoping he'd understood the command.

Obviously he had, because Brian's breathing got faster and more urgent, along with a muttered 'For Christ's sake, don't stop!'

Martyn savagely twisted the nipple ring again, feeling Brian's whole body convulse as the pain became pleasure and then, with a final hiss of 'Je-sus!', Brian came, erupting jissom all over his discarded shirt, almost crying out with pleasure, his breathing hard and laboured.

As they both relaxed, coming off the sexual high, they stayed in the tableau for a minute or two, Martyn's cock still ploughed deep inside Brian's tight arse. Neither said anything, as they recovered their strength and stamina. But both were also listening in case anyone else came in.

Then Brian eased himself forward and thus freed Martyn. The younger man stood up, breathing deeply, and then turned to face Martyn, his prick already drooping, a small glob of come gathered at the head of it.

'Thanks, Martyn,' he said. 'I needed that.'

Martyn reached over and pulled him to himself, ignoring the wetness as their two spent cocks pressed against each other, and kissed him again. 'So did I,' he said. 'And thank you.'

They kissed a bit longer, then parted, each dressing silently. Brian put on the new sweatshirt he had brought in, while Martyn got into his own clothes.

A couple of moments later, they left the changing room, Brian's original shirt rolled up tightly under his arm.

'Hey, Ralphie,' he called out as they emerged on to the large shop floor, 'I like this one.'

He dug a twenty out of his pocket and gave it to the store manager.

Feeling slightly self-conscious, aware that Ralphie knew exactly what had occurred, he guiltily bought one of the T-shirts he'd taken in, despite not having actually tried it on.

He followed Brian out of the store as nonchalantly as he could, back into the bright midday sunlight.

Brian smiled at him, dropping his old shirt into a waste bin at the side of the road. 'See you again?'

'Maybe,' said Martyn, deliberately vague. If he got his way, he might be spending the next dozen sex sessions with just Scott. He felt guilty for a moment – he'd just used a possible virgin as a sort of 'last chance' before getting 'involved' with someone. But if Scott didn't pan out . . .

'If not, when you get home, give me a ring, yeah?' He dug a card out of his wallet.

Brian nodded and took the card, leaving Martyn with the impression he regularly got cards along with the brush-offs. 'No, I mean it,' he added, rather lamely. 'It'd be nice.'

'Cheers,' said Brian and pocketed the card. 'Maybe see you for coffee one morning.' It was an empty statement rather than a question and Martyn silently got back into his car and drove away, wondering how such good-feeling casual sex had suddenly become a guilt trip. Guilt because Brian wanted more? Nah, if he used that shop like he said, then he must get fucked over, literally and metaphorically, quite frequently.

No, he felt shame because only a couple of hours ago he was deliriously happy over the flowers Scott had sent and yet, at the first opportunity, he'd buggered a stranger.

He had thirty minutes before his rendezvous and celebratory lunch, with Chad and Mickey.

Oh hell . . .

Brian Lawrence watched Martyn drive away – and probably for good. Shame – he seemed quite nice. Still, you never could tell what dark secrets seemingly wonderful people really hid.

You never really knew anyone that well, least of all in Los Angeles.

He started collecting a few empty cups and plates when, out of the corner of his eye, he saw a car that had been parked a while on the opposite side of the road do a sudden U-turn, bringing it around to park outside the bookshop. It crossed Brian's mind that he'd not seen anyone getting into it – they must have just been sitting in it for ages.

Perhaps it was a rental car and they were map-reading. Perhaps they were going to ask him for directions.

Not much point in that – Brian didn't drive in LA so he knew places only by bus route or doing that typically British thing which Californians could never get their heads around: walking.

A darkened window scrolled down, and a black guy in mirrored shades leant out.

'Excuse me, who was that customer you were talking to?'

Brian thought this was a bit odd, but shrugged. 'A friend from England,' he said.

'It's just we're supposed to be meeting him and we're running late, but don't know where. It took us a while to realise it was him and now we don't know where we're going.'

This seemed a bit strange, but Martyn seemed capable of looking after himself.

'Melrose and Larchmont.'

'Of course,' the black guy grinned. 'I knew it was Melrose. Couldn't remember which junction. Thanks.'

The window scrolled up but the car remained still while the back doors opened and two white guys, wearing tight T-shirts and sweatpants, got out. Only then did the car drive off.

'Coffee, gentlemen?' Brian asked.

One of the white guys nodded. The other just cracked his knuckles and grinned.

Seven

A ll Peter Dooken could think about was his defining sexual
encounter.

He'd been eighteen – just. The weekend after his birthday.
He'd spent the actual day with his father in Nottingham, and had
then flown out the next day to see his mum back home in
Holland.

Two days later, it'd been a chance to stay with Lisa and her
new boyfriend Phil in her flat in southeast London. Dad had
entrusted him with a hundred pounds to go out and enjoy himself. Peter was convinced that Dad expected him to pay for
a prostitute to 'make a man' of him – that was the kind of
guy his dad was. He came from that old-fashioned world that
decreed that, if you hadn't fucked someone by your eighteenth
birthday, you had to pay for it. A kind of ritual passing into
manhood.

Peter never knew whether his dad suspected he was gay even
then, but Peter already knew. He'd known since his early teens,
but he'd never actually had any kind of sex with another man
until his eighteenth birthday.

A shame that what came next was such a disaster.

Peter had returned to his sister's home after a day out with
Phil, not having spent his hundred pounds on a girl, but a fair

proportion of it on some CDs and pot, which he'd bought from a smelly guy in a park near Soho.

Lisa said nothing about the pot, but Phil was remarkably keen on it when Lisa had gone shopping, showing Peter how to roll his own ciggies and make a joint.

'It's your eighteenth, you should smoke some now,' Phil suggested, but Peter wasn't sure. It had been something rebellious, something big even to buy the stuff – but, now it came to actually smoking it, that was different.

Phil shrugged and said, unusually fairly, that it was Peter's choice, but suggested that he use it before he went back to his dad in case he wasn't quite as relaxed about it as Lisa or Phil.

Peter could see the point in this, and decided he'd try it by himself later.

'So, you didn't go for the girls then?' Peter raised an eyebrow at Phil's question. 'Oh it's OK. Lisa said that's what your dad would suggest. Didn't say this to her, but I don't think that's quite your scene, is it?'

Phil got up and headed to the kitchen to make some tea. It was probably a calculated move, and Peter went for it. He followed him.

'Why d'you say that, Phil?'

Phil was putting water into the kettle and, as he reached over the sink, Peter found himself observing his sister's boyfriend properly for the first time.

He was not slim, but not fat either. Quite average, but with a small bum and long legs. Lisa had once said that Phil rode a bike a lot and, as he stood there in cut-off jeans, Peter could see the powerful leg and calf muscles created by vigorous riding.

'Just a thought really, mate.' He plugged the kettle in and then hoisted himself on to the work surface, facing Peter, legs apart, showing a fairly sizable packet held in check by the cut-offs. His chest and shoulders were broad, but his middle a bit shapeless. He wasn't a particularly attractive man – Peter wondered what Lisa saw in him, actually – but he did have quite piercing eyes, and Peter felt that they were staring right through him, digging around inside.

Discovering secrets and years of teenage fantasies.

'If I were your dad, I'd say it's because you don't play much sport, or pin up pictures of Sam Fox on your walls. But maybe you do, I don't know. Personally, I see it in the way you looked at guys in the street in Soho today. You were trying not to, but I saw it all. Especially the guy outside the Stockpot.'

Peter didn't know what to say – Phil was right of course, but he suddenly felt very hot. He knew his face was flushing.

Phil jumped off the work surface and walked out of the kitchen, grabbing Peter's hand as he did, almost dragging him along.

They went into the master bedroom – Lisa and Phil's double bed was at the centre, unmade.

Phil pushed the door shut and pulled off his top, revealing a hairy chest, with two large nipples almost buried under the fur.

He undid his shorts and pulled them and his pants to the floor and Peter realised he was seeing another man's dick for real. It was completely different from how he thought other people's dicks should look, how he remembered schoolfriends' pricks in the showers after games. Yet it wasn't the exaggerated, powerful and perfectly formed cock you saw on the guys in the magazines he bought.

No, this was a squat, uncut dick, growing before his eyes into a long and wide lump of flesh. It had a slight kink in it, he noted, just below the head, which was like a mushroom as it pulled away from the foreskin, almost blunted and flattened, already moist at the slit.

Phil's balls were small but, again, mostly hidden by hair, and for a moment Peter was reminded of a gorilla he'd seen in an old Tarzan movie – a man in a fur suit.

That was what Phil looked like. And Peter suddenly felt ill – his own sister's boyfriend was coming on to him.

'I'll cut you a deal, Peter. You and me will have some fun for half an hour and I won't tell your dad.'

'Lisa . . .?' was all Peter could say, but Phil shook his head.

'You won't tell her. Because she'll find a way to blame you – I'll see to that.'

Peter was feeling really bizarre now. He knew this was wrong – he was being blackmailed into having sex with Phil, yet there was something inside him that wanted it.

'No,' he said, 'No, I want to do this,' he said to Phil.

He stripped off, his body a complete contrast to Phil's, with his thin physique, lack of much body hair and paler skin.

All they had in common were their cocks: up and ready for each other.

Phil roughly pushed Peter on to the bed and dropped on top of him, kissing him hard. Peter returned the kiss but there was no doubting that this was Phil's show. He was stronger, more powerful and more urgent. Peter wondered how long it had been since he'd last had a guy, how long he'd been forced to deny his bisexuality or whatever.

But he didn't ask. He didn't want to. This, for the next few minutes, wasn't going to be Phil, his potential brother-in-law. This was just a man with a ready cock, prepared to have sex with him without any preplanning, without any thought to the outside world.

He let himself go, lose himself in Phil's bearish figure, feeling his cock being pummelled and sucked, roughly twisted one minute, gently caressed the next. Whatever made Phil the way he was seemed irrelevant now.

Peter got Phil's cock into his mouth eventually, the older man fucking his mouth ferociously, his balls slamming against Peter's chin. At one point, Peter nearly gagged, choking on the huge dick in his throat, but refused to give in to that, refused to appear weaker. He stayed there, taking all of Phil's pent-up aggressiveness alongside his own.

He worked his finger up Phil's arse as he sucked him, widening the hole slowly, concentrating on imagining it as being in the front of a train, watching a dark tunnel get wider as he got nearer, wondering what it would be like to put his hot and ready cock inside it, to feel Phil's arse close tightly around it, holding it there as he spewed spunk inside.

Then Phil suddenly jerked back, wrenching his cock out of Peter's mouth, shaking his fingers from his arse and savagely pushed Peter on to his back, grabbing his legs and pushing them apart.

Oh God, Peter realised, *he's* going to fuck *me*, not the other way around.

He barely had time to realise that Phil at least had shoved a condom on before he felt his world explode in a sudden blinding flash of pain as Phil roughly, without any foreplay at all, entered him. Yet, almost brutal as it was, it was also amazing for Peter. He felt both violated and complete and, with each savage pump from Phil, he felt the pain giving way to an amazing feeling of pleasure as his insides flowed with the movement, sending powerful waves of joy throughout his body.

He looked up at Phil's face. The older man had his eyes screwed up, as if each thrust was somehow causing him immense anger or terrible anguish. Yet he carried on, getting faster and faster, and Peter could feel his arse widening as it became used to the extra-hard flesh buried inside it.

Although Phil never made a sound, Peter knew he had come: his prick seemed to change suddenly, and he could imagine the spunk shooting out of it, pretend he could feel the whole thing ripple as it let go of all that pent-up emotion, transformed into liquid gushing inside him.

As suddenly and as harshly as he'd fucked Peter, Phil pulled his cock out, yanking the condom off him as if it was somehow corrupting him, some strange unwanted evil that had attached itself to his prick.

Peter realised he'd stopped breathing while Phil was inside him, and almost began hyperventilating as the pressure inside him returned to normal.

And then he realised how different this was going to be.

Phil was already dressing, ignoring Peter and his own unused cock.

'But . . .' Peter started to say, but Phil was across the room, backhanding him on the side of he neck.

'Never, ever talk about this again,' he spat, the playful friend replaced by a demonic powerful corruptor. He finished dressing and left the room.

Peter couldn't believe it — he'd just had the most amazing experience of his life and seconds later it was gone, lost in whatever guilt and frustration made up Phil's psyche.

Confused and hurt, his arse starting to throb with the pain of the fuck, Peter dropped back on the bed and began wanking himself, letting tears of hurt and frustration, rage and bewilderment run down his face.

He wanked harder and harder until it hurt him, until his prick told him to stop, but still he carried on.

He was still wanking, without any hope of coming or finding any other release for his angst, when Lisa returned to the flat.

Panicked, Peter rolled off the bed, and hurriedly put his clothes back on.

He heard Lisa call to Phil, and, in reply, Phil yelled, 'Oi, twathead, you found that bloody CD yet?'

As he zipped up his flies, Peter spied a pile of CDs on the bedside cabinet and grabbed one at random.

He marched into the front room, planning what he would say, detailing how he would expose Phil as the lying, abusive cunt that he was.

But as soon as he saw Phil, with Lisa kissing him, wrapped in his huge arms contentedly, Peter's mouth went dry.

'Well, that took you long enough,' laughed Phil, taking the CD from him.

To Peter it was as if, during the time in the bedroom, an alien had come down and possessed Phil's body, turning him into a wild sexual berserker. And here, in the flat's comfy living room, was the Phil that Lisa loved, the Phil Peter thought he'd spent the day with. Friendly, good-humoured and pleasant.

Peter knew that he'd been cheated. No way could he rationalise Phil's behaviour. It wasn't assault or rape or anything else – Peter had been a more than willing partner right up until the end.

But now he felt cheap. Used.

He caught Phil's eye and, for a second, wanted to hit him. But there was a flash in the other man's eyes, a warning.

You wanted it as much as I, the eyes said. Say anything and I'll make it ten times worse for you than it will be for me.

Systematically over the next few years, whenever he went to London, Phil would manufacture a way to get Peter alone and fuck him relentlessly. Sometimes they smoked pot first, or had a couple of drinks. But Peter, ashamed and angered as he was, was always willing because he needed to be fucked just as much. And in time he became used to the briefness and lack of fulfilment of

the whole thing. Occasionally a third person would be involved –
and about eighteen months ago, shortly before he left for California, Peter had let himself get buggered by a skinny, pock-marked
Scotsman who smelt of piss, while Phil took photos as he wanked
himself off. It had been those shots that Phil had given him when
he had first arrived at his and Lisa's place in New Cross.

But after coming home from America, from Scott and everything that had happened there, he was ready to face up to his life,
his past, and move on.

Telling Phil that morning to fuck off had been just the first
movement in a symphony that heralded Peter Dooken's new life.

The past was the past. Broken and abandoned, he had a new
purpose now. And that meant he needed to be free and alone in
London.

Eight

It was 1.40 and there was no sign of Chad or Mickey. Typical dizzy queens.

Martyn had parked his car easily (parking in LA was always easy) about half an hour before, and quickly walked to the corner of Melrose and Larchmont. He'd found the record store – a fantastic cornucopia of vinyl and cassettes (not a CD in sight) and Martyn spent a good fifteen minutes ploughing through the racks, nostalgia for some embarrassingly bad records he'd once owned sinking in. Some of them were worth considerably more than he'd guessed when he'd given them to a jumble sale. He almost bought a scratchy copy of a Thompson Twins album, but then he thought he could probably find it on CD, and that was easier to carry home.

He left the store and returned to the heat outside, glancing around for other stores of interest.

Melrose was an odd area. Because of the association with Aaron Spelling television shows about beautiful people, Martyn was amused to find that the area he was in was as far from plush as you could get. It reminded him of a wider version of Brewer Street or Rupert Street in Central London, odd shops nestled together, a real mixed bag of customers patrolling the streets, tons of litter and a general air that suggested the eighties and nineties had passed the road by. If it weren't for the huge painting of

David Bowie – a copy of the cover to his recent *Earthling* CD, complete with Union Jack coat – beautifully adorning a vast brick wall opposite, he might be an extra in an episode of *Starsky and Hutch*. Or some other cop show set in seedy Los Angeles.

As people wandered past (most of them of the overweight, heavily bearded sort with Whitesnake T-shirts and sweat stains under the arms), they tended to stare at him. And, for the first time, Martyn became aware of his tourist status in the city – Melrose was 'their' area and, despite Beverly Hills at one end and Paramount Studios at the other, the middle was clearly designated an 'inhabitants only welcome here' site.

He was about to give up waiting and head back to the car when he saw Mickey in the distance, emerging from a comic store on the opposite corner.

Mickey waved limply, causing half a dozen people to look at Martyn and see who this comic store geek was signalling to.

Martyn opted not to return the wave in the vain hope that no one had actually guessed he was the recipient of Mickey's greeting.

There was little doubting it when, dodging a green four-by-four that trundled along Melrose, Mickey dashed across and hugged him.

'Sorry. I was supposed to meet you ages ago, but I got caught up in there. New issue of *Astro City*. You read comics?'

Martyn said he didn't, and hoped that the conversation would not become so dull that he would have to ask what *Astro City* was about.

Mickey started to tell him anyway, so Martyn switched half his brain off, alert enough only to nod or grunt 'Oh, really' whenever a relevant pause required him to do so.

Where was Chad? Mickey was OK but, despite being about twenty-three, he did tend to act like a fifteen-year-old at times.

'Chad's going to meet us in the food hall.'

'When?'

'Oh.' Mickey glanced at his watch – one of the Animaniacs pointed out that it was ten to two.

Martyn was relieved that he didn't know which Animaniac it was.

'Five minutes ago. Got a car?'

Martyn led the way to the car and Mickey gave him surprisingly accurate directions to go about three blocks towards the Paramount lot. They parked outside a small Italian restaurant, complete with white picket fence and candy-striped sun blinds.

Chad got up as they went in, and offered Martyn his hand in a curiously British way of greeting a friend.

As they sat, Martyn glanced around for a menu.

'Oh, I ordered for all of us. Hope that's OK.'

Martyn said it was – Italian food was Italian food, and it saved time.

Except that, when it arrived, the meal proved conclusively that Italian food is not the same the world over – Martyn had never, ever, tasted better, he was sure of that.

Some wonderful meatballs wrapped in a cheese skin, surrounded by puff pastry and very spicy fuseli – Martyn was very satisfied with that.

The three talked for a while and then Martyn decided he needed a pee and excused himself.

He found the restrooms at the back, in an outhouse down a small path away from the restaurant. How quaint.

He entered the outhouse and relieved himself, washed his hands, and straightened his hair in the mirror.

And froze.

Behind him, seated in an open toilet cubicle, was the big black guy from the club who had been following Scott, dark glasses in place, arms folded.

Martyn, rigid with fear, tried to speak.

The black guy spoke first. Softly. Almost a whisper.

'Tell your new friend that we haven't forgotten anything.'

The black man then stood up and came up close behind Martyn. 'Me? I've no problems with what you two get up to in bed. But my friends . . . they're not fond of fags. And they're not fond of your friend Taylor. Put the two together and we have a . . . problem. So I want to keep my friends calm. You, presumably, want to keep your new friend in one piece. I think you and I should help each other. Yeah?'

Martyn wanted to shit himself. If being on the street had

reminded him of a bad cop show, this was frighteningly real. All he could do was mumble and nod.

The black guy adjusted his shades and nodded. 'I hope we don't need to speak again.' He turned to go, then returned. 'By the way, the stunt in the club last night – good one. But you won't catch us out again.'

And he was gone.

Martyn fell to the floor, ignoring the dirt and the dust and the cold tiles and . . . everything.

All he could think of was the dark glasses, the face in the mirror, and the smile that wasn't smiling at all.

How long he sat there, he wasn't sure, but he became aware of the toilet door opening and Mickey stepping in.

He was at Martyn's side in a moment, easing him up.

'You OK?'

Martyn shook his head. 'I . . . I don't know . . .'

'Did he hit you?'

'Who?'

Mickey was straightening Martyn's clothing, brushing him down. 'Daniella, the owner, saw this huge black guy walk through from here to the road. She went white as a sheet and asked if this was where you'd gone. When Chad said it was, she started panicking and said we should come and find you.'

Martyn started to focus again. 'No. No, he didn't hit me. He didn't do anything but . . . well, talk. A warning, I s'pose.'

'Who is he?' said Mickey, suddenly excited. Maybe he thought it was like something out of a *Spider-Man* comic. 'What did he want?'

Martyn waved him aside. 'Right now, I need to sit down with a drink. A stiff one.'

If Mickey even thought of a double entendre to that, he didn't bother. Instead, he became calm again and left the toilet with Martyn.

The fuss started again as they re-entered the restaurant, Daniella the owner fluttering around like a dragonfly on water, touching Martyn, the wall, the chair, the bar and finally Chad's shoulders, full of apologies. Chad held her hand, saying it was hardly her fault.

'That man,' she said to Martyn, 'my husband says he's a bad one. Lots of the people around here, they say he is bad, too.'

'Who exactly is he?' asked Martyn eventually.

There was a pause. 'Oh,' said Chad finally. 'We thought you might know.'

Martyn shook his head. 'Although,' he added, 'he is linked to what I wanted to tell you. It's a bit weird.'

Daniella seemed pleased that no harm had come to her customer, that maybe he didn't seem the kind to threaten to sue the restaurant for not looking after its clientele, and so, leaving a complimentary carafe of Chablis, she scuttled off, shooing the waiters away as well, to leave the poor Englishman and her delightful regular 'boys' to their lunch.

He outlined the previous night, and Chad nodded sagely. Mickey's reactions hovered between outrage, amusement and thrill.

After Martyn had finished – with the roses – Chad leant forward and, for the very first time, Martyn saw something different in him, a seriousness that had previously lain dormant under the camp *savoir vivre* and double entendres.

'What do you actually know about this Scott Taylor, Marty?'

Martyn shrugged. 'I don't know ... but I guess I like him. You know, when you can just tell someone is really nice. A bit like I did with you.'

Chad shrugged away the compliment. 'And yet Scotty has some rather dangerous buddies that even Daniella here has heard of. And recognises. Sorry, Marty, lovely as last night sounds, I'd want to check into Scott's background a bit.'

'How? Without seeming ... tacky?'

Chad looked at Mickey and a silent understanding seemed to pass between them. Mickey, too, seemed to grow up in that instant, and got up, took a mobile phone from his jacket and walked out of the restaurant.

'You leave that to us, Marty. You have a ball tonight at Dive! and fuck his brains out.' He smiled. 'Leave us to do some digging.'

'Why? And how?'

Chad reached over and kissed Martyn very lightly on the cheek. 'Because I took an instant liking to someone too, last night. Not in a passionate way like you and this Scott, but you're nice, for a Brit boy. And I don't like it when not-nice things happen to my friends. And how? Mickey and I have been around, yeah? If we don't know someone on the scene, someone else that we know must do.'

Mickey came back in and sat. He said nothing until Chad turned to him. 'Well?'

'Benny said to call him at five.'

Martyn started to shake his head. 'This is getting more and more like a bad Clint Eastwood movie, guys.'

'That's LA, sweetie,' said Chad. 'Deal with it.'

They finished their meal mostly in silence, Mickey breaking it occasionally with irrelevant comments about anything that took his fancy as it walked past the restaurant.

Martyn couldn't stop thinking that Chad was constantly staring at him, looking for something, yet, every time he looked at his companions, their attention was elsewhere.

After finishing (Chad picked up the bill, which was nice), they suffered a further round of fussing from Daniella before escaping into the warmth of the afternoon sun.

'Fancy a drive?' Chad said, and, as Martyn had nothing else to do, he took them to his car. 'Where to?'

'Just drive,' Chad ordered. 'I'll play guide.'

Mickey clambered into the back and started flicking through his comics, although Martyn noted that, every so often, Chad would point out some landmark or relate a piece of history and, without looking up, Mickey would correct him, or add another pertinent fact.

It was like a well-rehearsed double act, neither of them ever living up to his facile exterior.

Martyn wasn't sure whether Chad and Mickey were the kind of friends he wanted after the vacation was over. He didn't think they had enough in common to stay in touch long-distance. And yet there was nothing unpleasant about them – in fact they were the height of friendliness. There was just something he couldn't put his finger on.

OK, they were scene queens, which Martyn wasn't, really. And they obviously liked a bit of gossip, a bit of casual shagging, and could flounce with the best of them. All of these were not within Martyn's normal remit of friends. But, right now, he appreciated their company.

'This is Century City,' Chad was saying. 'Built on the old Twentieth Century studio lot where all the westerns were made. Over there is the Century Plaza Hotel – looks nicer at night, all lit up.'

Martyn listened but took little in. He was aware that they were turning on to the famous Sunset Strip, Mickey delightedly pointing to the spot where River Phoenix coughed his last outside the Viper, and the famous Whiskey A Go-Go, where so many bands had received their first West Coast fame during the last three decades. As they moved into Beverly Hills and down some of the side roads, Mickey was enthusiastically pointing out houses. 'That's where Madonna lives,' he shrieked. 'I once camped outside there for three days hoping to see Madonna and Child!'

'Bet you did,' Martyn muttered, sounding a little nastier than he meant.

But the others did not, or chose not, to notice and Martyn decided to make more of an effort. He could challenge Scott about the black guy later.

'So, where'd you two meet, anyway?'

Taking this as a cue, Chad pointed out a coffee house on Wilshire and they pulled up.

Moments later, they were gorging themselves on mocha-chocolates with all the trimmings (Mickey managed to charm his way with the male server to getting triple the amount of cream on top than Martyn or Chad), with Martyn finally feeling relaxed again.

'Us?' Mickey said after Martyn prompted his question again. 'Gay Paris!' he said, using the French pronunciation.

Chad nodded. 'I was there on holiday – shit-for-brains there was with a school trip.'

'College, thank you, granddad! I was with my friends Annalise and Courtney at Sacre Couer. Annalise is a good Catholic girl and, when we went in, she opted to sit through the mass.'

'It was very beautiful, that place,' Chad said. 'Full of candles. Everywhere you went, there were candles. I'm not a believer myself, but I tell you, Marty, the whole building had a . . .

something about it. No matter how cynical we can be – and I'm fucking cynical – that building felt "holy". So there I am, enjoying a little holiday by myself, backpacking (and screwing, naturally) my way around Europe, when I see this cute, adorable little imp scamper into the church with these two really attractive girls. Got to be a fag, I immediately thought, then wondered if one of the girls was his girlfriend – in which case, I decided, she was in for a let-down one of these days. Anyway, I thought nothing more about it and followed a party around the praying masses and went up this awful old staircase to the upper levels.'

'You could see the whole of Paris from up there,' Mickey added. 'One of only two places I liked in the whole city. No, three, actually. I forgot the Eiffel Tower, which is nice.'

'The other?'

'Oh, the Defence Arch. Stand at the back of it and look down toward the Champs Élysées and you have a good view. Turn around a hundred and eighty degrees and it's like someone's cut civilisation off with a meat cleaver. Desolation. A graveyard and a few rusty railroad tracks. I think they're building it up now, but three years ago it was like something out of a bad science-fiction film. Civilisation just stopped.'

'Looked good from the top of the arch, though,' Chad said. 'Kind of windy.'

'Anyway, getting back to us –' Mickey drained his cup and signalled to his tame server that he'd like another '– we met walking around Sacre Couer, up on the white balconies.'

Chad nodded. 'He'd got rid of the chicks and was taking a photo of the tower when I oh-so accidentally bumped him and spoiled his shot. And this little camp voice went "silly bitch" and I knew then that the girlies had no chance!'

'You know what, Marty? The bastard then spoke French to me – pretended to apologise in French so I smiled and called him every name under the sun, making out I was fine. Then he spoke in this gorgeous Californian accent and I melted. And laughed.'

Chad also ordered another drink, asking Martyn if he, too, wanted a refill, but he'd barely touched his first. 'So, anyway, we talked, what we were doing, why, who we were with. Turns out the girls were bored of Mickey already and couldn't wait to see him cop off.'

Mickey stared open-mouthed in mock hurt, and Martyn finally managed a smile. He could see that, beneath the banter, the insults and the pissing around, these two guys adored each other. It was a well-rehearsed bitching session they'd done hundreds of times before when telling this story and was now second nature to them.

Martyn ached suddenly for Scott, to have that kind of rapport with someone must be so . . . complete. So perfect.

Chad was carrying on his tale, but quite quietly now. 'So, we went back downstairs and stood at the back of the church, watching the people all praying, or thinking, or reading or whatever. And then this mincy voice says in my ear, "Is it blasphemous to have an erection in a cathedral?" and pushes against my ass, so I can feel it – like someone pushing a gun against you. I just laughed, reached back and just groped at it through his pants. And you know what Marty? The moment I touched that cock, I knew. Not just that I wanted sex with Mickey but there was something . . . special that went through me. I knew this was going to be more than a one-night fuck.

'So we slipped away from the crowd and snuck into a confessional-box thing. Christ knows how immoral it was but I just removed his pants and stood, looking at the most perfect cock I'd ever seen. Smooth, long, perfectly cut, with a tiny curve upward. A pair of cute little balls behind and these fluffy pubes – not the scratchy normal kind, but it was like looking at cotton candy.

'And I knelt down and took it in my mouth and began sucking. Real slow. Neither of us made a sound, and I just went on and on at this gorgeous piece of meat, so slowly, taking it right down into my throat, feeling that soft hair in my face. I tell you, Marty, my own cock was up and ready by then and Mickey tried to kneel too, to free my cock, but I stopped him – and I've never done that before. I just wanted that cock so much, I didn't care about my own. We must have been like that for ten minutes possibly.

'Gradually I worked my finger around to his ass, massaging that tight hole, just as slowly, and I could feel it relaxing. I knew it was opening like a flower bud. I let my finger penetrate and worked and worked his ass with my fingers, his cock with my mouth, and he stood there, taking it without a sound. When he came, it was the sweetest-tasting thing ever and we must have stayed like that for a good fifteen minutes afterward, sucking and gently fingering. I know I came inside my pants, which I'd never done before, but it didn't matter in the slightest. I knew how brilliant knowing this boy would be.'

Martyn just watched Chad as he told the story – the second one he'd heard from his new friend in twenty-four hours. It was mesmerising – Chad's own eyes were just staring at Mickey, who was grinning back. All the childishness had gone from Mickey's face and these two lovers gazed at each other adoringly, but never sickeningly so.

Chad stood up, a hard-on proudly signposting his pleasure. But that was Chad – he made no attempt to hide it. 'Just going to put some money in the meter and get some cigarettes – Mickey, you finish our sordid little life story, yeah?'

As Chad walked out, Mickey shook his head, smiling. 'If he goes around the corner and wastes a good jerk-off, I'll kill him.'

'You two are both gross,' Martyn said.

'Uh-huh,' said Mickey. 'And it gets worse! That night I got the girls to go out and Chad came round. The hotel we were in was nothing fancy – hell, it was a dump really, around the back of the Pompideau – but we met in the lobby and went upstairs. It might as well have been Buckingham Palace or overrun with roaches for all we knew. I took him into the room, and you know what – how tacky is this? – I locked the door behind us.

'Neither of us spoke – we didn't need to. We just stripped and stared at each other, naked. Then Chad hugged me, sort of wrapped himself around me and hugged me until we kissed. How long did we hold the kiss for? I can't honestly remember, but it was a long time. Then we went to the bed and I made him lie on his back and I began to kiss his body. All over. Started on the neck, the chest, his fantastic nipples, down to his tummy, his sides . . . everything. I used my tongue to just trace every line, every contour of his body.

'I'd never realised before how much another man tastes, how

91

that taste stays with you for ever. It's like a scent. Whenever you get something approaching that taste or that smell, your cock is up and ready, no matter where you are or what triggers it. That skin of Chad's did it for me – I was in love. So smooth, so sweet. I explored his arms, his legs and then I headed for his balls. He knew what I was like from earlier, but he was so fresh, so wonderfully unexplored to me. I'd not had anything like the sex in the past that he'd had, but I knew it'd never be better than this.

'I remember as my face got near those balls, they smelled so . . . attractive, so compelling. I must have licked them all over and under and around before I took them in my mouth and just played with them, teased them inside my mouth. Then I let them go and explored his dick. It was the biggest I'd ever seen, and solid too, like a piece of wood. I licked up and down again and again. I knew it was driving him crazy – his dick was twitching like mad, and wet at the end – but I really wanted to do this properly.

'I finally crouched on top of him and took his cock into my mouth and it felt fantastic. I worked up and down on it for ages, all the time massaging his tits, while he played with my balls and ass. Finally I knew I couldn't wait any longer and I asked him to fuck me. He didn't move much and I just lowered myself on to that solid dick, him pushing up, me forcing myself down, feeling it grow inside me, getting even larger and stronger if that was possible.

'It felt like, oh I don't know, as if I was blind and could see again – like some new part of me had just started existing inside my body but it felt it should always have been there – and, although I'd never noticed it missing before, ever since then, when it's not there, I notice it. And I always want it, back inside.

'I must have ridden him for about half an hour, really slowly, feeling every movement either of us made. It was like his cock had gone straight up into my chest – I felt so good, so happy. When he came, it was a wonderful feeling. Each time he shot it up, I felt his cock tense and swell, which made everything inside me tingle. Afterward I climbed off and he just rolled on to his front. I bent over, pulled his cheeks apart and I think he thought

I was going to fuck him, but there was something else I wanted to do first. I'd never felt relaxed enough to rim anyone before, but I was virtually eating his ass within minutes. My tongue was going in as far as it could and that was a marvellous thing. Then I did get round to fucking him. I can't begin to explain what it was like, watching my own cock going in and out, feeling him tense inside as I just pushed back and forward, watching him sweat. I remember pausing to lick the sweat off his back, which he thought was gross, but it wasn't. It was just more of him, another taste and smell I could take away with me.

'He rolled over and threw his legs around my shoulders and told me to keep fucking. Every time I entered him, I watched those fantastic balls swing back and forth against me, and I couldn't believe I was doing this to the most beautiful person I had ever seen. I must have come four or five times – I just couldn't stop fucking him and he didn't want me to.

'We were still fucking each other time and time again all night. The girls came back about four in the morning and took it so casually. I mean, they came in, and the first thing that greeted them was this guy they'd never seen before, shooting his spunk all over the bed while I was kneeling behind him, pumping myself dry.

'In the morning we woke up – the girls had gone for a walk. They told me afterward they assumed we'd just start again and, as neither of them had got a lay that night, they just didn't want to know. I can't remember whether it was even a minute before he started jerking me off with both hands and I remember I came into his palms and he smothered it all over himself, crouching and looking like someone had tipped glue on to his chest and face.

'I asked him to bring himself off – I just wanted to watch those hands around that cock – and I held my breath as he began to climax. I wanted to see the exact second that he came, wanted to see the first explosion of come shoot out from him. It was like watching a dam burst – I can still see him go rigid for a split second and this come going everywhere, on to me, the bed, the pillows. I remember sucking it out of the pillows and sheets – he was so disgusted, but at the same time loved what he called the seediness of it. I just didn't want any part of him to go to waste.

'Then we took a shower and, oddly enough, didn't have sex! We were naked, together, and all we did was wash each other and have a smooch. We met up with Annalise and Courtney later at the catacombs. Everyone got introduced properly and, since then, we've spent, oh, about three, maybe four, nights apart. Sometimes there's been other people with us, admittedly, but I can't remember many times I haven't fallen asleep with him and woken up with him still there.'

Mickey sighed and finished his second drink just as Chad came back, taking the last drag of a cigarette. 'Well, I can't smoke in here, can I?' he said to explain his delay.

Although Chad's erection was long gone, Martyn knew he'd be revealing his own if he moved – until Mickey whispered, 'It's all right, me too. We'll just sit a few more minutes till they've gone, OK?'

'You know Chad asked me to have sex with the two of you within minutes of us meeting last night.' Martyn hoped Mickey wouldn't be too alarmed. But he nodded.

'What a surprise. And, as I think I said between puking up too much beer in La Diva, I'll be very disappointed if we don't before you fly off and abandon me to him for the rest of my life.'

And something inside Martyn at that very moment made him promise himself that he would do that. Maybe not this trip – and it would depend on Scott – but, if he came back and was young, free and single(ish), the first thing he would do would be to have a night in with these two very sexy young guys.

'This city is doing my head in,' he said. 'Because the answer is "yes". Sometime, OK?'

'All right!' beamed Mickey and he stood up, no erection in sight.

Gingerly Martyn did likewise – his was still there, but, if Chad could walk out with it up and proud, so could he.

So long as it was gone by the time he had to drive.

Nine

After Martyn dropped them off outside Mitzi's, a bar-cum-coffee shop on the edge of West Hollywood's gay area, Mickey and Chad made a few calls and waited for their friends to arrive.

'D'you think he's getting in over his head?' Mickey asked. 'I mean, he's only known the guy one night.'

'We've only known Martyn one day, and we like *him*.'

Mickey shrugged. 'We're not saying we're going to spend the rest of our lives with him. And. if we were, I'd do some checking out as well.'

Chad agreed with this, although he felt it necessary to remind his boyfriend that their sources were rather biased. 'Let's face it, if this Scott guy has so much as given Ben the wrong look or once ignored one of Dolly's flirtations when she's been on door duty at the Whiplash, he's evil personified. No one is very forgiving around here.'

'No one's very forgiving in any gay scene, let's be honest,' boomed a massively overweight mountain sitting down beside them, having some difficulty forcing his bulk into the seat. He had prominent buck teeth, a small goatee that failed to hide his treble chin and long black hair streaked with grey pulled back tightly into a ponytail, making him look like a cross between a sumo wrestler and a beaver.

'Hi, Ben,' said Mickey. 'You look well.'

Ben shrugged. 'Yeah. Right, thanks.' Ben wasn't well, every-one knew that. The general belief was that his heart was dodgy and carrying all that weight around merely speeded up his impending doom. Ben, despite this, never showed any interest in dieting or changing his ways. 'If I'm gonna croak,' he was once heard to say, 'then I'll go as I am. Happy and fat.' No one bothered to argue with that kind of fatalism.

'So, who is this Scott Taylor guy you asked me about?'

'That's what we want you to tell us, *ma cherie*,' said Chad. 'If you or Dolly don't know, no one does.'

Ben harrumphed at the mention of Dolly. There had long been a semi-joking feud between them about who knew more people, more gossip about those people, and who was better at feigning complete innocence when gossip got out and they began blaming the other.

Of course they both also knew that neither had managed to get a good screw in living memory, but on the whole this wasn't something that many people chose to point out.

The door to the café was pushed open and a tall, lanky figure with sunken cheeks and rather doleful eyes minced in, waved at a waiter and sat beside Chad's table, crossing his legs overdramatically.

'Afternoon, dolls,' he rasped in a voice that implied too many cigarettes. 'How's today's council of war getting on without me? Badly, no doubt. Oh bless you, hon.' He nodded as the waiter plonked a cup of black Java in front of him. 'Late night on the door,' he added by way of explanation to Chad and Mickey. 'Some cunt wouldn't go home unless his stupid boyfriend went with him. At some point during the evening they'd become exes and it all got a bit tawdry. Bastard ripped my wig off and took half my extensions with it. I ask you, what's hostessing coming to these days when you have riffraff to deal with?'

No one dared answer in case they said the wrong thing. Dolly drained his Java in one go and ordered two more. 'Now, who are Ben and I researching for you two lovely cupids?'

'Scott Taylor,' Ben answered. 'Mean anything to you?'

'Mean anything to you?' Dolly came back.

'Nope,' said Ben.

'Hmmm . . . well, I think it does. But not directly. Let me think.' Dolly placed his hand over his eyes and leant back theatrically. 'Yes . . . yes, it's coming to me now. Young Dutch guy, very cute, bit nervy.' Dolly reached out and touched Ben's arm. 'Think, sweetie, about six months ago, came over. Hated the Pet Shop Boys – oh, sacrilege! – and Eurotrash. Didn't drink.'

'Gotcha,' Ben said suddenly. 'Was Scott the blond little one he picked up? Come from some rich place like Bel Air?'

'No, not here. No, I'm sure it was Santa Barbara or somewhere beyond Malibu at least. Solvang perhaps – he looked a bit Nordic.' Dolly suddenly clicked his fingers. 'And now it all comes back. They were banned from Axis and Rage and I think even Gold Coast.'

'Gold Coast? What did they do?' Mickey laughed. Gold Coast was really easy-going – it didn't ban anyone!

Ben and Dolly both leant forward conspiratorially. 'Well,' said Dolly, 'as I understand it, it went like this . . .'

Martyn swung the car into the first parking space he could find – luckily lots of US car parks had spaces reserved for 'compacts' and his rental car certainly fitted that description.

Another nice thing about driving in LA was that car parks connected with malls and restaurants never charged for the parking, which made a welcome change from London, where you were lucky if you could even *find* anywhere to leave your car, let alone come away with change from a fiver for an hour's worth of parking.

He wandered up some concrete steps and found himself on a paved walkway a couple of levels up, facing a blue door with a porthole in it.

This was Dive!, Steven Spielberg's contribution to Century City's eateries. A themed restaurant, based on a submarine, which Martyn decided would be either cute or crap. He'd visited the Rainforest Café underneath the Trocadero in London's Piccadilly. That was the best restaurant in London, he'd decided a while back, despite the alarming propensity for the animatronic elephants, gorillas and antelope to suddenly come to noisy life while you were trying to have a quiet tête-à-tête, or a rainstorm complete with lightning thrashed its way through the plastic undergrowth, most likely causing a seizure in anyone who was even mildly epileptic and had to avoid strobe lights. But the food was ace.

Somewhere, Martyn just guessed that Dive! would, every so often, do just that. He could imagine the warning klaxons, the red lighting like something out of *Voyage to the Bottom of the Sea*. So long as gallons of water didn't crash through, washing the waiters and his food away, he wouldn't mind.

Besides, it was his first meal (hopefully not the last) with Scott. That alone would excuse the restaurant any number of annoying gimmicks.

Breathing deeply and wishing his legs would stop turning to jelly, Martyn pushed the door open and found himself in a tiny anteroom where a tall, bronzed man who ought to have been in *Baywatch* (huge muscles, no brain, shrivelled cock – that was how Martyn always justified the existence of the people in that programme, and why he didn't have a chest like David Hasselhoff) stood next to a computer. He smiled with two rows of artificially whitened teeth and watery blue eyes and his tight trousers actually revealed quite an impressive packet. Oh well, scratch one *Baywatch* cliché. At any other time, Martyn might have wanted to find out how much bigger the packet got, but tonight it hardly crossed his mind.

'I'm here to meet a friend,' he said. 'Name of Scott Taylor.'

The host consulted his computer and nodded. Another host, a dreadlocked young woman, walked up. 'Mr Taylor is already seated,' she said. 'Follow me please.'

With a last glance at the man's crotch, Martyn shoved a momentary flash of sucking him off in the car park right out of his mind and headed towards the main restaurant, a level down.

The hostess pointed to a table in the far right corner, near a railed-off area meant to represent the engines of the submarine.

Earlier that evening, Martyn had allowed himself a few self-doubts. What if Scott was stringing him along and didn't turn up? What if he wasn't as cute as he'd seemed the previous night? What if he'd brought someone else with him, just in case the evening was a social disaster? What if he was really ugly, with pustulating zits, a huge nose and bad breath?

As soon as he saw Scott sitting there, reading the menu, his mind washed those thoughts away, his heart jumped a bit faster and his cock started to swell.

Scott was beyond being cute. He was beautiful. He was everything Martyn could ever imagine wanting in someone.

As if sensing someone was focusing on him, Scott looked up, and immediately stood. As Martyn got to the table, Scott enveloped him in a huge hug, pulling him closer, regardless of what anyone else there might think.

'You've got a real hard-on, haven't you, Marty?' he whispered.

'Thank you for pointing that out,' said Martyn tartly. 'How flattering it might have been if you'd had one too.'

'Have now.' Scott eased himself down into his seat, letting his hand fall into Martyn's and pulling him down too. Rather than sitting opposite, Martyn sat to Scott's left, meaning Scott didn't have to let the hand go. Indeed, Scott squeezed it a bit tighter, brought it up to table height and thus made sure everyone could see they were holding hands. He then brought the hand to his lips and kissed the back of it. 'Thank you for coming.'

Martyn slid his hand away to adjust his crotch as subtly as he could. 'Thank you for the roses.'

Scott froze. 'Roses? What roses?'

It seemed an eternity before the meaning of that question sank in. Martyn's face flushed, his heart rate increased and his stiff cock wilted faster than if he'd fallen into a swimming pool of iced water.

'I . . . you sent . . . this morning . . . ohmygod . . .'

Then Scott laughed. A lovely, sweet, cheerful laugh that somehow still had a Californian accent to it.

And Martyn knew he'd been had. 'You . . . bastard . . .' he stammered.

Scott was enjoying himself. 'I've never seen anyone go bright red quite that quickly. Wonderful.' He applauded loudly, making Martyn go even redder. 'Still, if you can cope with that, you can cope with anything.'

Martyn just wanted to crawl away and die of shame and, at the same time, throw his arms around Scott and hold him all night, never letting go. He hated feeling so completely swamped with affection for this man he barely knew and yet he adored the freedom he felt that allowed him to think like that.

'Have you two lovebirds decided what you want yet?' A short, smiling waitress stood by their table, putting down a jug of drinking water.

'Yes,' said Scott, without giving Martyn time to even look at the menu. 'We'll both have the calimari to start, followed by Surfer's Paradise, again for both of us. I'll have whatever your equivalent to a Margarita is. Marty?'

'Oh well,' Martyn said quietly, 'if I'm allowed to make my own mind up, I'll have a glass of house white, thank you.' With a big grin, the waitress picked up the menus and left.

'Thank you, good sir, for choosing my dinner. What the fuck is a Surfer's Paradise?'

'Billy Warlock with my cock up his arse and yours coming in his mouth.'

Martyn just gave him a look and Scott waved towards the waitress. 'Can't remember, but it looked nice on the menu. She's taken them away, so we can't check. Anyway, you'll eat what you're given.'

'Promises, promises,' said Martyn quietly.

Scott leant towards him. 'Oh, that is a promise, Martyn Townsend. Unless we work out that we actually can't stand each other, tonight you and I are going to have a lot of fun.'

'And if we do hate each other, or don't want to go that far?'

'Then we say so. Honesty is very important to me, you know.'

'Me too. D'you mean it? No pretence, no going through the motions because we think it's the right thing to do rather than what we actually want?'

Scott nodded. 'Had too many of those nights, especially over the last few months.'

'Oh?'

'Tell you some other time. This evening, the conversation is light, flirtatious and fun. In-depth soul-baring comes when we know each other more and are better relaxed around each other. Fair?'

Martyn stroked Scott's hand. 'Very fair. Oh, and by the way Mr Taylor, I fancy the arse off you.'

'Mr Townsend, the feeling is entirely mutual.'

The waitress bought their deep-fried squid and they spent ten or so minutes laughing and joking together as they munched through it, without even noticing there were other people in the restaurant. By the time the Surfer's Paradise arrived, neither of them cared what it was, and just ate and laughed and talked and drank. After his wine, Martyn went on to Coke and, not wishing to be left out, so did Scott, which Martyn thought was a nice touch.

Neither of them took any notice as the restaurant went through its 'Dive! Dive! Dive!' drill, just as Martyn had expected it to. Neither noticed as, slowly but surely, more customers left, fewer replaced them. And neither of them realised the time until their waitress made a polite but indiscreet cough at a half past midnight.

'We're the only people left, aren't we?' said Scott.

'Uh-huh.'

'You'd like us to leave right now, wouldn't you?' said Martyn.

'Uh-huh.'

'Can we have the bill . . . er, the check?' he asked her.

The waitress pointed to a piece of paper Martyn dimly remembered her placing there an hour or so ago.

Scott paid with a platinum VISA card – Martyn noticed two names on it. S. J. Taylor and P. P. Dooken.

After Scott signed the bill, they made their way out, apologising to everyone they met. The same white-toothed guy was up by the exit and was the last person to see them.

'Sorry,' said Martyn, 'I'm not drunk, but forgive me: I have to do this.'

He cupped his hand on the guy's crotch, ignoring the shock on his face.

Scott howled with laughter and ran out of the door.

Martyn stepped back, staring at the palm of his hand and how stretched out his fingers were. 'Fucking hell, you've got a huge lunch box. Gay or straight?'

The man was too shocked to do anything other than mutter, 'Straight.'

'Well you tell your girlfriend she is very, very lucky. And, if you ever change your mind, call me.' And Martyn followed Scott outside. 'And I'm not even pissed! I don't believe I did that!'

Scott could barely speak. 'I can't believe you did it either! He was cute, though, wasn't he?'

Still deliriously happy, they wandered back to Martyn's car and got in.

Martyn was going to start it, but stopped. A wave of seriousness washed over him and he took a deep breath. As if sensing this, Scott calmed down immediately.

'What now?' said Martyn.

'Normally, I'd say let's hit a bar or a club or do some late-night shopping. Some of the Third Street Promenade stores stay open real late, you know.'

'This late?'

Scott checked his watch. 'Oops. No, not this late. But you know what I'd really like?' Martyn shrugged. 'A coffee. Some good music. And you and I alone together. Just talking. No sex, not even a kiss. Just getting to know each other. A bit like we did last night over Mulholland, but inside a home.'

'Yours or mine?'

Scott shrugged. 'What music have you got in your place?'

'Bugger all.'

'Mine then.'

And Martyn drove them back to the Valley, back to Scott's place without once having to be reminded of the way – it was indelibly burnt into his memory.

They drove in silence, the windows down, letting the warm air of the Californian night keep them awake.

God only knew what Scott was thinking. All Martyn could focus on was imagining a thousand different scenarios that could be played out as a result of the one question he wanted – needed – to ask Scott. Who was P. P. Dooken?

Chad and Mickey sighed simultaneously and looked at each other.

'He's not coming back, is he?'

Mickey shook his head. 'Not here, anyway.'

Chad thumped the steering wheel in sudden anger and frustration. Mickey touched his arm affectionately, trying to calm him. 'There's nothing else we can do except try calling him tomorrow. Let's go home, yeah?'

Chad gave Martyn's rented condo one last furious glare, as if the structure itself was to blame. 'If only we knew where this Scott lived.'

'I know, hon, but we don't, so let's leave it.'

Chad smiled at Mickey. 'I'm so lucky to have you. Do I say that often enough?'

'Nope.' Mickey reached over and kissed Chad, then slipped his hand to the side of the seat and tugged on the handle. The seat dropped right back, taking a yelping Chad with it. Quick as a flash, Mickey dropped his own seat back and undid his seatbelt, leaning over and undoing Chad's.

'Not here . . .' Chad started to say, but Mickey's teeth were already attached to his zipper fly, pulling the metal tag down. Chad tried to push him away half-heartedly, but Mickey knocked his hands away, tugging Chad's cock out through the fly and pumping it vigorously with his hand.

Chad gave in and undid the top of his pants, giving Mickey time to pull them down. Mickey then slowly but deliberately removed every item of his own clothing, as Chad's eyes grew wider.

'This is fucking illegal, boy! We're on the side of the road.'

But Mickey said nothing, his eyes glistening as they caught the glare of the street lighting. He smiled his sweet, boyish smile and Chad gave in, taking his clothes off as well, but more slowly, as he wasn't in the easiest of positions to do so.

Mickey suddenly knelt astride him, his cock tapping at the end of Chad's, then reached over and pulled all the seatbelts down, attaching the front ones to the slots in the back seats and vice versa, effectively pinning Chad into his seat, his body crisscrossed with straps.

'Oh no . . .' Chad started. 'Oh no no no . . .'

And Mickey reached into the glove compartment and took out a set of handcuffs.

'No, Mickey, don't . . . not here for Christ's sake . . . no!' It was too late: Mickey had the cuffs around Chad's wrists with the speed of an experienced boyfriend and then began licking Chad's naked body, ignoring the slight quiver as Chad felt the cold.

'You stupid asshole,' said Chad, half angrily. 'I don't know where the goodamn 'cuff keys are!'

Still not speaking, Mickey just shrugged and placed his lips around Chad's cock, going up and down on it vigorously, pumping his own cock at the same time.

Chad wriggled, but that just made the seatbelts tighten and Mickey work harder. He sucked so hard that Chad started to think his cock was going to disappear for ever down into Mickey's guts. Trapped, cuffed and naked, he could do nothing except let his boyfriend get on with the job at hand. Soon – too soon – he felt Mickey's hot come spurt on to his thighs and balls, soaking into his hairs. Still Mickey kept jerking himself, harder and harder, sucking faster and faster, until Chad released his come into the waiting mouth, sending surge after surge down Mickey's throat. He cried out, surprising himself at the volume of his ecstasy, but still Mickey kept pumping and sucking, evidently determined that they were both going to come twice, and as quickly as possible. Chad knew his limits – he'd seen Mickey achieve multiple orgasms within the space of about ten minutes, but had never done so himself. When he came, he shot out everything he had and that was that. It needed a good two or three hours before he could find some reserves to get rid of. But Mickey never seemed to run dry, so Chad just decided to relax and let Mickey get on with it – knowing that if a cop stopped them (hell, if anyone happened to walk by, see them and report them) they'd get the book thrown at them.

If Chad was already surprised at Mickey's behaviour, it took an even more astonishing turn when he stopped sucking Chad and sat right back, straight on to the gear shift.

Chad watched open-mouthed as Mickey seemingly effortlessly let it penetrate his ass, taking the bulbous grip and quite a length of the stubby shaft inside. Mickey came a second time almost instantly, spraying his seed on to the ceiling of the car, which immediately rained down in thick globules on to Chad's chest and neck.

He stopped rocking himself at that point, but stayed attached to the shift and began breathing deeply.

Chad wriggled a bit, desperately wanting to scratch his balls, which were beginning to itch as Mickey's come began to dry. All this did was make the seatbelts constrict further.

'Hey, Mickey, this is starting to actually hurt some,' he said.

'How much?' That was the first time Mickey had spoken since this bizarre ritual had started.

'A lot.'

Mickey kicked at the seatbelts, making them tighten even more.

'Now that's just plain perverted, Michael DiCastillo,' Chad warned. 'I might have to punish you for that later.'

Mickey laughed. 'But how, O masterful one, when I'm being fucked by the car and you've been tied up to watch?'

Chad sniggered. 'Tell you what. Untie me, and I'll show you.'

Mickey was off the gear shift and unclipping the seatbelts instantly.

Freed, Chad managed to stagger up, and held his hands forward. 'Unlock these.'

'I don't know where the key is!'

'I warned you . . . Jesus, what are we going to do?'

But Mickey had a glint in his eye as he said, 'Guess you'll have to punish me even harder.' And then he squealed as Chad leant forward and snatched at one of his balls with his mouth, his teeth just nicking the skin.

Mickey didn't move away when Chad made a second attempt and just began moaning quietly as Chad took one ball, then both, into his mouth, chewing gently yet determinedly on the tiny balls deep inside their protective skin.

Mickey manoeuvred himself slightly so that he could reach over Chad's back and, without any preamble, shoved his right thumb up Chad's ass, stabbing relentlessly, and each time Chad bit a little too hard on his balls, Mickey tried to widen his ass crack and insert a second or third finger.

Chad suddenly let the balls spill out of his mouth and snarled at Mickey, 'Go the whole fucking hog, why don't you?'

Mickey was moving around and settling behind Chad instantly, cramming himself against the back seat. Chad was on all fours, his handcuffed hands gripping the gear shift as Mickey slowly massaged his asshole and pushed. Round and round his fingers went, and Chad bit his lip and slowly his muscles relaxed. 'How much lube are you using?' he said slowly.

'Lube?' said Mickey as if it had never occurred to him, and, with a final thrust, every finger, his thumb and most of his hand were penetrating Chad's welcoming ass.

'Oh fuck, fuck, fuck!' Chad almost screamed as Mickey went in up to his wrist.

And, despite his earlier doubts, Chad shot his second load of the night, even more than before, into the floor of the car.

Simultaneously, he felt a small amount of Mickey's come slap against his asscheeks.

Then Mickey withdrew his hand slowly and kissed Chad's asshole as it began to relax, before flopping down in the back seat.

Chad counted to about thirty before he felt he dared move – his ass felt like it had been ripped open, twisted inside out and put back again, but upside down. It felt agonising but incredibly exhilarating as well.

Eventually, he let Mickey guide him into the back seat, tentatively sitting beside his boyfriend, allowing the cold of the vinyl seat to sooth his aching ass.

Still cuffed, he wiped a tear away from his eye and sniffed. 'That really fucking hurt, boy,' he said slowly.

Mickey reached down with his left hand and wiped away a last dribble of come from Chad's drooping dick and licked his finger. He held up his other hand. 'Dad, I think I need to wash my hands.' He grinned like a five-year-boy might who has spilt ice cream down himself. 'Oh, and the key to those is in the back pocket of my Levi's.'

With a sigh of relief, Chad crawled back to the front of the car and rustled through Mickey's clothes.

And stopped. 'When did you take the keys, Mickey?'

'Yesterday . . .' He trailed off. 'When I was actually wearing my Levi's, but now, of course, I'm not. I was wearing my Diesels, wasn't I?'

And Chad turned to look at him with something resembling

first-degree murder in his eyes. 'I think, young man, you're about to have your first ever driving lesson. And then, when we get home, believe me, shoving my hand up your ass is going to be the most comfortable thing that happens to you all night . . .'

Mickey laughed. Then apologised.

He was still apologising when they pulled up outside their apartment twenty minutes later, miraculously not having hit any other cars, not having attracted the attention of any traffic cops and not actually having broken any laws other than the fact that Mickey didn't hold a licence.

And he was still apologising an hour later when he and Chad settled down to the most aggressive sex they'd ever experienced.

And the next morning, he started apologising again, hoping that Chad would start fucking him again.

And it worked.

Ten

'**B**it of a late one, Scotty?'

Martyn nearly died of fright at the husky voice. He and Scott had parked quietly, locked the car quietly, and quietly opened the wrought-iron gate into the little courtyard that Scott's and all the other condos were built around.

But they'd obviously not been quiet enough for one resident.

He was in his fifties, leaning on a cane, dressed as if he'd just come back from Sunday worship. Indeed, Martyn's initial impression was of the leader of a gospel choir or some small ministry in Peckham or Lambeth. His dark skin was wrinkled, his tightly cropped hair shot through with grey.

Weaving around his unsteady legs were two white cats, quite friendly and looking well kept.

'Evening, Mr Terrell,' said Scott unlocking his front door. 'Weren't waiting up for me, surely?'

'No, no, no,' said Terrell, adjusted his weight so the other side of his body leant on his stick. Martyn had the oddest feeling the old neighbour was lying through his teeth – that he'd been watching and waiting for Scott's return.

Nevertheless, after giving Martyn the visual once over, he retired through his own front door, trailed by the cats, and, seconds later, his lights went off.

'Nice neighbour?'

Scott shrugged. 'Don't really know him. I get cat food for him a couple of times a week, but he keeps himself to himself most of the time.'

Martyn followed Scott into the condo, taking it in.

The main room was spacious, or would be if it was not cluttered up with books, dirty mags and dirtier vids. Every so often the book and video shelves had unnatural gaps – as if someone had arbitrarily selected odd volumes and removed them.

His eyes hit upon the CD racks, and the similar small gaps were evident. Scott had struck Martyn as a bit of a Virgo – everything ordered and uncluttered – yet this betrayed exactly the opposite.

A short flight of steps went up to the far right of the room, over the tiny kitchenette underneath. These steps led to the bedroom, which then doubled back over the main room, open-plan, like a converted loft, so that anyone lying on the bed, which he could see from here, would be able to watch the TV, albeit from quite some way away.

'The bathroom is off the back of the bedroom,' Scott explained, following Martyn's gaze. 'All en suite. Bit posh.'

'And you afford this how?'

Scott was in the kitchenette. 'Tea? Coffee?'

'Tea please. Milk, not lemon.'

'I know how to make tea,' snapped Scott suddenly.

'Sorry,' said Martyn quietly.

'Pick some music,' Scott said, as if the previous two sentences hadn't happened. 'But not Dire Straits or goddamn Aqua!'

Martyn noted that there wasn't an Aqua or Dire Straits in the collection, but thought better of pointing this out. Instead he found an imported copy of the first Daft Punk CD and put that on.

'Excellent choice, Marty.' Scott emerged with two mugs of tea, made in the perfect European way. 'Welcome to my home.' He sat on the couch next to Martyn, resting his arm on Martyn's shoulders and tucking his legs under him. 'Isn't this nice?'

Martyn grinned. 'Yeah. Yeah, nice is a nice way to say nice.'

Scott was about to say something when the phone rang. There was one beside the couch, but Scott unfurled himself and ran up the stairs to, presumably, another one in the bedroom.

Martyn couldn't hear who it was or what Scott was saying over the thumping dance music, but that didn't matter. He'd be back soon.

Martyn got up and began thumbing through some of the books on the shelves. A selection of quality reference books, some erotica, a couple of Gay Guides to Life and a copy of *The Cat in the Hat*, scuffed by age.

Below that was an eclectic fiction list including Carrie Fisher, Umberto Eco, Nick Hornby, Paul Magrs, Amy Tan, Peter Carey and even a Norman Mailer. He began to glance through what appeared to be an unread copy of Guterson's *Snow Falling on Cedar* and saw the inscription on the inside front cover.

FOR YOU, HON
THANKS FOR THE FIRST THREE MONTHS,
HERE'S TO THE NEXT THREE DECADES!
LOVE
P xx

Poking out from a page, almost like a bookmark, was a photograph of Scott and, presumably, P, taken at what appeared to be Disneyland. Guiltily, Martyn slipped the picture into his back pocket, intending to ask Scott about it later. He then shut the book, feeling that he was nosing around in business that wasn't his. P was obviously an ex. Why shouldn't Scott have exes? He was beautiful, young and highly lovable. And why did the fact that he did upset him? Was Martyn Townsend really so insecure that he wanted to find a virginal lover? Someone previously untouched?

'Wanker,' he told himself and started flicking through one of the Amy Tans instead.

He was on page six when Scott's chin suddenly rested on his shoulder. 'Boring book,' he said quietly.

'Have you read it, Mr Critic?'

'Nah. Most of the books are gifts, there for show. I'm Mr Shallow at heart – I want things to display, to say I've got them, but Christ, I never read them.'

'How many of the videos have you watched?'

'Now,' Scott said as he sat on the couch and waved a finger at him crossly, 'you are my mom and I claim my fifty dollars.'

Smiling, Martyn drained his tea and held out the mug, Oliver Twist-style.

Taking the hint, but with a cartoon sigh, Scott got back up and returned to the kitchen.

'Who phones this late, Scotty?'

No reply, and Martyn was about to ask again when Scott emerged.

'Sorry, did you say something? Couldn't hear you over the kettle.'

'I just wondered who was phoning.'

'My brother. Lives in Illinois – forgets he's two hours back from me. Thought it was eleven thirty and wanted to know if I'd seen the game.'

'Game?'

'Yeah, the baseball. Apparently if you live in LA and don't watch the baseball religiously, they throw you into the La Brea pits.'

'And do you?'

'Do I fuck! My bro's a big sports jock – thinks of nothing but baseball, football and basketball. Boring bastard.' Then Scott shrugged. 'Mind you, he's got the biggest, thickest cock I've ever seen. Hangs down to his goddamn knees – well, nearly. He doesn't just shag girls, he bloody spears them!'

Martyn frowned. 'Do I want to know how you know that?'

Scott sat on the couch again, fresh tea held out for Martyn.

'When I was about thirteen, we lived in Poughkeepsie, New York. I could never understand why Dale used to lock his bedroom door all the time, so one day I snuck in ahead of him and hid in his closet. Everyone would have thought I was asleep in bed – all I had on were my briefs because I couldn't bear to sleep in anything else; it was too stifling. Anyhow, I watched and waited and he came to bed later and, sure enough, locked the door. It never occurred to me that I had no chance of getting out and back to my own room, but, when you're thirteen and wondering what your seventeen-year-old brother does behind locked doors, that doesn't really occur to you, right?'

111

'Anyway, there I was, watching through this crack in the door when he just stands in the middle of the room and strips down to his shorts and starts doing push-ups and sit-ups and such like. I don't really remember seeing my brother without clothes on before that – not since I was about six, anyway – and I remember being amazed by his body. Every single muscle was defined, really standing out. Not like Schwarzenegger, but just beautiful. He worked up quite a sweat but I thought this was pretty weird – why lock the door just to work out?

'Then he whipped his shorts off and I saw his cock. I mean, fuck, just dormant it was huge, it really swung between his legs. Then he started jacking it and sat on the bed. His face was going red, but all I could do was watch as this beautiful tool hardened in front of me, growing longer and thicker. It was like some kind of monster growing and it seemed to be taking tons of effort to get it up – no wonder he needed to work out. He lay back, using both hands to pump it harder.

'This was an epiphany for me – previously I kind of thought my dick was just for pissing with. We had that kind of upbringing, which explains why he locked the door. Anyway, now I found I could do the same as him. As I watched him build up to his coming, I tugged my own briefs off and I spewed out jissom all over his neatly folded-up T-shirts and sweatpants. It took him a long time to come. I could see each bead of sweat on his shoulders and arms dripping on to the floor. I could see his face in screwed-up effort as he desperately wanted to come. And I could see his balls, probably huge but in proportion to his cock they looked stupidly tiny, clenched tight in their sac as they prepared to explode.

'He was using long, practised strokes, but never quite reaching the mushrooming cockhead, always stopping short, and I just wanted to yell at him – when I'd just jerked off, even though it was my first time, I knew that taking it to the head had done it for me.

'But luckily I kept quiet and finally realised that he was building up. He went crazy for a few seconds, thrashing on the bed, arching his back and pumping real fast with both hands, but right near the head now, and then he came, a huge jet of come splashing up and raining down on him. I came again on the spot without really trying. God, I remember my balls were aching for hours after – but it was a spectacular feeling.

'He lay there for about five minutes, panting as his cock started to deflate until it was lying flat and lifeless on his stomach, the head resting just below his ribs.

'Then there was a knock on the door and it was Mom – he nearly died of fright. He grabbed his shorts and stuffed his cock right down into them and threw his shirt on, letting it soak up all that gorgeous spunk, and unlocked the door all in about ten seconds. If Mom guessed what was going on, she was very good at ignoring it. I still don't know what she said, but, when she left, he seemed nervous and locked the door again. Then he stripped off and towelled himself down, each muscle buffed to a sweatless sheen, every hair around his navel plucked clean of any stickiness.

'I just watched with my hard-on aching to be played with again as this guy I'd previously only ever thought of as my annoying, slightly bullying elder brother was now like some kind of God of Sex to me. Then I realised he was going to get dressed, and that meant coming to the closet. I buried myself to the back of the thing as far as I could, slipping behind the few collared shirts and good pants and jackets he owned, hoping he'd not pull the doors open and just take what he wanted. Which of course would be the sweatpants and tops I'd just come over. And they were. I closed my eyes – by now my cock was so deflated it might as well have dropped off, I was so frightened – and hoped he'd not see me, never guess how something sticky got on to his clothes. I assumed he didn't because he just threw the ruined ones on the floor and dug out some others. I presumed he'd got dressed and I heard the lock go and the door close.

'I counted to twenty and then made my way out of the closet, my briefs in my hand. And he was standing there, fully dressed, the soiled clothes in his hand, glaring furiously at me.

'It was bad enough that I was naked, my shrivelled thirteen-year-old cock dangling uselessly, my balls clawing their way back inside me in fear, but that look turned me to stone. I just apologised really stupidly and begged him not to tell Mom. I started to cry – I began thinking what I had done was really dirty and evil and I would be punished. Hell, I remember promising never, ever to touch myself ever again.

'And then he threw the clothes at me and told me to get them cleaned and pressed without anyone knowing and we'd never mention it again. Either of us. And you know what? To this day, we never have. But, honestly Marty, even though he's my brother and I've grown up to realise that what my thirteen-year-old eyes saw was not maybe what I'd now call reality, I still think about that cock. It might not be the length of hose I imagined, but, fuck, it was huge. And there have been times when I've mentally taken that cock off him and put it on someone else, wondering what it must be like to have something as big as that up my ass.'

Martyn just shook his head slowly. 'Wow. I never had any brothers or sisters to watch or think about. Not sure I'd want to, either . . .'

'Taught me one thing though, Marty,' continued Scott. 'That moment of panic as Mom knocked on the door, my hard-on was still there. Harder than ever. And as I went through the next few years jacking myself off every night, I'd made sure I did it whenever Mom or my brother or friends were around − the possibility of being discovered was a far bigger thrill than actually coming, you know? I always made sure that I let my wad go just as Mom's hand was on the bedroom door. Or, if I was doing it in the swimming pool or the back yard, I always managed to shoot less than a second before someone would be close enough to see but never actually catch me. That element of danger has remained with me ever since. Have you ever had sex in the open air?'

Martyn nodded. 'Yeah, my first real boyfriend. Richard. I was twenty-one, he was about eighteen or nineteen. Our parents lent me their second car and we went hiking around the Isle of Wight, off the south coast of England. Gorgeous island. We took a tent and pitched it in this field late at night − legitimately, but we thought the owner would find us in the morning and get the field rent off us then. But no. About ten at night we hear him calling out. Trouble is, Richard's got my cock rammed up his arse, shooting everything I had into it. He pulled away before I'd finished, and most of it caught the back of his hair as he jumped forward and stuck his head out of the tent to greet the farmer, and kept him talking long enough for me to scramble into my sleeping bag and feign waking up.

'The next day we made out on top of this cliff, right under what we thought were telephone lines. Jesus! As if BT were going to put phones on top of a cliff! But Richard was beautiful, really angelic-looking. So . . . unblemished, so boyish. He had fair hair, deep-blue eyes and a body that he had no right to own. I mean, if he was twenty-five and had spent years in a gym, it'd be fine. But he had this natural physique ever since we met at school when we were about eleven. A broad chest, with really big, permanently erect nipples surrounded by blond hair that was like gossamer when you stroked it. He had really small hands – it was like a baby grabbing your cock, you know? It felt . . . different to anyone else ever. And, Christ, he knew how to wank me off, really slowly but tightly.

'Well, we were naked, thinking being on top of this cliff we'd be away from prying eyes. God knows how stupid we were – I mean, there's a *cable* up there, people, you know? Needless to say, we were sixty-nining, fingers exploring arses, the whole thing. He was mouth-fucking me and just as he came down my throat, pumping really sweet-tasting spunk into me, I rolled away, screaming at the top of my voice how good it was, and promptly shot my come up and over myself. And stared right up into about ten pairs of eyes as these people on a chair lift were hovering above us, aghast. And they were close enough to measure our dicks – no way could we even pretend one of us was a girl.

'In a rare moment of comedy, Richard rolled on to his back to see why I'd screamed and there we were, two poofs, come all over us, pricks pointing straight up at these horrified people. And the chair lift trundled them away, down to the bottom of the cliffs where they could purchase little tubes of famous multicoloured sand and snowstorms showing the Needles, but with the image of two young boys doing it burnt into their minds for ever. I've never had sex anywhere other than behind closed doors since.'

Scott hugged Martyn suddenly and intensely, and Martyn felt really good. Both of them had hard-ons after discussing all this and Scott nibbled on Martyn's ear. 'Let's go to the *relatively* behind closed doors of my bed and let me see if I can get you to scream like that all over again, yeah?'

Detective O'Malley shook his head at the report that had just been passed through from the labs.

Great – it was a suspected homicide after all, not a suicide. Just what he wanted at one in the morning.

'Do the papers know?'

His sergeant nodded. 'They were on the scene before we were, Lieutenant. The anonymous caller that came through to us must have called them.'

O'Malley shook his head again, as if constant denial would make the case go away. 'Someone wants the world to know about this, then. Any trace on the caller? Because I'll lay odds they're connected to this.'

The sergeant frowned. 'Bit of a jump that, sir?'

'No, Sergeant, just gut instinct from twelve years in the LAPD homicide. When you've been here longer than five months, you can pass judgements on my instincts, but not before, all right?'

'Sir.' Chastised, the sergeant slunk off to get his lieutenant a coffee. The little experience he did possess meant he knew that a one-in-the-morning murder that was going to be in the morning papers before the police had even informed the nearest and dearest required jugs of black, sweet coffee for the lieutenant.

' "Body found",' O'Malley read, ' "at twenty-one thirty-seven at Venice, apparently washed up by the sea." Yeah, right. Probably dumped there . . . blah, blah, blah,' he continued, glancing through the salient points. 'Oh, how typical – died of drowning, but shot up first with enough heroin to kill a horse.' He checked some photos, then the autopsy report from the coroner. 'Typical, not a regular user, no puncture marks bar the new one. Poor kid. Where're you from? Oh great, Sunderland, England. Sergeant?'

'Sir?' came the reply from down the hallway.

'Where's the ID? I've got his address but no name.'

'On my desk, sir. His name was Brian Lawrence.' The sergeant came back with the coffee and placed it on O'Malley's desk along with the Lawrence file. 'Worked at Rainbow Bookstore, a waiter in the coffee house.'

'We looking at a fag, Sergeant?'

'Yes, sir. Came over with another English guy, but he's been back home for a couple of months.'

O'Malley sighed, long and hard. 'Murdered gay boy then, drug-related, probably not a user. Clean-cut, steady job. Yet dead. Dealer? Runner?'

'Could be. You don't think so?'

'No, Sergeant, I don't. This has all the hallmarks of a warning. This Lawrence kid was known to someone and they've ensured that his death gets in the papers tomorrow as a warning. I doubt we'll ever solve this one.' O'Malley closed the file and swigged back his hot coffee in one. 'Time for home, Sergeant. He'll still be a corpse in the morning and maybe someone will do us a favour and come forward.'

'To confess?'

'No, but to explain the connection.'

O'Malley barely gave the sergeant enough time to put his jacket on before he flicked the lights off.

Eleven

Martyn stood in the overlit expanse of Scott's bathroom, checking his face and neck for blemishes, making sure his body was as clean and perfect as it could be. Within reason.

'God, I look rough.' He'd have liked to shave. Hell, he'd have liked liposuction and three job lots of that famous LA plastic surgery, but beggars can't be choosers. 'Make the most what God gave you,' his mum used to say. He doubted that she was referring to the way he considered his own vanity and the effect it would have on screwing someone, but, as she would always say afterwards, 'There's not much you can do if God's made you that way.'

Funny how she never remembered that when he told her he was gay. Mothers are like that, he thought. When you're a kid, they fill you with vacuous sayings and philosophy from the back of cornflakes packets that sounds really meaningful and essential. Then, as you hit adulthood, you realise what a pile of shit it really was – particularly if you're gay.

Then, fuck me, five years later, you start saying the same things to five-year-olds belonging to the neighbours who've asked you to babysit while they go the cinema.

God, how he hated kids. At least the neighbours' ones he could give back, like a borrowed drill or stepladder. 'Thanks, it was fun,' or 'Sorry, I chipped a bit off the knee but I think it'll still work if you tell it you love it.'

He sniffed his armpits. Not too bad – bit of manly sweat, nothing extreme. He stuck his tongue out. Bit furry, but the tea had helped. He breathed on to his palm, then sniffed. That was bearable, too.

He wrapped the robe that Scott had lent him tightly around him, took a deep breath and flicked the light off before going back into the bedroom.

Scott was asleep on top of the duvet.

Bastard!

God, though, he was beautiful. Naked, lying on his side, facing Martyn, breathing shallowly. He had an impish little grin on his face, and looked so peaceful. And his cock had retracted into his groin, and just dangled limply downwards.

Ahh, sweetheart.

Martyn let his robe drop to the floor and gently eased himself on to the bed, noting over Scott's shoulder that it was now 2.30 a.m. He wondered if Scott had set the clock to wake him up for work.

He eased himself on to the duvet – the warm night meant he didn't want to get under it either. He slipped his arm carefully under Scott's neck, and eased his sleeping head on to his own shoulder.

He turned his head and smelt Scott's hair. His whole body had an aroma of coconut – had to be his shampoo or shower gel. Or both. Either way, it was the sweetest, most wonderful smell Martyn could think of. And he decided that he wanted to fall asleep thinking of coconuts and beautiful Californian guys and hard, passion-driven sex and –

'I hope you weren't planning on spending the night sleeping, Townsend.'

Scott pushed himself up from the shoulder and rolled on top of Martyn's naked body, letting the Englishman take all his weight.

'Not originally,' gasped Martyn, but I thought you'd fallen aslee–'

He stopped as Scott kissed him violently but pleasurably full on the mouth, no preamble, no gentle massaging of lips. The tongue was in and thrashing about, the cock was rock-hard and jabbing his stomach, the knees were forcing Martyn's legs apart.

They kissed hard for a minute or two, and Martyn broke free, wiping saliva from his chin. 'Foreplay not in your vocabulary, then?'

Scott just grinned that heart-melting grin, his eyes wide with excitement and pleasure. 'And the last day and a half has been what exactly?' was his only reply and he focused his mouth on the side of Martyn's neck. Martyn felt an impulse to mutter, 'Don't leave a mark,' as some fourteen-year-old might, but what the fuck! Tonight, Scott could chew Martyn's entire body up and spit it out again, and he'd be in heaven.

All his life, Martyn realised, he'd wanted to feel this connected, this relaxed. Hell, this was the first time they were going to have sex, and yet all the usual fears about whether he would be good enough, whether his cock would stay up, whether he would satisfy, whether he was attractive enough – they were all dormant. Martyn knew that Scott was right for him. And he knew, not through ego or arrogance but simple instinct, that Scott thought the same way.

'One thing, sweetheart,' he said, feeling that Scott just might be a vampire sucking most of his lifeblood out through his jugular right now, 'let's make this last the night, OK?'

'You think I'm going to let you sleep?' Scott came up for air, licking his lips. He flicked Martyn's cockhead viciously, sending both pain and exquisite pleasure down the shaft and vibrating through his balls. 'You, hon, ain't gonna be coming for hours yet. I don't care if I have to tie a knot in it, I'm keeping you up and waiting, OK?'

Martyn smiled his agreement. 'By the way, flick me again.'

Scott did so and Martyn squirmed delightedly. 'I like you, Mr Taylor, d'you know that?'

'Feeling's mutual, Mr Prissy Stuck-up English Fuckwit!' Then Scott was on Martyn's right tit, sucking and chewing at the same time.

For the first time, Martyn could see Scott's smooth back, glinting in the light through the window above the bedhead – he didn't possess curtains, presumably another of his exhibitionist traits. On his right shoulder blade was a tattoo – a tiny lizard, like a newt crawling up his back. Ouch – shoulder blade! That must have been a painful hour or so having that done. He traced the outline of the lizard, and got a sensual moan out of Scott for his effort, and his tit was chewed on a bit harder.

Martyn looked down the back, at the buttocks, clenched and compact, not an ounce of fat on them. Tiny fine hair was caught in the moonlight, curving down towards the concealed arse crack that Martyn just knew he needed to explore later. In great detail. With each slight movement of Scott's body, Martyn could see more flesh, more unexplored square inches of his body that Martyn wanted to stroke, to touch. To make love to.

Not have sex with, but make love to.

Oh fuck, it was a bit early to be thinking that.

He wriggled slightly, and Scott shifted his attention to Martyn's other nipple, sending fresh spasms of delight running from his head, via his heart and straight to his cock, which fought valiantly against the pressure from Scott's body to stand upright.

Martyn slowly dragged the tip of his finger around the back of Scott's ears, then ran his hands through his blond mop, feeling it fall through his fingers, each gentle stroke setting off passion alarms throughout his body.

Scott began dragging his tongue down the centre of Martyn's ribs, around his navel and to the star of his pubic hair, letting his chin, slight stubble bristling there, brush the tip of Martyn's cock, and getting smothered in pre-come for its trouble.

Scott dragged his stubble around the cockhead, and Martyn lay back and let his body shake in anticipation. A gentle brush of Scott's lips where the foreskin was attached to the head was his reward before Scott moved down to his thighs. Freed from its weight prison, Martyn's cock twitched furiously with each passing of Scott's breath over his skin. He let his legs widen, offering Scott the opportunity to go further under his balls, towards his own crack if he wanted to, but Scott ignored this, concentrating more of his vampiric sucking on Martyn's calf.

Then suddenly he reared up and dropped down beside Martyn, burying his face into his armpit, sniffing and snorting like a love-struck warthog, tickling Martyn, but he was determined not to let

Scott know this. Instead, he tugged Scott over so he now lay on his back, leaving Martyn free to begin exploring his friend's tits with his teeth this time.

'Chew,' he heard Scott mutter – so he did, violently, and Scott was moaning with excitement. Scott's chest was almost hairless – just a slight fuzz in the dip between his pecs – but Martyn licked the little hair there was flat against his smooth, babylike skin. He then returned to the pronounced nipples, feeling the tough flesh tugged through the slight gap in his front teeth.

Trails of pre-come were being spread across his hip as Scott moved every so often, his rock-hard cock slapping against Martyn. Martyn slid down the body, taking the cock into his mouth in one fluid movement.

'No,' breathed Scott, 'not yet . . .' But Martyn ignored him, taking it as far down his throat as he could, then let it drag out again, brushing his teeth against the solid flesh. Before the head could escape, Martyn swallowed it again, bringing a fresh series of sighs and gasps from Scott, moving his mouth up and down along the shaft, without ever letting the cock escape entirely. He flicked his tongue around the head, discovering its complete shape in the semidarkness, imagining what it would look like in the morning light, and knowing that he would still adore it, still want it as badly as he did now.

Still, he finally let it go and moved to Scott's balls, matting the hair back with his tongue before swallowing one bollock, then the other, letting them move themselves within his mouth, reacting to the new environment, a part of Scott's body exploring him as much as he was learning about it.

He slid a finger under the balls, towards that beautiful arse he'd watched moments earlier. Scott was clenched tight, but, as Martyn's finger made its first furtive enquiries of the hole, he felt everything relax, a welcome mat for his invasion. He began massaging his hole, feeling the normally tight muscles there relax and soften, enabling entry for his finger. Martyn eased his finger in gently, while still rolling Scott's balls around in his mouth. Then he used his tongue to lever them out, and they reacted with the sudden rush of cool air, causing his arse to tighten again, his finger well inside, massaging his prostate, causing Scott to convulse pleasurably, his cock twitching angrily, anxious to erupt spunk everywhere, but refused the additional physical stimulation it required.

Something flew through the air, bouncing off Martyn's forehead. It was a condom.

'Now?'

'Now,' Scott confirmed. 'And I mean now!'

Martyn tore the package open and eased the rubber around his own cock, feeling a bit strange to be touching it after touching Scott's.

'How?'

'Hard and aggressive' was Scott's unhelpful, although quite enticing, reply.

Martyn grabbed at Scott's legs, dragging them on to his shoulders and straightening up. Scott arched his back, lifting his arse slightly, and grabbed either side of the bed, and Martyn let his excited cockhead touch Scott's hole, baiting himself as much as Scot.

'Fuck me, Marty. Fuck me. Now!'

And Martyn stabbed in, hard and sure, pushing and pushing, unrelentingly, feeling Scott's initially unyielding tunnel open and accept its new inhabitant.

The wall of flesh felt good and warm and tight against his cock and he finally stopped when his balls slammed against Scott's arse. The American had spread himself as wide as he could – almost looking as if he might tear apart any second – but the expression on his face was serene, almost rapturous, and Martyn began pumping, drawing himself in and out slowly, slowly getting used to the feel of being inside the most beautiful man on earth. With each stroke in either direction, the ball of pre-come gathering on the eye of Scott's cock grew larger as more and more began squeezing its way out and Martyn wanted to break off, to reach over and flick it away on the end of his tongue, feeling that light, saltiness wash around his mouth.

But instead he kept pumping, going faster and faster, slamming against Scott, who in turn thumped against the pillows and wall, crying out in pleasure at the movement, begging Martyn to go faster, harder and deeper. All three were impossible – but he tried nevertheless. If he could have found a way to get his entire body inside Scott at that point, he would have.

Scott was holding on to one side the bed, flailing about and slapping the other side, crying out louder and louder.

When Martyn came, it was with more force, more energy and, frankly, more juice than ever before. It poured out of him like a running tap, caught by the rubber but, he imagined, in danger of spilling out of it. But Scott didn't seem to care. 'Keep fucking me,' he yelled. 'Keep fucking my ass!'

Christ, if the neighbours heard . . . Oh, of course, Scott would *want* the neighbours to hear. Part of his exhibitionism.

Spent and aching, Martyn disobeyed Scott's orders and wrenched his engorged cock out of his arse savagely, causing Scott another screech of agony/ecstasy. And just as Martyn thought it was time to relax slightly, Scott sat upright, grabbed his head and shoved his mouth roughly on to his cock. Martyn barely had time to breathe as Scott threw his groin upward, stabbing into Martyn's throat, exploding come inside Martyn's mouth – huge wads of it splashing down his throat. He didn't need to swallow – it just shot down there like water down a pipe. Thank God it didn't go the wrong way and choke him to death.

After what seemed like ten minutes but was only about twenty-five seconds, Scott went limp, his whole body slamming back on to the bed in exhaustion and delight, his prick pulling out of Martyn's mouth, leaving a trail of come connecting the cockhead and Martyn's throat. Martyn slurped it in, then reached down and replaced the cockhead in his mouth, sucking hard and draining every last drop of warm liquid from the eye.

He sat up, breathing out. His heart was racing, his cock still draped in come-enveloping latex, but all he could focus on was that he wanted to do it again.

'Well,' Scott said between deep breaths, 'that was great.' He casually reached forward, his hand wrapped in tissues, and eased the condom off Martyn's prick, throwing the whole package over the end of the bedroom, where it landed with a soft plop somewhere on the coffee table downstairs. 'Sorry it was a bit quicker than we planned,' he breathed, 'but, fuck, that was marvellous.'

'Next time,' said Martyn, scooping Scott's limp body up into a bear hug, 'bagsie I get fucked first!'

'Deal,' said Scott, who then kissed him.

Martyn knew he tasted of spunk but Scott didn't give a toss, his tongue thrashing about in Martyn's throat as energetically as ever. Gently, Scott eased Martyn down on to the bed and, wrapped in each other's body, sweat and lust, they drifted into a deep, exhausted and happy sleep.

The arrival of morning was announced by the smell of fresh Kenyan coffee wafting into Martyn's nostrils.

He rolled over and it took a minute for him to remember whose green-striped duvet he was sleeping under. And alone.

Dimly he could hear Scott downstairs talking. On the phone. He crawled out of the bed and scooped up the spare robe from where he'd discarded it late last night. Wrapping it around himself, he went down the steps into the main room.

Scott had his back to him, and was listening to someone on the telephone while crouching in the open doorway to his apartment, stroking what must have been one of Mr Terrell's cats.

The fresh, clear air gave Martyn goosebumps, but that wasn't the only thing. Scott was stark-bollock-naked, displaying everything he had to the outside world.

Martyn wasn't sure what shocked him more – Scott doing this or the fact that Martyn was jealous. He wanted to slam the door shut, scream at Scott, 'That cock is for my eyes only from now on, OK?'

Oh, hell, what a way to start the day. Angry at the supreme exhibitionist. Ah, sod it – he wasn't going to stay here for ever, and it was best to live a bit.

Martyn let the robe drop and, equally naked, walked behind Scott, who was still talking, and rested his cock and balls on his shoulder.

Let the world see. Who cared anyway?

He ruffled Scott's hair, but the young man jerked away and stood up, waving Martyn away. Not unkindly, but enough to suggest he didn't want the caller to know what was happening.

The cat scampered off and Scott eased the door shut, mouthing 'bastard' at Martyn, but smiling.

Grinning likewise, Martyn again wrapped himself in the robe and draped himself on the couch, picking up the TV remote and flicking channels, keeping the sound muted. Loads of traffic snarl-ups, a report on the Governor's recent trip to Hawaii, a couple of local murders and a store hold-up.

One of the murder reports seemed to feature a grumpy-looking police lieutenant down at Venice Beach, but Martyn lost interest in that. Tragically, murders seemed to occur with alarming frequency in LA.

'Paper?' he mouthed to Scott, but the blond shook his head, his cock swinging beautifully in time.

Having got Scott's attention in between his 'Yeah, OK' and 'All right, I'll do that' and 'Yes, I've seen to that', Martyn flashed his own cock at Scott, waving it at him alluringly.

Scott pretended to vomit and finished his call. After hanging up, he nipped into the kitchenette and returned with two black coffees, placing them on the table and switching off the TV.

'I do the exhibitions round here, smart ass, not you.'

Martyn cupped Scott's balls in his hands. 'Yes, O masterful one. Whatever you say, O God of Fucks.'

Scott sat astride him, both their cocks growing hard but neither bothering to do anything about it. Scott just tweaked Martyn's left nipple and for the first time Martyn noticed a raised scar just under Scott's right armpit, going about tree inches down.

'That looks nasty. What happened?'

Scott paused before answering. 'D'you want to know about my exes yet?'

Martyn nodded. 'Why not?' He remembered P. P. Dooken.

Scott touched his scar. 'For about five weeks I went out with an older guy I met at Revolver. He seemed nice – he was more of an exhibitionist than me, if you can believe it. He used to collect knives – big fuckers, all wholly illegal. He was mixed up with some dodgy people and I got a bit frightened of some of them. One day, he turned on me, cut me up, said he was marking me as his property.'

'Christ.'

'Yeah, well, I fled. Never saw him again, although I gather he moved to the city a couple of months later. But I still have his "brand". I feel like a bloody cow sometimes.'

Martyn pointed to a photo showing Scott and a dark-haired young guy laughing by a waterfall. The same guy as on the Disneyland photo he was too ashamed to admit he'd stolen last night. 'That him?'

'No,' said Scott quietly. 'No, that's my most recent ex, Peter Dooken.'

Yes, P.

'Ah. Of the credit-card fame.'

'Sorry?'

Martyn explained what he'd seen in Dive!, but didn't mentioned the inscribed book.

Scott shrugged. 'That's been bugging you all night, hasn't it? Why didn't you just ask? Peter's history.'

'Bad break-up?'

'Sort of. Peter was more trouble. He was into drugs – big time. Nasty people were always trying to get him and it began to spill over into my life. I broke it off and threw him out. He went back to Holland, I assume. Or maybe London, I don't know. I don't really care. I'm glad to see the back of him.'

Suddenly it clicked into place. 'The guys at the club – they were those "nasty people", right?'

Scott settled properly on the couch, hugging a cushion, looking Martyn straight in the eyes. And Martyn wanted nothing more then than to hold him, for ever, and tell him everything would be all right now. Instead, he listened.

'Peter was smuggling all sorts in and out, I think. Especially bad crack. I think he did a bum deal. Those guys still want him and wanted to get his address out of me. If I knew it, believe me, I'd tell them. But I don't – he was a shit and he's out of my life. They aren't convinced.'

Martyn told Scott about the events yesterday at the Italian restaurant, and Scott's mouth dropped open in horror.

'Fucking hell, I'm really sorry, Marty. Oh God, I'm so sorry you got caught up in this.' He angrily threw the cushion away. 'That bastard Dooken still has his claws in everything. Even you!'

Martyn offered his hands and this time Scott took them, allowing himself to be lowered on to Martyn, and he hugged him. 'No big deal, Scotty.'

'Yes it is. God knows why they want to involve you. How they know you, even.'

'The big black guy? He saw me at La Diva. Knew I'd rescued you. But I think I satisfied him that I knew nothing else.'

Scott looked at Martyn, tears in his eyes. 'I'm so sorry,' he muttered and then savagely kissed Martyn, full on.

As if to work out all the anger, fear and frustration that Peter had put him through, Scott became sexually aggressive and Martyn let him. There was no foreplay this time, not even really any emotion. It was simple frustration and Scott was letting it out in the way he knew best.

Martyn barely even registered the build-up – or that Scott had miraculously produced a condom and hurriedly unrolled it down his prick – until Scott rolled him on to his front and, with his hardened, angry cock, penetrated him in one powerful thrust, pumping again and again.

Martyn wasn't really into mechanical sex, especially after the beauty of the previous night's romp, but he was surprisingly turned on by the silent abuse his arse was taking. He enjoyed the powerful strokes. He could feel the contours of Scott's cock, from the wide base up the slimming trunk and then the mushroomed head, as it pushed and squirmed inside his guts. He liked the fact that he wasn't put off by Scott's sudden need for domination, for soundless, unromantic fucking. It was unusual for Martyn not to be in charge of sex, or at least to be perfectly equal. Yet right now, in the sweat and pent-up angst of Scott's relentless buggery, he was really getting off on being truely servile.

He felt Scott come inside him, conjuring up an image of jets of angry jissom entrapped in latex, wanting to escape into the freedom of his body, as bitter and twisted as the man who had so feverishly produced it.

And he came himself, drenching the robe he was lying on, feeling his own wet sex seeping into his navel and spreading into his pubes, trickling into the crack between his groin and thighs.

Roughly, he was rolled on to his back again.

'Sorry,' Scott said quietly, but Martyn didn't want an apology. He just wanted to be turned on like this again, to be abused.

But only by Scott. Only by this gorgeous, perfectly sculptured young man. 'I thought that was terrific,' he said simply.

Then he reached forward and grabbed the base of Scott's proud shaft, peeling back the condom and then holding it in his hand, tipping it up and squeezing it, sending the captured sperm cascading down on to his own cock, mingling with his own juice. He wrung it out, turned it inside out and smeared the last few patches into his pubic hair, running it around his balls, under his legs. Then he dropped the condom into his cooling coffee.

Scott's eyes were alight, incredulous but seemingly enjoying the bizarre spectacle. He lay down on Martyn, squishing the come between them, running his hand in Martyn's pubes, making sure he got as sticky as his partner.

Martyn kissed Scott then, but this time gently and charmingly, wanting this to be as much of a contrast to the previous moments of fevered lovemaking. Scott reacted equally tenderly, and together they massaged each other's body, stroking, touching, moulding flesh and muscle, never a hint of physical pressure, just tender feeling and gentle manipulation.

'I called in to work,' Scott said as he licked Martyn's earlobe. 'I don't have to be in until two this afternoon. Do you want to stay here and fuck or go out and spend some time together?'

Martyn said he didn't mind – but it depended on whether or not Scott wanted him to come back that night.

'Tonight, tomorrow and every night until you go home.'

'And then?'

'And then, my beautiful boy,' said Scott, 'we'll face that bridge together.'

'Let's go out then,' said Martyn, caressing Scott's pecs. 'Let's just have a laugh and not give a damn about anyone or anything else.'

'OK,' Scott said, 'but we need to shower, eat and dress. Oh, and one other thing.'

'What's that?'

'Hon, I want you inside me again. Like last night. Before we move from this couch, I want to feel you hard and strong inside my body.'

Martyn grinned and took a deep breath as Scott began rolling a condom on to his inflating shaft once more.

Twelve

'You need a holiday.'
     'I've just had a holiday. I've just had eight months in California. How much more of a holiday do I need?'

Andy Hepworth shrugged and placed a large mug of tea in front of Peter, stepping over the disarrayed bags to get to his seat opposite.

Between them, Andy's wooden occasional table was scattered with photos, brochures and other memories of his friend's excursion. 'That wasn't a holiday, Peter. That was a trauma. You and Scott. Trouble. No relaxation.'

Peter let himself sink further back into the comforting surroundings of the vast sofa. One of those three-k jobs from some smart shop up Tottenham Court Road that no one normally dared actually sit on in case they damaged it. Not that Andy gave a toss — he had enough money not to. If the sofa got damaged, get another one.

Peter imagined the sofa was his mum, twenty years ago. Huge, all-encompassing comfort, where he could burrow into the folds of her skirts or jumpers and feel secure and safe.

Andy had been lovely — he'd given Peter a few weeks to get his head together and a place to sleep. A small but nice little back room in which Andy and his boyfriend stored their books and videos. So long as Peter could cope with the fear that one night the shelves would fall off the wall and burying him for ever under a complete run of *Star Trek* (all the films and various TV series), *Doctor Who* and *Babylon 5*, everything would be cool. Actually, Peter suspected that every third *Star Trek* video was really hardcore Euro porn but didn't feel he could bring himself to look. Hell, if anyone saw him with a crap science-fiction video . . . oh, the shame!

Andy slid a copy of *Boyz* over. 'Look, love, it's August. It's party time. My friend is renting a villa in Ibiza during the danceclub season. There's only him and his boyfriend going – he's got three spare rooms and buckets of cash to spend. Let me sort it out for you, eh?'

Peter didn't know what to do. It sounded great. But he didn't want to feel indebted to Andy.

'I know what you're thinking,' Andy said suddenly. 'I'm chucking money around, saying, "Ooh, look, I'm loaded", but I'm not. I'm just acknowledging that I can, you can't, and I'd be happier if you were more relaxed. Leave your stuff here, get on a plane and get some sun, sea and sex in a nice place with nice people. You've been before – you know your way around.'

Peter gave in. He always did with Andy. Once, they'd shagged – a brief fling when Andy and Jon were going through a few problems. Frankly Andy had been lousy in bed – selfish, cold and precise, but nevertheless they liked each other and remained friends. Jon, as one of Peter's best friends, had also been pleased because it meant he and Andy had someone in common when they eventually banged their heads together and sorted out their differences. Andy was about fifteen years older than Jon (and Peter and most of their other friends) – he'd been a city lawyer or something and made enough money to be able to go freelance. He did so for about two years, making enough to buy this huge house in Blackheath overlooking the parkland and two hundred paces from the best Indian restaurant in London. Now he was 'retired' – he lived a life of leisure, doing charity work (he was a major mover in Lighthouse) and keeping Jon in sad videos, plastic toys and cheap books. Jon, of course, was in seventh heaven – he worked in a bookshop in Greenwich and earned enough to buy cat food, but, with Andy to rely on, he didn't care. Jon and Andy, despite this slightly unequal financial situation, were more in love than ever before and Peter felt jealousy.

That's what he thought life with Scott would have been like.

Except for one major obstacle . . .

'So, what do you say? Shall I call Stevie and tell him to air one of the villa's guest rooms?'

Peter nodded dumbly. 'I'd like that, Andy. Thank you.'

Andy stood up. That's sorted then. 'You go for a wander around the block, get some air, and some dinner for both of us, and I'll make some calls.'

Moments later, Peter was out in the late-afternoon sun, on one of those rare English days when it actually looked like a picture postcard from the fifties – blue sky, bright sun, people laughing and smiling and a slight shimmer on the horizon.

He walked over the road and on to the Heath itself, staring over at the small church at the centre. To the right was the village, no more than a large circle of shops, with a road going around it. The road forked twice – one fork taking cars towards the South Circular, either for Greenwich or the Blackwall Tunnel, the other going in the opposite direction, down past the circle of shops and off towards Blackheath station and Eltham. That road was also lined with shops and estate agents and Peter decided that looked a better bet for lunch. He walked down towards the fork, past the Indian, past a very good pizza place, and stopped outside a pub with a wood fascia. He remembered this from his last jaunt to southeast London – a friendly place, not too smoky, and divided into little sections. Weaving around was a bit like getting lost in a maze, but all roads led to the bar and it was, as usual, packed with students from Goldsmiths, the college over on Lewisham Way.

Today, as he went in, it was quite empty – the evening rush hadn't started, and so it was mostly locals. Blackheath didn't really offer much in the way of a class system for those who lived there – you were either stinking rich or you lived in Charlton. Therefore, most of those in the pub tended to look like they were on the committee for the Women's Institute or would have been happier messing around on a yacht near Cowes. But the beer was always good and he had ninety minutes or so before the shops packed up for the day.

He ordered a pint of bitter (his first since returning from the country of warm lager and bottled dog pee) and sat down in an alcove near the window, watching the outside world go by.

'You all right?' said a female voice in his ear. Distracted, Peter glanced up at a young woman in a white blouse and dark skirt, cleaning out the ashtray.

'Yeah, fine,' he replied. 'Been a while since I was here. I'd forgotten how nice it is.'

'Goldsmiths?'

Peter must have looked very confused, so she added, 'I thought maybe you used to be a student there. We get a lot of business from the students.'

Peter shook his head. 'No, I've friends who live across the way. It's just been a while since I visited them. I like it here. This pub, I mean.'

'Good,' she said simply, smiled again and wandered away.

Peter watched as two guys got out of a car they'd parked opposite the pub and ran over to the building on the nearest corner – an estate agent. They were pointing at various properties, the blonder one of the two scribbling notes down on a pad he had clearly brought along for the purpose. They knew what they were doing; they knew what they wanted.

They had about them that mysterious 'thing' that gay men have that enables other gay men to spot them. It's not a campness, or a walk, or a flounce or any of the things straight people immediately look for. No, with this pair, it was a subtler form of body language. The way they enthused about their task without any concern about who was watching. The way that, when they did look at each other, they held the gaze a second or two longer than two straight guys would.

It was in the way they carried themselves.

One of the men, the darker one, was wearing a tight red polo shirt and dark-blue jeans. Huge arm muscles stretched out of his sleeves, his bum firm and small, and a waist slim without being skinny. His fingers as he pointed were firm and direct – he was assured and calm. The blonder guy was a few inches shorter, clearly the more precise of the two, perhaps a bit anal. He wrote everything down, it seemed. He was in a dark jacket, so Peter couldn't see his shape, but he was nimble – he kept darting back to one particular picture, like a bird on a food table, pecking away at a favoured piece of bread, but trying to get a morsel of all the other bits, just to be sure his was the best after all.

The estate-agency door opened and a power-dressed woman with neatly cropped hair and owlish spectacles emerged and offered them her hand, then waved them in. She gave a furtive glance behind, as if checking that no one had noticed she was doing business with faggots.

Stupid bitch, she's blown the whole deal. The guys would spot her anxiety now and their enthusiasm would probably dampen and they'd go to another agency – one that didn't mind if a gay couple encroached into Blackheath's hallowed territory.

Peter wanted to be in a couple. He wanted to go to estate agents and choose a flat or a house. He wanted to have a partner, someone to trust, to care about. Someone to love and be loved by.

He thought again about Scott. How close he had come to persuading Scott to come back with him, get a job and find a future with him. But no, that was gone for ever now. Scott has his agenda, Peter had his, and they couldn't find enough common ground upon which to compromise.

With a sigh, Peter drained his pint.

Obviously the sigh had been louder than he intended, as the barmaid wandered over with a tray. 'That sounds like a man in need of another drink.'

He laughed. 'No, but I will. Just a half, please.'

She nodded and headed off to the bar.

Just the half, then over to get dinner and back to Andy and Jon's place.

The drink was brought over and he paid.

'Penny for them?' she said brightly.

'You got a few spare hours, then?' It came out ruder than he intended, but she didn't seem to mind.

'A minute or two, at least.'

Where to begin. 'Well, I've just come back from Los Angeles, where I met the man of my dreams, I suppose.'

'Ah. It didn't work out?'

He laughed, humourlessly. 'You could say that. We met in a bookshop, in Burbank.'

Peter remembered his first sight of Scott. Small. Blond. Compact. A toothy grin that seemed to reflect light. They had both been rummaging through books in Barnes & Noble, behind the shopping mall.

Peter's attention had been drawn away from the local-history book he was flicking through as, looking straight at him, over the top of the shelves, was Scott. He was in the fiction section, and their eyes just met in that way they do in bad postwar movies starring Trevor Howard and Celia Johnson or Alec Guinness and Sylvia Syms.

Scott had then walked away, two novels in his hand, and Peter had watched him move to the cash registers on the right-hand side of the store. He walked like Jesus must have walked on water, with a perfect fluidity, almost as if he wasn't touching the floor but was suspended a few centimetres above it. His body exuded sex, without being blatant or seductive. He covered the relatively short distance, aware that Peter was still watching, but with a confidence that actually dared Peter to turn away, knowing he wouldn't.

Normally Peter avoided cockiness, but Scott's wasn't borne out of arrogance, just instinct.

Having bought his books, Scott crossed back across the shop to the coffee area and ordered a drink and then sat down.

Was he waiting for Peter? Had Peter misread the situation? Hell, did he want to know someone who so evidently understood is attractiveness and knew how to flaunt it?

When Peter spotted the discarded carrier bag, with three CDs in it, just where Scott had been standing, he made his choice. He picked the bag up, slotted his unbought book back into its shelf and walked straight over to Scott.

'I think you left this behind,' he said. 'Deliberately.'

Scott stared at him for a moment, seeming to read his face as if there was print all over it saying 'Yes, Dutch Boy Seeks Cute All-

American Hunk For Fun, Games, A Future Or, If Nothing Else, A Damned Good Ramming'. Then he offered the seat next to him. 'Then I thank you for falling into my evil trap and you are now the slave to my every whim and will buy me three more mocha chocolates before we leave.'

Peter said he doubted this very much and said Scott owed him a double-creamed latte.

Scott acknowledged that this was the case and agreed to a compromise – he gave Peter ten dollars and told him to buy the drinks.

They left the shop an hour later, both buzzing from the caffeine of four coffees, and went shopping in the mall. Scott wanted some special climbing boots and they headed to a big sports store, but, after trying a dozen pairs on, they left without buying a thing.

'You didn't want climbing boots at all, did you?'

Scott just shrugged. 'Not much gets past you, does it, Mr Windmill.'

They had agreed to meet again the following day and see the sights.

Scott had arrived early, catching Peter in the shower. The phone in his hotel room had buzzed angrily and, sopping wet, Peter had answered it. 'Morning, Tulip Man, I'm in reception.'

'I'm in the shower,' Peter had snapped back. 'I'll be ten minutes. Oh, and I want breakfast before we go anywhere, OK?'

He had gone back to finish his shower rather annoyed that Scott had interrupted his routine.

He was just soaping his legs and groin when he heard a strange noise and looked out through the shower curtain.

Scott was sitting on the closed lid of the toilet, naked, his cock up and rigid, his clothes on the floor.

'Consider me breakfast,' he said simply and then joined Peter in the shower.

Astonished, all Peter could say was 'How . . .?'

'Fifty dollars and a lot of charm works wonders on a concierge who thinks I'm picking up my cousin from Holland whom I haven't seen for eight years.' And with that he kissed Peter on the lips. Instinctively, Peter's mouth parted and took in the tongue, pulling the beautiful American towards him, his own cock solid and now pushing against the newcomer.

Scott eased away from him and picked up the soap from the dish, lathering up his own body and then turning his attention back to Peter, turning him around and washing his buttocks and the small of his back. 'I know how difficult it is to reach these . . . awkward little places.' He let his finger massage copious amounts of soap around the top of Peter's legs, around the perineum and up behind his balls. Then he drew his hand back again and his finger moved towards Peter's arse. He started gently, fingering Peter's hole and the Dutchman sighed loudly. 'Do you normally do this after just one date?'

As an answer, Scott inserted not one but two fingers into Peter's soft flesh, lubricated by the soap, pressing against the wall of his arse, gently easing himself in.

Peter reached back, taking Scott's other hand and firmly placing it on his cock, and Scott began slow but powerful strokes, from base to tip of the shaft, and Peter relaxed completely.

He leant back a bit, letting Scott take most of his weight. 'You know,' he said between deep breaths as he was slowly being brought to climax, 'I don't normally go for sex first thing, but I can't possibly tell if you really like me unless you get inside me.'

'Oh,' said Scott. 'Oh, I'd hate to give you any false impressions.' And he withdrew his fingers, slowly, without breaking his stride as he jacked Peter off. A moment later, Peter winced as he felt the head of Scott's prick on the edge of his tunnel.

'Now?'

'Now.'

With the sleight of hand of a stage magician, Scott reached through the curtain to his jeans and produced a rubber, which soon sheathed his eager cock.

'Now,' he repeated and eased his way in, Peter doing his best to offer no resistance. 'I love being fucked standing up,' he said.

'It's not easy,' was Scott's reply, 'but incredibly satisfying.' He stopped manipulating Peter's cock, needing both hands to hold Peter's slippery skin as he pushed his way inside. Then Peter leant right forward, his hands pressed against the tap wall, unable to spread his legs any wider than the bath, but at least giving Scott full range to go all the way.

For about a minute, they stood there, Scott fully inside him, Peter staring straight down at the floor of the bath, the blood rushing to his head as he tried to imagine what it must look like to see yourself being fucked. Oh for a mirror within arm's reach that he could demist and use to watch the action. Instead he just had to imagine. 'Well, go on, fuck me,' he snapped, rather aggressively.

And Scott did, powerful movements sending his hardness further and further into Peter with each shove.

Peter threw his head back and shook it, scattering water everywhere, like a dog trying to dry itself after falling in a pond.

'Hey,' moaned Scott.

So Peter did it again. And again.

'Right, fucking stops now!' Scott announced playfully and started to withdraw.

'Hold on a mo, Scotty,' Peter said, 'I want to try something.' Very carefully and gingerly, he started to turn himself round, reaching up to grip the top of the shower rail with one hand, telling Scott to keep pushing in all the time.

Scott helped lift his leg over his head and rest it on his shoulder, so that Peter could then grip the soap tray embedded at eye level in the opposite wall, and bring his other leg on to Scott's other shoulder.

Still joined, they now faced each other, Peter's weight taken entirely by the shower, the tray and Scott's shoulders.

'Now fuck me properly.'

And Scott did, harder than ever, his balls slapping hard against Peter's cheeks with every thrust until, with a small yell, he came, panting hard as he did so and slowly eased himself out. He then lowered Peter's feet to the base of the bath and, before Peter could say anything, took his cock in his mouth. Peter stood there, water raining on his back, imagining it was some exotic waterfall on a jungle-infested island, while the beautiful local guy was bringing him to climax without a care in the world. He was about to come, but desperately didn't want to – didn't want this moment to end – ever. All Peter could focus on was the pleasure racing through his body, brought on entirely by the gentle but confident motions up and down his prick being made by Scott. With a gasp, he let it all go, a waterfall of his own cascading down Scott's throat, releasing all the tension in his balls, and bringing with it a euphoric tremor of happiness.

He eased Scott off him and pulled the young man upright, and they kissed under the spray. After a few moments, in complete silence, they lathered each other again and then washed the soap off, cleaning each other, intimately where necessary. Scott, Peter noticed, had discarded the condom with the same dexterity he had employed to produce it.

Moments later, they lay naked on Peter's bed, letting the Californian morning dry them off.

'I called in to work,' Scott said as he licked Peter's ear. 'I don't have to be in until two this afternoon. Do you want to stay here and fuck again or should we go out and spend some time together?'

Peter had said he didn't mind – but it depended on whether or not Scott wanted to come back that night.

'There's always my place,' he replied.

'It's a bit quick for that,' said Peter. 'Call me an old-fashioned type, but I like to fuck on the first date, *then* take it slowly!'

'Fine by me, Mr Clogs.'

Peter hugged him, smelling the cleanliness of his neck, watching his chest rise and fall as he breathed, those lovely nipples, that tiny scar by his armpit.'

'How did you get that?' he had asked, but Scott had gone quiet, and just said it was a boyhood accident. 'My brother used to knock me around a bit and one day it got out of control. He was a drop-out and our mom died when we were very, very young – truth is, I don't remember her – so my dad had to bring us up. We moved to a farm in Winona, but it soon went under and Dad couldn't cope. My brother was a complete shit-for-brains and got in with some bikers and drank a lot. He attacked me with a knife when I told him I was gay. I had to tell someone, but he turned nasty so I fled. I came here when I was about fifteen and worked in bars and things, lying about my age. Now I work at Universal Studios.'

Peter didn't know what to say, but he could sense Scott was on the verge of tears. He was a sucker for stray dogs and injured kittens and Scott brought out that need to protect, the desire to look out for the vulnerable. He hugged Scott tighter and asked how often he wanted them to see each other.

'Tonight, tomorrow and every night until you go home.'

'And then?'

'And then, my beautiful creature,' said Scott, 'we'll face that bridge together.'

And Peter had thought that was the rarest and most romantic thing he'd ever heard.

Of course, he didn't tell the attentive barmaid all of it, and missed out most of the salient details in what he did say, but she got the gist.

'What happened?'

Peter watched as the two gay men emerged from the estate agent and moved about ten paces before they spoke, shook their heads and got back into their car. He watched until they pulled up outside another, and started again.

'What happened? Reality jumped up and sucker-punched me right in the bollocks.' He drained his drink, thanked the barmaid for listening and headed for the door. 'And now I'm back in the real world, for better or worse. Still, that's life.'

And with a cheerless wave, he left the pub and headed for the grocery store near Blackheath railway station.

Thirteen

The sun was microwaving Martyn's skin, he felt sure. God knew how much damage it was doing, irradiating his flesh, giving birth to a trillion melanomas all over his exposed body.

Still, right now he didn't care. He was lying on his front, while Scott massaged various oils and protective creams into his back and shoulders, regardless of the looks being given by the seated denizens and lunchtime joggers of Beverly Hills Park. A couple of rangers gave the two a filthy look but didn't approach them.

Martyn watched them wander away. 'Bit visible, aren't they? I didn't know this was a crime-ridden area,' he said.

'Ah,' Scott said as he moved away from Martyn's back and began smothering his own bare chest, 'this is the Will Rogers Memorial Park. Home to the rich and famous, and one of their favourite haunts.'

'Come again?'

'George Michael,' Scott said, by way of all the explanation needed.

'Oh, really? Where was that, then?' He sat up, and Scott pointed to some restrooms nestling to one side of the park. 'Bit primitive, isn't it? I mean, this is California of 1998?'

Scott shook his head. 'No, *outside* these bits of shrubbery is California 1998. In here it's Beverly Hills, 1958. I remember someone in the papers pointing out that you don't see the police arresting all the het couples humping each other senseless on Mulholland – but then they're probably at that themselves, so they wouldn't.'

'Didn't they say George Michael only found it on the Internet or something?'

'Dunno. It's listed on one of those cruising sites, but so are hundreds of places. Mind you, as a result of the publicity it's become a bigger game now.'

Martyn frowned. 'You what?'

'Well, now all the local cruising queens head down here for a fuck in between the ranger patrols. It's just become a dangerous game – who can get the longest fuck before a ranger patrol or undercover cop turns up. Whole groups take turns in playing lookout while others get on with it. I once saw eight people have a fairly lengthy orgie in the toilets once before a ranger came into sight. Everyone was dressed and out by the time they got within hollering range.' Scott indicated with his head. 'Guy on the seat over there, paper and sandwich box, right?'

'Uh-huh?'

'Undercover squad. Bit of a shithead actually, as I've seen two sets of guys get behind him and go the long way round, and they're probably nursing raw but satisfied asses right now.' Scott suddenly started to get up. 'Fancy a go?'

'What? Here? In a toilet?'

'Think of the risk, the danger. Oh, where's your sense of fun?'

'I left it at my place, along with my passport and other documents I'll need to produce before they expel me from your wonderful and tolerant country.' Martyn settled down again. 'No thanks.'

'Suit yourself – I'm going to see what action is going on.'

'You can't,' pleaded Martyn. 'Your undercover cop will see everything. We've not exactly blended into the background here already.'

Scott just grinned evilly. 'I'll get rid of him. Then it'll take a good twenty minutes before they can find a replacement. Watch.'

Before Martyn could stop him, Scott was up and off, walking

straight towards what he claimed was an undercover vice cop. Jesus! If it wasn't, this could be even more embarrassing.

'Hey, you, Mr Vice Squad Man, you're not fooling anyone you know. No one reads their paper that much and doesn't eat their sandwiches,' Scott shouted at the top of his voice.

Lots of people turned to look, and the man started protesting his innocence, so Scott grabbed the lunchbox, tugged it open and displayed a two-way radio. He then turned to two little old ladies – undoubtedly the Beverly Hills Recreation and Parks Department's preferred choice of customer – and said, 'Hell, he might have been listening in on everything even you said!'

With an exaggerated bow to the ladies, he turned away and walked back towards Martyn, winking. 'Told you.'

Martyn looked up and saw the cop depart rather rapidly and with very little dignity, and one of the old ladies glowered at his departing back.

'Give it three minutes while the ranger gets out of sight, and let's go.'

'I'm not sure . . .'

Scott sighed. 'And I bet you loved Mom's apple pie when you were a kid and did all your homework before dinner.'

Then he got up and wandered off.

Martyn flopped back on to the grass and closed his eyes. Watching other men cop off wasn't his idea of fun.

He'd lain there, humming songs from a Garbage CD to himself, when he realised Scott had been gone a while now. Shit, surely he hadn't got himself arrested that quickly.

With a deep sigh, Martyn got up, tugged his T-shirt from his jeans' belt and went in the direction of the famous restrooms, noting that the two old ladies had vacated their seat.

The first thing that he noticed about the public toilets in Beverly Hills was that they smelt sweet and clean. None of that urine and antiseptic smell most public toilets reeked of.

A little uneasily, he ventured in – no one was there and just one cubicle had its door shut.

He was about to leave when he heard someone coming in and so he dashed into the second cubicle and locked the door, his heart beating. Why was he acting like a scared rabbit?

He made the pretence of using the toilet and after a minute or two, flushed it, unlocked the door, deliberately leaving it wide open to prove he was alone, and exited to wash his hands.

Facing him was the big black guy in the mirror shades, his two white accomplices with him.

The other cubicle was now empty, the door open too.

'Sex is banned in these toilets,' said the skinnier of the two white guys.

'Yeah, to stop you poofs breeding,' added the other.

The black guy sighed and Martyn was sure that, behind those impenetrable glasses, he had to be rolling his eyes at his friends' stupidity.

'He's not here,' Martyn said simply, adding rather truthfully, 'Actually I don't know where he is right now.'

The black guy nodded. 'Then pass on a message. By lunchtime today or there'll be some bad days and nights ahead for him.'

Another man walked in to use the cubicle and the stupider of the white guys put a hand up to suggest he leave.

But the black man slapped the hand down and led them out.

Martyn stood there shaking and then let himself drift back to the cubicle door for support as he thought his legs were going to give way.

'Trouble?' asked the new man, cheerfully relieving himself.

Martyn didn't reply – he just went back into the cubicle and threw up in the bowl. When he finished, he went back out to clean himself up and then fled the restroom as quickly as possible, searching for Scott, part angry that he'd been left to deal with these thugs again, part wanting the comfort of Scott's presence.

But there was no sign of Scott by the bundle of clothing and oils he had abandoned.

A ranger walked over. She was about eighteen stone and wobbled alarmingly – Martyn thought that, in the event of a crime being committed, beyond actually rolling on the perpetrator, there was going to be bugger all she could do except puff and pant at them. And here he thought all Californians were obsessed with the body beautiful. How nice to see that wasn't true.

'Problem, sir?'

Martyn shook his head. 'No, my friend wandered off about ten minutes ago and I can't find him.'

The ranger raised an eyebrow and started to look towards the restroom.

'No,' Martyn said firmly, 'tried that. Not there. Bad luck.'

Without a reply, she walked away, her huge arse swinging from side to side, and it crossed Martyn's mind to wonder how they found a uniform to fit her.

Admonishing himself for such politically incorrect thoughts, Martyn gathered their stuff up into Scott's abandoned duffel bag and began to walk about, looking for visual clues.

About five minutes later, he spotted an enclosed area. It looked like somewhere old people in England played bowls – but did they do that in America?

Whatever was going on in the zone, it was unlikely to be bowls – Scott was kneeling down, staring intently through the hedges.

Martyn tapped his friend on the shoulder, but Scott waved him down, as if he'd been waiting.

Indeed, 'Took your time' was the hissed greeting.

'Oh, well, thanks for the easy clues,' Martyn said almost angrily without actually meaning it. 'We need to talk. Urgently.' It was about time he mentioned his latest visit from the black guy in the shades.

But Scott made him peer through the bushes.

It was a grass tennis court and Martyn realised it wasn't part of the gardens at all, but was connected to a huge powder-blue house next door – the hedge was laced with chicken wire to stop anyone getting through.

But Scott's attention had been caught because there were two adorable guys playing. Both were white, tanned and slim but with taut musculature. The most astonishing thing was that they were playing naked, believing themselves to be secreted from prying eyes – but they hadn't reckoned with Scott's unnerving ability to seek cock.

And what cocks they were, swinging about with every serve, both long and thick, uncut and heavily veined. The most notable thing was that both guys were totally shaved – no hair on their chests, armpits, balls or groin. Both had heads of dark hair, one long, one crew-cut, but that was their only concession to follicular activity. The one with the crew cut, who was nearer to the hedge, also had a tattoo on the underside of his cock – they noticed it only when it was his service and he reached back, swinging his tackle in the air.

'That must have hurt,' Martyn muttered.

'Yeah. I mean, I thought having mine hurt, but it must have been a picnic compared to that!'

The two friends watched as the players served and smashed expertly. This was no practice game: these two were playing for something major. The tattooed-prick man lost his service and, with a cry of 'Game, set and match', the long-haired guy punched the air in delight.

The tattooed man shrugged and placed his racket on the grass, picking up a towel to dry the sweat off. Slowly, almost deliberately, he mopped down his body except his crotch – leaving that to last. Then he threw the towel to his approaching friend, who then used it on himself, again leaving his hairless balls and prick sweaty.

'OK, now?'

The tattooed guy suddenly held his hand up. 'No,' he said. 'Change the deal. I want to bring something else into play.'

'No deal,' laughed the long-haired guy. 'You lost fair and square.'

'I think we could both be winners, Mitch, actually.'

Mitch frowned. 'What is it, Carlos?'

Carlos turned and looked into the hedge. 'Spies, my friend. Two sweet, untouched little spies.'

Martyn stood up and prepared to go, but, when he looked round Scott was standing up and smiling at Mitch and Carlos!

'Scott . . .?'

'Come round,' Carlos shouted: '3267.'

Scott grabbed Martyn's hand and dragged him towards the edge of the park, almost running.

'Hold on . . .' Martyn had a sudden memory of a song he'd been thinking about earlier 'This is not my idea of a good time,' chanted the Garbage singer in his mind.

Nevertheless, Scott was about to hammer on the white front

147

door of the big blue house and Martyn shook his head. 'I'm in bloody toytown,' he decided.

The front door was opened by Carlos, hiding his nakedness behind the wood, and Scott sauntered in.

'Coming?' asked Carlos of Martyn.

With a sigh, Martyn entered.

The hallway was vast, everything he expected of a house in Beverly Hills – more Gloria Swanson than Jason Priestly – and he had a sudden flash that he probably wasn't far from the house where Mickey had said Madonna lived.

Oh God, they were chatting up two hunks a stone's throw from his heroine's back window.

The hall was decorated in mahogany everywhere, and a plushly carpeted staircase went up the right-hand side, across and further up the left. Five or six doors led off to various rooms, all wood-panelled and classy-looking. The whole place reeked of decadent millionaires.

'Do you play tennis?' Carlos broke Martyn's concentration.

Scott shook his head, and Carlos looked enquiringly at Martyn. 'Oh, sure. Like all Englishmen, for two weeks a year when Wimbledon is on, we rent an hour on a clay court and feverishly hope we can be spotted as the new Tim Henman. But, for the other fifty weeks, not a touch of a racket.'

'Good,' said Mitch. A silk kimono was wrapped around him as he emerged from the kitchen, a jug of orange juice and some glasses held on a tray.

Scott took one and drank it in one go. 'Nice place. Lived here long?'

Carlos nodded. 'I inherited it. Mitch has been here, what, eight years now?'

Mitch nodded. 'Nearly nine.'

'So, why were you watching us?' asked Carlos.

Martyn started to say, rather feebly he had to admit, 'We like tennis . . .' when Scott interrupted.

'I liked your cocks. Especially the tattoo.'

Martyn wanted to die. They knew nothing about these two – it could be Dennis Nilsen's American cousin and his psycho partner.

148

'Right answer,' said Mitch, still naked. He lifted his long cock up and showed Scott the image. It was a devil's pitchfork. Martyn winced at the Freudian imagery that inspired.

'Want to play with us?' Mitch drained his own drink. 'Doubles. You two versus us two.'

'And the prize?' asked Scott.

'Well,' Carlos said, 'we had agreed that the loser gets fucked for the next month. I think we can adapt that ruling. We win, we fuck you. You win, you fuck us. OK?'

Martyn felt like asking why they didn't just fuck him and Scott now and save all that energy and sweat. Then he remembered the towelling off, the crotch left sweating. These two probably got off on exercise-induced sweat.

'You're on,' Scott said.

Martyn opened his mouth to protest, realised it was a waste of time and decided to go with the flow. He was going to get fucked again – knowing his luck, by the pitchfork. 'Thanks, Scotty,' he muttered.

Mitch shook Scott's hand. 'Scott and . . .?'

'Marty,' said Scott. 'My boyfriend.'

Martyn's shock at that statement must have been very obvious. He actually took a slight step back.

'Does Marty know that?' laughed Carlos, but, before either could answer, he pointed at their clothes. And ordered them to strip.

Scott needed no second command; Martyn was slightly more hesitant, but then complied.

'One other thing, guys,' said Mitch. And he produced a razor from his kimono pocket, letting the robe drop to the floor.

Scott's face was alight with excitement at the prospect; Martyn was appalled.

Carlos led them into a room behind the staircase – a gym. A table-tennis table was set up along one side, but no net.

Scott jumped on that, lay flat and winked at Martyn. Mitch sprayed shaving foam on to his balls and stomach and armpits and began shaving. Scott stayed very still, even when Mitch lifted up his already swelling cock. Martyn was astonished at how little wincing or grimacing Scott did. He was either brave or insane. He was coming around to thinking the latter.

After a few moments, Mitch told Scott to roll over and then smeared his arse crack with foam, shaving the whole of his arse. He then pointed to a far door and said, 'There's a shower in there.' Obediently, Scott scampered off and it was Martyn's turn.

He lay down, biting the inside of his lip. Mitch was very good, though, and very relaxing. Martyn's cock stayed remarkably flaccid as the older man lifted it, cupped his balls and scratched the razor around him. It itched every so often but on the whole didn't hurt. Mitch did his armpits next and even the few stray hairs that protruded around Martyn's nipples.

'Bum?'

Mitch nodded, so Martyn rolled over and the deed was done. He followed Scott into the shower and found his friend standing there, dripping wet but with the foam washed away.

Without a word Martyn showered, came out and buffed himself dry with a towel, wishing he could stop the stinging that had started on his balls and above his dick.

'You look like a nine-year-old,' Scott said, but Martyn didn't reply. 'Oh c'mon, Marty, it's just a bit of fun.'

'You're supposed to be at work in an hour, Scott Taylor.'

Scott's mood suddenly changed. 'Oh fuck you, "Mom". I want to have some fun. OK, we're gonna lose and get fucked by these two. So what? Anyway, let's play to win – that might be fun.'

Martyn didn't reply, just went back out into the gym, followed by Scott.

Carlos approached, something behind his back, and then grinned. 'Smile, boys.'

Scott evidently thought he was going to take a photo, because he struck a camp pose.

Instead Carlos produced a bottle of aftershave and splashed some from a presoaked wad of cotton wool on to his balls and groin.

Martyn wanted to hear Scott yelp in pain but didn't have a chance as Mitch did the same to him.

It stung like nothing had ever stung before. 'Stops the sweat giving you a rash on your naked little dicks.' As if that excused the pain!

They then followed their hosts on to the tennis court, Mitch giving them rackets.

And the bizarrely uneven game of doubles started.

Martyn and Scott were simply dreadful, barely able to get a volley going, but Martyn did find it quite liberating to try, stretching his body, feeling his cock and balls flying fast and loose, unrestricted and airy.

It took only fifteen minutes for them to be one set and another five games down.

'Match point,' Carlos yelled and performed a superb ace that left Martyn speechless.

And then it was as if a switch had been turned – both Carlos's and Mitch's cocks swelled and rose, both jutting straight forward, veins pushing their way through the shaft, their balls tightening in preparation.

Martyn watched as Carlos's foreskin just peeled back and a huge mushroom cockhead in various shades of purple burst out. Mitch needed to give his tighter skin an extra hand – his cock was far slimmer and less bulbous than Carlos's, but probably longer.

'You're mine,' Carlos said to Martyn, who just watched as Scott eagerly let himself be led away.

They were escorted upstairs into a massive double bedroom. The centrepiece was a huge round bed, covered with a white fur blanket, which Mitch tugged off. The walls, ceiling and back of the door were covered by hundreds of different shards of mirrored glass and Martyn wanted to laugh. It was a collage of glass, each reflecting at a slightly different angle, making their naked bodies seem weirdly angled or, in some cases, missing bits if the glass was embedded in the wall at a different angle from its neighbour.

Mitch crossed to an ornate, lacquered Chinese chest of draws, bringing out two extra-large lube tubes and a pack of condoms. He passed a condom and tube to Carlos and silently applied one to his own cock, rolling the latex down his shaft very, very slowly, as if just the feel of that was enough to turn him on.

'What, no foreplay?' asked Scott. 'Not even a blow job?'

Carlos began adding wads of lube to Martyn's freshly groomed arse and his own engorged cock.

'Lie face down,' he said, pointing to the bed.

Martyn sighed and did as told. Before he'd even settled, Carlos was above him on all fours and then he was there, that purple mushroom head, pushing at Martyn's stinging arse. Carlos gave no quarter, no hint of tenderness. Martyn knew he was about to be buggered rather than fucked – there was no emotion, not even a feeling of anticipation. Carlos might just as well have been jacking himself off for all the intimacy he was getting. Martyn's guts were just somewhere for Carlos's cock to rest while he pumped it.

And pump it he did, furiously. Martyn thought he was going to be pushed through the bed and on to the floor until Carlos wrapped his hands (Martyn only then noticed just how big they were – he could get both his hands into one of Carlos's) around his waist, heaved his buttocks up and started buggering him really, really fast.

Martyn didn't know where Scott was until he thought to use the mirrored walls and realised his friend was over by the door, pushed up against a glass wall, being similarly fucked very fast and very aggressively. The image of Scott's face rebounded off every surface in the room, and, for the first time, Martyn could see a look of something other than cocky self-gratification on him. He wasn't frightened or hurt, just . . . surprised. Scott wasn't in control of himself, or his body. And that was probably very unusual.

There was a sudden feeling of euphoria then, as Carlos yanked his cock out of Martyn's arse without any warning. But, before Martyn could think or move, Mitch's cock took its place and a startled cry from Scott told him that he was now with Carlos. This was working like some kind of well-oiled machine – Carlos and Mitch did this a lot, that was clear.

Mitch's cock was far less painful than Carlos's, and he used it far more seductively. Slow, hard penetration as opposed to constant ramming, and, for the first time, Martyn's cock began to respond to the stimulation – Mitch was by far the better worker. Martyn watched in the glass as Mitch slid in and out calmly, watching the latex glisten as it withdrew and then preparing himself for the re-entry. He focused on that, making himself think only about the glistening rubber rather than the cock inside it, imagining himself in the same position, working Scott's arse as he had last night.

Then, as abruptly as he'd started, Mitch too stopped, withdrew and stepped back.

'Which of you two wants to screw the other?' he asked.

Scott spoke first. 'Let Marty take me.'

Scott was led over to the bed and made to crouch rather than lie down. Carlos slid a condom on to Martyn's cock, stroking his balls as he did so – but, nope, still Carlos didn't do anything for him.

Martyn stared at Scott's shaven, reddened arsehole. Last night, he couldn't wait for it. Last night it had been a treasure trove of pleasure. Now it was just a hole he was being ordered to fill.

No. Concentrate on the fact that it's Scott. Ignore the other two guys.

He pushed his way in, Scott's tunnel giving easily because it hadn't recovered from the savage pummelling Carlos and his thick prick had given it. Martyn stood behind the bed, Scott crouching on it. Were the others just going to watch? Take pictures?

His answer came by way of Mitch, who eased his ankles apart, spreading his legs and then quickly entering him again, this time pumping vigorously in time with Martyn's fucking of Scott. Like cogs in a machine, Mitch went deeper into Martyn and he in turn went deeper into Scott.

Martyn wondered what Carlos was going to do until he knelt on the bed, facing Scott, slipped his condom off and began fucking Scott's mouth – the final piece of the mechanism.

Mesmerised, Martyn felt the whole thing turning into a bizarre dream – Mitch into him, he into Scott, Carlos into Scott. And Scott?

Taking it silently.

But his shoulders – those beautiful, smooth and sweet-smelling shoulders he had rubbed last night, admiring the lizard etched into his shoulder blade – were tense. Scott was angry, furious and humiliated all in one. He was taking this out sexually, a repeat of what he had done to Martyn that morning on the couch. Martyn watched in the mirror, not thinking about either his or Mitch's movements, just thinking about how much he wanted to get Scott away from these two weirdos and safely into his arms. Maybe this would teach Scott a lesson – teach him not to live quite so close to the edge.

Scott was eagerly sucking on Carlos's huge cock, twisting his head from side to side like a dog with a bone. Carlos was enjoying the savage jerking off he was getting, pumping furiously whenever Scott stopped moving enough.

Mitch pulled out suddenly and Martyn's attention was drawn back to the mirrored wall: the guy was peeling the rubber off his thin cock – and just in time. It twitched suddenly and spat copious amounts of white liquid over Martyn's back, again and again, making Martyn shiver slightly.

Then it was Carlos's turn. He pulled out of Scott's sore mouth, convulsed, and rained down his come on to Scott's sweating back.

Freed, Scott pulled away from Martyn's cock and rolled on to the bed, jerking himself off and instantly spraying upward, drenching Carlos's hairless balls and wiping the come off his back all over the pristine sheets.

Freed from his duty at both ends, Martyn too pulled his condom off and wanked hard until he came, splattering down on Scott's taut stomach.

Panting and exhausted, Martyn flopped down into his new lover's arms and the two hugged each other, finding solace in their own company, trying to forget the two strangers. As their breathing became more regular, Martyn lifted his head and disentangled himself from Scott's sticky body. Carlos and Mitch were standing by the chest of drawers, snogging passionately.

'This is too weird,' he said quietly.

Mitch opened a drawer, and Martyn hoped he wasn't getting fresh condoms out – he knew he hadn't the strength to do any more and thought Scott would have a seizure if he tried.

Instead, Mitch was carrying a tiny plastic bag, the white, powdered contents of which he emptied on to the top of the chest of drawers.

Carlos took a drinking straw from the drawer and started snorting the coke. Mitch did likewise.

'Anyone else?'

Martyn had never touched drugs in his life, and had no intention of starting now. He was about to refuse on both their behalfs, when he saw the look in Scott's eyes.

Hunger.

His pain, anguish and anger had gone, replaced by a startling expression of appeasement.

OK, so maybe Scott used drugs. Big deal. But the look was more than that – like someone was waving a million-dollar cheque in front of him.

He was across the room, taking a snort, before Martyn could say a word.

He wasn't angry at Scott, or upset. Yet he found himself walking out of the room, down the stairs and back to the gym, where he showered. He soaped the come off his back, and rinsed his arse with the jet spray. Normally, it felt good. Now it just felt necessary. He had to wash Carlos and Mitch right out of his body.

When he had finished, he dried himself and retrieved his scattered clothes where they'd been discarded earlier on the gym floor.

He picked up Scott's stuff and carried it back upstairs, going back into the room.

But Scott wasn't there.

Carlos and Mitch were on the bed, Carlos fucking Mitch's arse harder and faster than he had either Scott or Martyn – high on coke, and feeling powerful and excitable. Mitch was spraying his seed everywhere as Carlos pumped him – both men were ignorant of Martyn's presence. He simply didn't exist for them while they were in this state. The empty drugs bag was on the chest of drawers, every grain gone.

'Let's go, please,' said Scott from behind. He was naked, shaking and looking ill. His cock had withered to a tiny little lump of skin. He looked hunched and pathetic. Martyn wanted to hug him and protect him, but just handed him his clothes. Scott had obviously found an upstairs bathroom and showered, but his skin was still glistening from the damp. He took the proffered clothes and silently dressed, still shivering. Cold or the coke, Martyn didn't know. Maybe Scott wasn't used to coke after all. Maybe this was the effect it had on someone the first time. Either way, he wanted to go, and said so.

Scott nodded dumbly and they started to go downstairs. 'Shit,' Scott said suddenly, 'my watch must still be up there.'

He dashed back up the stairs and returned a minute or two later, proudly brandishing it. 'OK, I want to go now.'

They didn't bother closing the door behind them – let someone break into the house and rob the two sick guys.

'Please,' said Martyn after a few moments walking back to Scott's car. 'Please don't let's ever do anything like that again.'

Scott just nodded. 'Sorry – I didn't think it'd get like that.' He seemed to be recovering quickly now, his skin getting back its colour.

'I'll drive,' Martyn said, but Scott refused.

'I didn't touch the coke, Marty, honest. I just let them think I did, knowing they'd get higher quicker that way and we could escape.'

'You were shivering . . .'

'I was fucking in shock, you asshole!' Scott screamed loudly. 'I'd just been virtually raped by those two bastards, forced to have sex with you and God knows what else could have happened under the influence of drugs. Jesus Christ, Marty, give me a break!'

Martyn took a step away from the car, and breathed deeply. 'Finished?'

Scott glared angrily at him, then threw the keys over to him and walked around to the passenger side. He then grabbed Martyn tightly, burying his face in his shoulder, and burst into tears, saying he was sorry, and how he'd been so frightened and he never wanted to lose control again.

Martyn held him fast, that old feeling of need and mothering flooding into him. 'I'm not going to let you go either, Scotty. Ever.'

He eased Scott into the car and walked around, and a moment later they pulled away.

'Where to?' Martyn asked.

Scott glanced at his watch, wiping his eyes. 'I need to be at

work in forty-five minutes. I want to go somewhere else first.'
They continued up Sunset and along to the 101, which they
crossed, and into Griffith Park.

Scott directed Martyn to park outside the Observatory. 'I want
to show you something.' He seemed completely calmed down
now and was clearly getting back to his old self as, not caring who
was looking, he happily took Martyn's hand as they walked, and
then hugged his arm, leaning his head on Martyn's shoulder,
gripping his hand tighter.

They walked around the Observatory. It was a massive, white-
domed structure, built on the very edge of a jutting piece of cliff
side. To the right were the famous Hollywood Hills, the giant
white letters looking a bit battered but still impressive. This was
the nearest you could get to the sign these days, and Martyn was
pleased to have finally seen it. Below them, the ground dropped
away into grass and prickly bushes.

'Look, there's a chipmunk,' Scott said as something furry and
striped scampered through the long grasses. 'You don't have those
in England, do you?'

Martyn said they didn't. 'Nor raccoons, unless you believe Walt
Disney.'

Scott led the way through the arches of the front of the
Observatory, where they stood alone on the balcony, and Martyn
gasped at the view.

Los Angeles is a bowl, a city surrounded on three sides by
mountains, the fourth, the Pacific. And, from the Observatory
platform, Martyn could see everything. To the left, streets and
houses stretched away like tiny villages built from matchboxes.
Cars were just minute moving blobs. Straight ahead, the day was
clear enough to see out to Long Beach, and the Palos Verdes
Peninsula. Straight ahead, planes could be seen like tiny seagulls
taking off from LAX over the water, where the runways ended
rather suddenly for Martyn's comfort! And, to the right, LA
stretched away until it became one with the Santa Monica
Mountains or disappeared along the Pacific Highway towards
Malibu and ultimately Santa Barbara.

Los Angeles was not pretty, attractive or colourful. It lacked
any real historical importance or culturally significant buildings

and, from street level, could be a harsh, angry city, not particularly cleaner or dirtier than anywhere else but always living, always breathing. And just a bit edgy.

But, from up at the Observatory, it looked peaceful and beautiful, a panoramic view of humanity's achievements during the twentieth century.

Martyn felt good about the city and found he was hugging Scott tighter.

'I thought you'd like this,' he said simply, and Martyn just nodded.

He looked deeply into Scott's eyes and, for the first time, thought Scott was revealing himself, his true self, in the expression that stared back.

They let themselves kiss, deeply and passionately, regardless of the swarming crowds that might encounter them, and separated only after four or five minutes.

'Take me to work,' Scott said simply, 'then you can have the car for the rest of the day.'

'Ohh . . .' Martyn feigned the voice of a small child. 'Take me to Universal.'

'You wanna see where I work?'

'Sure I do.'

Grinning excitedly, Scott led him back to the car, taking the keys and driving himself.

They took Barnham Boulevard back towards the Universal complex, and Scott parked in the employees' car lot.

He waved at a couple of people and they walked in past all the crowds milling about trying to buy tickets.

'Hey, Taylor, you bastard, you're late.' The speaker was a tall guy, about forty with a huge grin and bright eyes.

'Martyn, this is Grant Austen, my boss. Boss, this is my friend from London, England.'

Martyn and Austen shook hands, and Austen gave Martyn a plastic card. 'It's a pass – gets you on all the rides while Scotty here actually does a bit of work.'

Martyn thanked him and he and Scott walked past the shops and into the main area. To the right was the Universal Studios Tours bus lot. To the left, a long flight of steps led to a bridge.

'*Jurassic Park*'s thataway,' Scott said simply. 'Miss it and regret it for the rest of your life.'

They were on the bridge by now. Behind them was the magnificent view of the San Fernando Valley, reaching from Burbank right around to Northridge. The good weather was again allowing excellent visibility.

'I gotta go and work, lover,' Scott said.

Martyn nodded and cupped Scott's face in his hand, kissing him on the lips, but avoiding tongue work this time.

Scott pulled back from the kiss, grinning.

'I'm going to lose my job for sure, Marty. Thanks for that.'

Martyn shrugged. 'Come home with me. Leave all this behind. Forget all the trouble that Peter caused you, his drugs and everything.'

'You are joking. Aren't you?'

Martyn shook his head, realising how deeply he felt. 'No, sweetheart. No, come with me. My God, I can't believe I'm saying this, but I love you. I really, really love you.' He took a deep breath and carried on. 'Fuck, I used the L word.' He gripped Scott's shoulders even tighter, ignoring the looks of the people nearby, some tutting, some watching in quiet amusement. Two guys clapped. This inspired Martyn further.

'Yeah, I love you very, very much indeed. Come home with me. Give it a go.'

Martyn looked at the gathering crowd. In the distance, other Universal Studios workers were walking towards them, including Grant Austen.

Scott was smiling brightly at Martyn. A smile brighter than anything Martyn could imagine ever seeing anywhere else, and it lifted his heart even higher.

Scott nodded. 'OK. Why not? Guess you know what this means, Marty.'

'What?'

Scott stroked his hand. 'I love you too.'

Martyn closed his eyes and leant down to kiss Scott's neck, not giving a damn about anyone else.

There was a noise that made him stop and open his eyes. It was like a car backfiring, and everyone jumped at the suddenness of it. Then there was a second, identical sound.

Except they were a hell of a long way from either the car parks or the main road.

Simultaneously, Martyn was aware of what must have been a wasp or hornet buzzing past his ear.

'What the hell was that?' Martyn asked, looking around.

But Scott didn't answer.

Instead Scott slumped against the man he had just confessed his love for.

Instead Scott twisted jerkily, his back against Martyn's chest, his hands reaching blindly forward to nothing.

Instead Scott just gasped something incoherent.

Instead Scott dropped on to the concrete ground.

Instead, Scott said nothing.

And someone screamed.

And so did someone else.

And it took what seemed like an eternity but could have been only two seconds before Martyn understood what they were screaming at.

Scott was jerking spasmodically on the ground, blood gushing out of two huge wounds, one in the neck, the other right in his chest.

'Oh God . . . Oh God . . .' Martyn started shaking, wondering what to do. 'No . . .' he muttered, 'Nononono . . .'

Grant Austen had his mobile out, punching up 911.

The two other workers rushed over. So did a couple more.

Martyn was scrabbling around, covering the blood with his hands, willing it to go back inside. As he desperately tried to hold the wounds together, he could do nothing to stop the blood pouring out of Scott, soaking into Martyn's trousers and T-shirt.

Flooding the concrete.

'No,' he kept saying, 'No, no, no . . . I don't know what to do . . .'

He wanted to force his hands into the wounds, to stem the flow of blood . . . To do something. Anything.

But he couldn't. He couldn't do a thing. He was crying in fear and frustration.

More people were there, all trying to help. All in the way. All saying calming things. All saying pointless, idiotic things. No one was stopping the bleeding. No one was sealing the skin in his neck or chest.

No one was saving Scott.

'Marty . . . I really love you . . .'

Blood was gathering around Scott's mouth as he forced the words out, forced himself to speak.

And Martyn knew as Scott shivered once more that he was gone.

For ever.

But still Scott didn't stop bleeding.

And still Martyn didn't stop crying.

Fourteen

For Lieutenant O'Malley, it had been a tiring day – and it was only 8 a.m.

It had begun yesterday afternoon, with a reported shooting at the Universal Studios amusement park.

A single, white man, aged twenty-two, had been shot twice and died before the ambulance arrived. No one saw who did it, no one knew why and all his officers could glean from the witnesses and the staff was that the victim worked there, and was extremely popular. He was a fag, however – his 'friend' was with him when he died. He was brought to the precinct still somewhat hysterical, although the MO had cleared him for interview.

O'Malley had been on the force long enough to be suspicious about everything. No one deliberately shoots dead a young man, gay or otherwise, who has a spotless service record, is incredibly popular and has no criminal record.

Therefore, there had to be something wrong somewhere.

The coroner had already confirmed that the assassin was nearby, and the shots very accurate – which virtually ruled out accidental death. This was premeditated.

The shaken young Englishman hadn't been much help – until one of O'Malley's sergeants had abruptly pointed out that he was as much a suspect as anyone else. While not remotely true, it did sober him up enough to be interviewed.

After providing his relevant details, the English guy, a Martyn Townsend, claimed to have known the victim, Scott Taylor of Valley Village, just about forty-eight hours. They had met when Taylor had been pursued by some rather overly dramatic-sounding thugs who, Townsend believed, were somehow connected with Taylor's previous boyfriend, a Dutch guy called Peter Dooken, who, Townsend believed, was caught up in some kind of multinational drugs cartel.

O'Malley was similarly experienced enough to cut away the BS to get to the truth. This Dooken guy was probably some small-time crackhead who had screwed up a deal and had some unpleasant characters on his tail who, as he had left the country, had turned their attentions to the last person Dooken had contact with, this poor Scott Taylor.

O'Malley had wondered if the three pursuers had demanded money from Taylor, but Townsend had no idea, it seemed. He related two incidents where he alone encountered them, both of which required him to warn Taylor that they were around, rather than making demands. A typical war of nerves, presumably attempting to frighten the Taylor boy into helping.

O'Malley had already been to Taylor's apartment and gone over it, while his juniors talked to the neighbours, all of whom liked Taylor, especially some middle-aged guy who seemed to rely on Taylor to buy him cat food.

The apartment hadn't revealed very much, except that Taylor was a typical gay man in his early twenties – loads of magazines and videos scattered around, a few photographs of Taylor with other guys, couples or in groups.

One of his officers found a small bag of cocaine in the bathroom – barely enough for personal use, let alone worth being hounded by these mysterious dealers that Martyn Townsend claimed were after him. Hell, it wasn't enough to warrant an arrest if he'd been found in possession. He told the officer to flush it away – it would only create additional paperwork if they took it back to the precinct.

They gave up shortly afterwards, telling the nosy, but genuinely shocked, cat-owning neighbour opposite that, if anyone was seen going into the apartment, he should report it immediately. The neighbour looked the type who would keep a vigilant eye on things – although O'Malley was less amused to see one of his officers returning from the local shop with three cans of cat food.

They made a return visit to the scene of the crime – the public having long gone by now.

The man who met them was called Austen – he was Scott Taylor's boss. He explained that Scott had taken the morning off – no doubt to spend time with his new boyfriend, the poor young Brit. Nice guy, such a horrible thing to witness. No, Taylor didn't make a habit of bringing his personal life into work. No, Austen couldn't remember ever having seen Taylor with another boy-friend, although he knew from conversations that there had been one or two. Drugs? No, Scott Taylor was not the sort of person to go near drugs. Very anti-them, in fact.

OK, O'Malley wondered to himself, I'm getting two sides of the same coin. Hates drugs. Possesses coke. Sweet lovely guy who buys his neighbour cat food and is rarely late for work. Gunned down in broad daylight for no apparent reason.

Too many contradictions.

After leaving Universal, O'Malley headed back to the precinct and had another interview with Townsend, who had calmed down remarkably.

'How long do I have to stay here?' he'd asked.

'You're free to go whenever you want, Mr Townsend. But I would ask you to stay around for a while because we want to try to clear this up.'

Townsend had nodded and agreed. 'Nothing else to do.' He had twiddled with a pencil he was carrying. 'Anyway, he was buying dinner,' he laughed humourlessly. 'Fuck, I can't believe this.'

O'Malley suddenly had a brainwave. He collected a file from his desk and placed it in front of Townsend.

'Mr Townsend, can I ask you something that might seem irrelevant? Please open the file and tell me if you recognise the young man there.'

Frowning, Townsend did as asked. O'Malley knew from his reaction that he indeed recognised the smiling booth photo of the

guy whose heroin-shot-up body they'd dragged from Venice
Beach the day before.

'Brian,' he said simply. 'From back home. Oh God, what was
his surname?' He clicked his fingers furiously, finding something
else to focus on and be angry about. Working out his grief with
that typical lack of sentiment Brits were apparently famous for.

Poor kid.

'Lawrence. Brian Lawrence. I met him yesterday morning at a
café. He worked somewhere on Santa Monica Boulevard. Sorry,
I don't know the name. Why?'

'He's dead,' O'Malley said simply, wanting to gauge Townsend's reaction.

Townsend let the photo drop and looked straight into
O'Malley's eyes. 'It's me, isn't it?'

'I'm sorry?'

'It's me. Everyone I've met is dying around me. What happened to him?'

'He was found in the sea. He'd been pumped full of heroin but
actually drowned. We don't think he was a user.'

'I don't understand.'

'We've seen this sort of thing before, Mr Townsend. Usually
it's a warning – to tell people who know the victims that there's
trouble about.'

'But why me?'

'I don't think it was you. For some reason, these people that
Peter Dooken upset decided to deal with his "contacts" if you
like. You say they'd been threatening your friend Scott Taylor.
Then they came to you. Maybe they used Lawrence to frighten
you, so you'd exert influence over Taylor so he'd get back in
contact with Dooken. I'm sorry to put this to you, but maybe
Scott Taylor only told you enough to keep you quiet. There may
have been far more about Dooken's business deals that he was too
frightened to talk about to you yet. Did he know you had been
approached by your three mysterious men?'

Townsend shrugged. 'I told him about the restaurant toilet –
that's when he told me about that Dooken bastard. But no, I
never told him about the Memorial Park incident. It never came
up, although I was going to, certainly.'

O'Malley nodded. 'I think they got tired of verbal warnings and wanted to scare Taylor even more.'

And then O'Malley could see that it struck Martyn Townsend as it had struck him earlier. But, no matter how much O'Malley needed his job done, deliberately upsetting witnesses was pointless. He knew Townsend would see it himself eventually and it was far better to let him reach these conclusions without too much prompting.

'You think . . .' Townsend spoke slowly, averting his eyes and looking back at the closed Lawrence file. 'You think it really was me. I mean, you think they intended to shoot and kill me this afternoon, not Scotty?' His voice was breaking, partly, O'Malley surmised, because he was recalling Taylor's death and partly because it had dawned on him that he may have been the intended victim.

O'Malley could see he was working it out, his darting eyes, his frown, the way he licked his lips. It seemed to be falling into place as Townsend replayed the scene.

'I bent down fractionally. I kissed Scott's neck as they fired. Oh my God . . . they wanted to kill *me*. Then he'd finally tell them where Peter was.' He frowned. 'But I didn't know about Brian Lawrence being dead. How was that supposed to get me to bring pressure on Scott?'

O'Malley shrugged. 'I won't ask what you've been doing all day but it has been in the papers and on all the TV shows since this morning.'

'Oh my God . . . you were on the beach . . . I watched it but with the sound off . . . I remember . . .'

O'Malley could see he was remembering other things about this morning, and decided to not pry any further.

'Go back to your hotel or apartment or whatever, Mr Townsend. I'll get someone to drive you back. If we need to talk again, we can do it tomorrow, OK?'

And, dumbstruck, Martyn Townsend had been led out of the interview room where a female officer took charge of him and took him back to wherever he was staying.

O'Malley put the Lawrence file and the Taylor file together in his drawer – now inextricably linked. And he knew his instincts had been right. This was a major drugs incident – two lives that were actually irrelevant as far as the main guys were concerned. But, to people like Martyn Townsend, they mattered.

O'Malley decided it was time to think about retiring. He was getting too old to be a cop, and far too sentimental. Probably because his own boy, Lucas, was twenty-three. It could very easily have been him lying in the mortuary. And it could have been Sheryl, Lucas's girlfriend, he had just seen off the premises, her life ruined.

It was 3 a.m. and time for sleep. No point in going home now: he'd sleep on the couch in the ramshackle room he called an office. In the morning, it'd be on the breakfast news shows and his life would get more complicated.

He thought it could only have been two minutes later that the front desk phoned through. It was, he realised with horror, seven thirty in the morning. He didn't even recall sleeping!

'Lieutenant,' said the desk sergeant. 'I've got two . . . men here who want to talk to you about the Universal case.'

O'Malley could tell from the pause before 'men' that the sergeant assumed they were gay. 'Send them up, sergeant.'

Five minutes later, two young men were shown into the office.

One was tall, quite good-looking and well dressed. The other was a little younger, a bit nervous and constantly fidgeting.

The older one introduced himself as just Chad, his 'friend' was Mickey. 'We saw the news report about the shooting yesterday. Can I get it right – the victim was a Scott Taylor?'

'Why? Do you know a Scott Taylor?'

'Did he have anyone with him? Martyn Townsend?'

That was enough for O'Malley, and he called to the outer office for coffee. He was tempted to ask Mickey if he'd prefer soda, but thought he was probably not as young as he looked. Hopefully. He'd hate to arrest Chad for offences against a minor.

Then, without giving too much away, he outlined the case to Chad and Mickey. A glance passed between the couple, and then Chad spoke.

'Off the record, OK?'

O'Malley nodded, not entirely agreeing – and knowing he

could easily claim he didn't agree if asked later. But, for now, better to gain their confidence.

'We learned something yesterday that we needed to tell Martyn about regarding Scott. Trouble was, he didn't go home – he must have stayed at Scott's place and we don't know where that is.'

'You've never met Scott Taylor?'

'Nope,' said Mickey. 'At least, neither of us think we have. Maybe in a club or something.'

'But not consciously,' Chad finished off. 'Anyway, we said we'd ask around for Martyn, see if anyone did know him. And then we discovered he was seeing a guy called Peter Dooken, from Holland. So we followed that avenue up as well.'

'Why am I always astonished that the gay network in this state is vastly better organised than any other?' O'Malley mumbled.

'Because very rarely do we tell the police anything,' Mickey said. 'Otherwise, you just persecute us.'

Chad shut him up with a look. 'Anyway . . .' he said loudly, to make his point. 'Anyway, talking to people who knew Peter – very few knew Scott at all well, by the way, but everyone knew Peter –'

'I wonder why,' O'Malley interrupted and instantly regretted it. 'Sorry. Please go on,' he said, thinking that everyone would know Dooken if he sold them coke, heroin, whatever.

'And no one, but no one, had anything bad to say about him,' Chad finished. 'But, most importantly for Martyn, we found out why Scott and Peter split up and when.'

'When?'

'Yeah, like four days ago.' Mickey said. 'I mean, if we go by what Martyn said about Scott, it was pretty full-on for a guy whose previous lover had gone home the morning of the very night he met Martyn. And here's why . . .'

And Lieutenant O'Malley listened carefully, seeing the jigsaw come together. When they finished, he looked at his watch. 'Time to give Mr Townsend a wake-up call,' he said gravely.

'We'll go,' Chad said quickly.

O'Malley tried to tell them not to but they were already

leaving. He threw his hands up and dialled through to whoever was on duty in the car lot, telling them to find him a car.

Chad and Mickey arrived at Martyn's Studio City place to find a strange little Mexican man locking the door.

'Hey, mister, what's going on?'

The man shrugged. 'Guest call me this morning. He go home, he say. I say what about rent? He say he leave it on table, right up to next week, as agreed. I get here, money there, he gone.' With a shake of his head, the landlord wandered back to his dilapidated four-by-four and drove away.

Chad and Mickey looked at each other.

'LAX!'

As he started work for the day at the airport car rental booth, Dack Phillips was amazed to see the red Hyundai back in its slot as he marched through the lot. He was even more surprised to find the keys in the drawer when he got inside the booth in the airport arrivals lounge. He turned to Bob, who'd been on since six that morning.

'Who brought the Hyundai back?'

'English guy,' Bob said. 'Seemed a bit distracted. Said he'd finished with it early, but paid in full up to Monday. I thought it was odd and so I nipped out. Thought he might have damaged it – you know the way the English can't drive properly – and wanted to dump it back on us. But not a scratch on it.'

Dack frowned. 'Didn't leave any message?'

Bob shook his head. 'No, he was in and out real quick. His plane was going quite soon. Who for?'

But Dack shrugged, slightly disappointed. 'Doesn't matter.'

'Hell! We're too late.'

'You know, we could always go after him.' Mickey shielded his eyes from the bright sunlight as the flight took off over the Santa Monica Bay.

Chad shrugged. 'We don't know where to begin looking. I never got an address or phone number from him, did you?'

Mickey shook his head. 'But the cop may have one.'

Chad considered this. 'I doubt he'd help. As he said when we first saw him, we're not family – he's not obliged to tell us anything. Oh hell, let's try anyway.'

He opened the car door and got in, Mickey jumping in beside him.

As the car pulled out of the LAX road system and back on to the freeway, the plane taking Martyn Townsend away from Los Angeles, on the longest eleven hours of his life, became a speck in the sky as it turned northward and began its ascent up the coastline.

Fifteen

With relief Martyn let his luggage drop to the ground. Like LA, London was roasting in the late-summer heat. Unlike LA's humidity, though, the level here was high and Martyn was breathing heavily in the close atmosphere as perspiration continued to soak his already moist polo shirt. The journey on the packed tube from Heathrow to Green Park had been all but unbearable and Martyn regretted his decision to save his money and not get a taxi.

The walk from the tube station to Ryan's flat in Mayfair's Shepherd's Market was only a short one but, even so, his arms ached from strap-hanging and he longed to collapse into a chair with a strong, well-iced drink.

After ringing the bell, Martyn was relieved to hear rapid footfalls on stairs beyond the closed door, which, moments later, was opened wide to reveal Ryan Hardy.

'Hi,' he beamed. 'Welcome back to good old London town.' And, after a moment's appraisal of Martyn, added, 'You look . . . hot.'

Despite his exhaustion, Martyn couldn't help but think the same of his friend. Ryan was an actor by profession but he could so easily have been a model. Framed in the doorway wearing only an unbuttoned shirt and a pair of loose jogging shorts, Ryan could easily be the type of hunk you saw on the back covers of the glossy gay magazines, his evenly tanned, athletic, but not overly muscular, body enticing the susceptible reader to purchase a cologne or phone a chat-line. More than likely, though, those same readers would be massaging the growing bulge in their trousers. As the amorous thoughts went through his mind in a flash, Martyn felt his own damp cock give an involuntary twitch in his tightening briefs.

'Why don't you come on up?' suggested Ryan suggestively. A knowing smile played across his lips as he reached down to pick up one of Martyn's bags. His hand briefly brushed Martyn's leg as he did so – surely no accident.

His spirits lifting, Martyn grabbed the remaining bag and followed Ryan into the building, kicking the door shut behind him. Together they struggled with the cumbersome bags up the two flights of stairs and into the reception room of Ryan's flat. For Mayfair accommodation it was surprisingly dilapidated and uncared for. The Persian rug was frayed at the edges, tiles around the boarded-up fireplace were cracked and the ceiling sagged ominously in the middle. Martyn couldn't help but also notice the various unwashed plates and cups scattered around the room, as well as two champagne bottles that had been half-heartedly placed behind a cushion on the three-seater sofa.

A thin layer of dust covered the room's surfaces. Although washing and dusting seemed to be the fanatical hobbies of most gay men, Ryan obviously did not share them. Judging by appearances, nobody would assume that Ryan was anything approaching a slob but, nevertheless, he did appear to be comfortable in his own peculiar brand of decadent squalor. Somehow, though, thought Martyn, it suited him.

The whole place reeked of normality, complacency and homeliness.

And it was a complete opposite of Scott's home.

'Just drop your things anywhere,' said Ryan who did precisely that with the bag that he was carrying. 'You sit down while I get us a drink and you can tell me everything.'

'Great,' replied Martyn, flopping into the nearest armchair that wasn't covered in magazines and half-empty wineglasses. 'I hope you don't mind me crashing in on you like this. I just didn't fancy being on my own again in an empty flat.'

Ryan turned from the open door of the fridge in the kitchen area that was part of the living room. 'Of course not. I'm happy to have you here,' he answered genuinely. 'It's been a while since we've spent time together, anyway, hasn't it?'

Martyn knew that what Ryan really meant by 'spent time together' was that they hadn't had a shag in ages. Looking at the boyish blond, he wasn't quite sure why he hadn't seen more of him. However, it was perhaps their lack of recent contact that had made Martyn particularly keen to stay with Ryan and not with Miles, Gary or any of the other members of his immediate circle of friends. Ryan's detachment, coupled with his kind spirit and patient ear, made him the ideal choice to chill out with for a while.

Martyn knew that he would be able to unburden himself to Ryan and explain the events of the past week in the knowledge that Ryan wouldn't transform into a grotesque parody of a protective mother. As vulnerable as he felt, the last thing that Martyn wanted at this moment was some old queen fussing around him as though he were an invalid.

And, of course, if Martyn was being totally honest with himself, he welcomed the uncomplicated physical comfort that he hoped would be part of Ryan's warm welcome.

Ryan pressed an ice-cold triple gin and tonic into Martyn's hand and seated himself cross-legged on the carpet in front of him. The wide 'V' of his legs caused his shorts to ride up high on his slender, almost hairless thigh, the fabric pulled taut across the ample bulge in his crotch.

'So,' he said, sipping at his own glass, 'what's been going on? You didn't tell me much on the phone.'

Martyn took a swig from his glass and pondered on where to begin. Ryan looked on patiently, his deep-blue eyes never wandering from Martyn's face.

He told him of Los Angeles – from his picking up Dack at the airport through to his meeting Scott at La Diva, the growing adoration, the meeting with Brian Lawrence, his friendship with Chad and Mickey and, finally, Scott's relationship with the maleficent Peter Dooken, the three guys with the dark glasses, Scott's death and the inquisition by the police.

Martyn concluded his story with a long sigh and took another thoughtful sip from his glass, trying not to cry. Just the recounting of the events in LA had been draining, whipping up a maelstrom of conflicting emotions and feelings. The sense of loss, the guilt over Brian, the fear of loneliness after knowing Scott's love so fleetingly.

There was shame, too. Shame that he desired the company of others so soon after the death of Scott. It seemed so like betrayal but it also seemed right – an almost primal need that had been somehow awakened by the terrifying but exciting events of the past few days. Scott had demonstrated that himself the morning after their lovemaking, the morning he revealed the truth about Peter.

'And now . . . now I need to find this Peter. Confront him like the police won't bother to do. Tell him how he's caused two deaths, ruined my life, caused misery everywhere. Tell him it's all his fault. And then, if I'm very lucky, I can just walk away from him and never think about him again.'

Martyn was a different person now than he had been a week ago. Primitive urges of desire had been awakened within him. The desire for vengeance, for closure . . . and for company. He knew that, even now, just moments after telling how the potential love of his life had been murdered, he wanted Ryan. He was tempted to drop from the chair on to his knees and to push Ryan to the floor, pulling the already unbuttoned shirt from his torso and kissing his naked chest with a hungry mouth. Only shame held him in check. Even happy-go-lucky Ryan might be shocked at such behaviour.

There was a still silence. Ryan's head was bowed, his gaze sightlessly on the floor as he digested Martyn's tale.

'So, what now?' he finally said. 'You want to find this Peter but what do you have to go on?'

Martyn reached for one of his bags, unzipped a side pocket and produced the photograph of Scott and Peter at Disneyland which he had taken from the book.

The book that was still in the condo, a testament to false love, lies and abandonment.

A testament to betrayal and murder.

Martyn looked at it momentarily and then handed it to Ryan. 'Scott's on the right. Peter's on the left,' he said.

Ryan took the picture and studied it. 'He's gorgeous,' he said simply. 'They both are.'

A stab of anger shot through Martyn. Not at Ryan but at himself because he too had found himself admiring Peter, even though he knew that he was responsible for Scott's death.

'Yes,' replied Martyn awkwardly.

'So,' began Ryan, obviously choosing his words with care. 'Your plan is to do what? Go round the bars and clubs showing this to everyone you meet in the hope that someone might recognise him?'

Martyn knew that Ryan was doing his best to avoid sounding pessimistic but he could hear it in his voice. He too knew that there was no guarantee that his simplistic plan would provide the lead to Peter that he sought. There were dozens of gay bars and clubs in London and, even assuming that Peter went to several of them, the chances of happening upon someone who knew him was fairly remote. Nevertheless, he had to try. He had to.

'I don't know what else to do,' confessed Martyn sullenly. He must have looked crestfallen, because Ryan raised himself up on his knees, leant forward and hugged him, his head pressed against Martyn's chest. Martyn allowed his own head to rest on top of Ryan's, his nose nuzzling into his sweet-smelling blond hair. He could feel Ryan's crotch pressed against his right knee and found himself pushing lightly against it.

Ryan suddenly pulled away and rested back on his haunches. Martyn's immediate thoughts were that he had offended Ryan but the knowing smile on the younger man's face told a different story.

'Why don't you go and get a shower?' suggested Ryan.

Martyn laughed with his understanding of Ryan's subtlety. Of course, after his arduous journey in the moist heat of London he must stink of stale sweat.

'Good idea.' He grinned and got to his feet.

★

Moments later, the hot spray of the shower on his naked flesh seemed to cleanse Martyn's mind as well as his body. As he rubbed the creamy white liquid soap into his skin he felt his optimism returning. True, the chances of finding one person among the many of London were remote. However, he had to make the effort and do the best he could. He owed Scott that much, if nothing else.

He was pleased that he had come to Ryan for support and companionship – that had been a good choice. As he thought about his young friend waiting for him down the hall, Martyn found his soapy hands unconsciously caressing his crotch. His fingers slipped over his cock, which was now semi-hard and beginning to rise away from his balls, the foreskin slowly pulling back of its own accord. The sensation was warm, soothing and very welcome, as were the images of Ryan that filled his mind. But Ryan was only in the living room and Martyn had no need to rely on fantasy.

Martyn turned off the shower and stepped from the cubicle into the small bathroom. He dabbed himself dry with the white bath towel that Ryan had given to him and then tied it around his waist. As he brushed his teeth and combed his damp hair, Martyn felt the comforting sensation of his still swollen member now restrained against his leg by the towel. He patted it playfully and smiled in anticipation as he opened the bathroom door and padded down the hallway to rejoin Ryan in the living room.

'I've got an idea that might help you find this Peter,' Ryan was saying as Martyn entered. He was sitting on a typist's chair in the corner of the room. In front of him was a quietly humming computer. On the monitor a stream of text occasionally scrolled upward as new lines appeared at the bottom.

Ryan spun round in the chair and took a moment to appraise Martyn's almost naked figure before he spoke again.

'Have you ever cruised the Net before?' he said coyly. A strand of blond hair flopped down over a twinkling blue eye but he didn't brush it away.

'I've heard of it but I've never done it,' replied Martyn. Ryan turned back to the monitor and Martyn joined him, crouched down by the side of his chair and peered at the glowing screen.

'There are literally thousands of different chat channels on the
Net and loads of them are gay,' explained Ryan. 'You can join
any channel you want and chat live to people from all over the
world by typing in whatever you want to say. This channel,
though – ' Ryan gestured at the monitor – 'is called Queer
London, so you know that most of the people on here are local.'

Martyn looked at the screen and read a few lines.

<WantFuck> Anyone up for it in North London now?
<Hungry> Who wants to suck my fat cock?

and

<Muscles> I'm looking for a hairy top in W12

'Are <WantFuck> and <Muscles> people?' asked Martyn.
'Yes, they're their nicknames or "nics" as they call them on the
Net. There's a whole sort of shorthand language that people use
to talk to each other in. This is a list of all the people that are
talking on Queer London at the moment.' Ryan pointed to a
column of at least thirty names on the screen alongside the main
window of text. 'This is me,' he said indicating <Look4Guy>.

Ryan then typed a message and posted it.
<Look4Guy> then appeared in blue text saying,

<Look4Guy> Searching for cute guy I met in bar last night.
Anyone know his name?

And beside it, a picture appeared.
'I scanned your photo of Peter in. I thought, if anyone knows
him, they might tell us. Could take a while, though. And not
everyone on here has the ability to download pictures.'

'It's a bit blurry.' Martyn was squinting at the photo. He felt
sick – Peter had astonishingly nice eyes and this image didn't do
them justice.

What the hell was he thinking this for? Peter was a shit.

Ryan shrugged. 'It's good enough. Anyone who thinks they

might know him will contact me direct and I'll send 'em a better-resolution copy down the line.'

A tiny box appeared in the bottom corner of the screen – a personal message from <Allan> in Stratford.

<Allan> Don't know him, but I'd like to

'We'll get a lot of those,' Ryan said tartly. 'That's life.'

Martyn rested his head on the desk edge, closing his eyes and wishing he was . . . leading a different life.

A life without Scott, Los Angeles, Peter Dooken and anger dominating it.

A life less complicated.

His old life.

Martyn felt Ryan stroke the back of his neck, a gentle caress, no more.

But Martyn shook it off and regretted it instantly.

'Sorry,' he said quietly. 'I know you're trying to help.'

Ryan spoke quietly. 'You know, you are throwing yourself into this frighteningly quickly. I think you need to rest a bit. Did you even sleep on the plane?'

'It's ten at night for me,' Martyn said, 'and six here. I need to get back into London time, so I don't want to crash out yet.' He swallowed. 'You can . . . do that neck thing again if you want. It was nice.' He said the last bit too fast, in case he was tempted to stop himself.

But Ryan didn't put his hand back.

Instead, he eased Martyn's head up off the desk and turned it to stare into Ryan's own face.

'And I say, you're exhausted. OK, don't sleep, but lie down. Relax a little. I'll come and get you if we get a positive sighting, all right?'

Martyn nodded, all cock-heightening thoughts gone. Ryan's voice was almost hypnotic – he did need to rest a bit.

He knew where Ryan's bed was – he'd slept in it enough times a couple of years back. Slept and shagged.

Once in the bedroom, he let the towel drop to the floor – and smiled. Despite the almost student-like clutter of Ryan's flat, the bedroom was immaculate, kept like a palace. The sheets were silk – bringing back sights, sounds and smells of the first time he had found himself wrapped in Ryan's arms within them. And the second, the third . . . and every other time, including the last.

His parents had bought Ryan this flat – a tax dodge, Ryan said. Martyn could believe that, but guessed there was a degree of hand-washing and guilt-relieving too. Mater and Pater Hardy were wealthy socialites from the posh end of Colchester, always giving good garden parties and hobnobbing with the cream of the local bigwigs. A gay son who wanted to be a poncy actor was not something they could afford to be openly proud of. And they weren't. Ryan might convince himself that Daddy dearest had a few hundred thousand to get shot of before the taxman made enquiries, but Martyn knew there was far more truth in the theory that they wanted to buy Ryan out of their immediate lives.

And it had worked – Ryan took a perverse joy in the place. It was in the heart of London's snobbish area and he lived like a tramp. In many ways, when Ryan stood in the reception room, bronzed and beautiful amid the garbage of his life, his beauty was accentuated.

Martyn slid into the sheets and wriggled in their comfort, delighting in the soft sheen against his freshly washed flesh.

He closed his eyes and opened them only when he realised that Ryan must have silently followed him in and was now pressed against his naked back, his crotch pushed against Martyn's arse.

Martyn rolled back over and, with a quiet grunt, Ryan lifted his head, resting it on Martyn's shoulder, breathing down on to his chest, wafts of air tickling Martyn's nipples.

Just like he had been with Scott the last time he'd been in a bed.

He smelt Ryan's hair, and stroked his broad back.

Ryan's cock was growing, sliding up Martyn's leg as it grew harder and stronger, leaving a slight smear of dampness on Martyn's skin.

'Hello,' Ryan said quietly without opening his eyes.

'Hello,' Martyn said. 'I didn't hear you come in.'

'You didn't hear much at all.'

'I'm sorry?'

Ryan opened his eyes and moved, pushing himself up on his

elbow, his hand under the sheets, where it wrapped around Martyn's erect prick.

'It's nearly three in the morning. You went out like a light.'

Martyn was going to protest that this wasn't possible. He couldn't have fallen asleep, but the darkness outside the window and the clock on the far wall told him otherwise.

Instead, he just looked at Ryan.

'Ryan, will you do me a favour?'

'What?'

'Get inside me? I need to feel . . . connected . . .'

'Wanted?'

'No. Yes . . . well, I suppose so. I know it's a bit rude but –'

'Darling, I know why you chose to come to me rather than Miles or anyone else. Because you're in a slight state of shock and trauma. And, like with every other normal person in the world, sex is a great distraction and a great reliever. And everyone would treat you like a Ming Dynasty vase right now whereas you knew I'd treat you like a rent boy.' There was nothing but kindness in Ryan's voice, despite the words. Ryan was, as always, right.

And he had a cock to die for.

Ryan rolled over on to Martyn, crushing him slightly, but Martyn didn't mind, and their lips locked in an embrace, tongues piercing the darkness of each other's mouth, seeking comfort and assuaging hunger at the same time.

Ryan then rolled off Martyn again, and instead pulled him over, pushing him upright, so he was sitting astride him, his cock stabbing at Ryan's chest, while his own rested heavily against the small of Martyn's back, leaving a comfortingly damp patch of pre-come there.

With one hand Ryan casually stroked Martyn's cock without massaging, just a casual playing, while his other moved from one of Martyn's nipples to the other, teasing them one at a time, seeing which one could get harder and more pronounced.

Martyn was already sweating a little, a result of his delayed shock, and he was trembling ever so slightly.

Ryan moved his hand away from Martyn's cock and to a small silver box on the bedside table. He brought out a couple of rubbers and passed one to Martyn.

'Do the honours, yeah?'

Martyn moved quickly, tearing the packaging off, feeling the latex slip and slide between his fingers, smelling the lube on his skin.

He went down beside Ryan's rock-hard cock, looking closely at something he used to take for granted. He had never really studied it before, the straight lines, the slight bump of veins around the base, the way the pubic hair curled inward, as if stroking that beautiful skin itself.

He glanced at the head, a nice rounded blunt top, dark and attractive – he could almost feel the heat it was giving off in waves. Ryan was uncut, and Martyn leant over and kissed the rolled-back foreskin, letting his tongue just trace the base of the head.

More pre-come oozed out of the tiny slit as he did this, and so he used his tongue to flick that away, down into his stomach, and he smiled.

He then placed the teat of the condom on the top and slowly, carefully and precisely unfurled the rubber, massaging it down the shaft, watching each microscopic piece of flesh vanish under its new glistening coat of latex, as if giving it a new transparent raincoat. Ryan's cock was thick but not unusually long and there was a good amount of roll-up at the base of his shaft, meaning it was unlikely to slip off or split in the hard action Martyn knew was going to happen.

He hadn't thought about Ryan in ages, yet, as he gazed longingly at this magnificent tool, he remembered what being fucked by his old friend was like. As a purely mechanical gesture, it was unbeatable. Scott's fucking had been powerful and emotional and Martyn had desired him and wanted him and loved him to stay buried inside him for ever.

Ryan was just a sex machine, but a bloody good one. Ryan never fumbled, never slipped. Ryan knew exactly how to fuck, how to make an art of something as simple as putting one piece of his body inside a hole in another man's body. Ryan had frequently talked of having sex with women, but said that, when it came to fucking, a man's responses were far more satisfying to him. Sex with a woman, he said, was an equal partnership. With a man, the active partner was always in charge, no matter what the situation. No matter how many times you swapped over, no matter how often you discussed positions, pleasures and rules, the simple fact was that, when a man's cock was inside your arsehole, he was your boss and you were his slave.

Martyn needed to be enslaved and crawled back on top of Ryan. He let Ryan reach down and finger his arsehole without any preamble, without any heavy petting or build-up. He felt Ryan's fingers probe him, working him open. And then he felt the fingers move and that fantastic piece of meat enter him, pushing back his boundaries, his skin and muscle as it relentlessly ploughed inside him, setting off nerves and pain centres that through the miracle of sex became vast oceans of pleasure as he got in deeper. It was as if Martyn's arse cheeks conveniently grew wider apart, letting as much of Ryan's groin bury itself in him as it could, pushing and pumping right up until it could go no further. And then it stopped. For a second, nothing happened.

And then everything went mad!

Ryan gripped Martyn's shoulders and, pushing from his groin, sat up, sending stabs of gut-searing pain and pleasure into Martyn's middle. Martyn wrapped his legs around Ryan's thighs and bum and this enabled Ryan to get up, still embedded deep inside Martyn's arse, and walk away from the bed, each step pushing his cock deeper and harder inside Martyn. He reached the bedroom wall, and, with Martyn completely supported by Ryan's hold on his shoulders and his cock up his arse, fucked him violently, slamming Martyn's back again and again into the wall, breathing hard through gritted teeth.

Again and again Ryan slammed into Martyn's guts, Martyn slapped into the wall, and both men grunted with effort and pleasure.

Without any kind of physical stimulation, Martyn felt as if his cock was going to explode. His balls had tightened, and before he could warn his partner, his dick spewed out come into Ryan's face and hair. It came in fast and hard gushes, making Martyn shriek with pleasure, louder than he'd ever shrieked.

Ryan was crying out as well as he fucked faster and faster until Martyn thought his arse would split apart with the friction. But he didn't want Ryan to stop – all he wanted was for this to go on all night, to screw away the pain, the hurt and the anger.

Ryan had known what Martyn wanted. Needed. And Ryan was selflessly giving it. He felt Ryan come in that strange way he remembered, feeling as if Ryan's cock was actually rearing up inside him, like an attacking snake, and spitting out copious amounts of its venom, the shaft swelling and contracting for a split second with each explosion of lust.

They both dropped to the floor, Ryan pulling out.

Martyn rolled on to his front. 'Again,' he begged. 'Fuck me again.'

And, probably using every reserve of energy he could muster, Ryan speared his way back inside, violently fucking Martyn's upturned arse, his balls swinging below his legs and occasionally slapping against Martyn's. Never in all their past had either of them fucked for as long or as violently, and, before the night was out, they had both spent every drop of come from what reserves they could find inside them.

As they lay together, half awake, knowing the first shreds of daylight were easing around the blinds, their sore cocks both flaccid and drained, still pressed hard against each other, they kissed again, more powerfully and more savagely then ever before, neither wanting to be the first to let go, the first to admit to needing either sleep or a second's respite.

But Martyn gave way first, sheer exhaustion catching up. As he drew back suddenly from Ryan's chapped and scratched lips, everything was let go. All the anger and hurt and resentment of the last forty-eight hours of his life exploded in a cascade of hot, salty tears and sobs that tore from his chest, each one hurting more than the last, and accompanied by a mixture of self-deprecating apologies and empty, pointless but understandable admissions of undying love for Ryan. He finally succumbed to sleep on Ryan's tear-stained shoulder, the other man stroking his hair and kissing the top of his head with a passion and adoration borne out of a loving friendship and not even a hint of lust.

Sixteen

'M y name is Joe, pleasure to meet you.'
'Peter, Peter Dooken. Where's Stevie?'

Joe pointed towards the swimming pool, which Peter could see to the left of the villa, raised up and above the garage.

Joe took Peter's bag from him – and nodded towards the pool. 'You go and say hi to the others, I'll put this in your room.'

Peter thanked Joe and walked up the gravelly path around the villa, past the parked car in front of the garage and up the brick steps to the swimming pool, and, on getting there, took a moment to inhale the view.

The villa was situated on a hillside just outside San Antonio, the mainly modernised tourist bay on Ibiza. Taking a cab from the airport at Ibiza town, he had been driven past San Rafael, down a long road that seemed to have no lights, no marking, nothing, but which the driver joyously pointed out was the main road across the island. At some apparently random moment, the driver had taken a right and driven up a bumpy road that seemed to be no more than a pathway – and Peter thought his life was over. A quick cosh on the head and the cabbie would be off with his passport, cash and cards, leaving Peter just another dead tourist, a statistic on the local Poliza notice board. But no: a sharp left followed by another right had taken him towards two or three villas nestled in among the trees and hillside. Stevie's villa was the uppermost and the driver had deposited him just at the end of the driveway, taking his generous tip with pleasure, and had begun reversing.

And now Peter stood by the pool, looking down a sheer drop to the orchard owned by the next villa down. Across the way were hills of greenery, dotted with tiny farms and the like. Little plumes of smoke drifted out of tiny white chimneys – the buildings all had the typical Mediterranean white plasterwork and red roofs.

Peter could not believe the view – the peace, the quiet and the beauty.

'Wotcha,' said a decidedly East London voice from a deck chair nearby.

'Stevie?'

'Peter?' Stevie looked like a tiny version of Grant Mitchell from *EastEnders* – crop-haired, pug-faced and rough-looking, but with a white smile that could melt the coldest of refrigerators. He wasn't short or tall – everything about him decidedly average.

They shook hands and Stevie introduced Peter to the others. An attractive man in his late fifties but with the body of a twenty-five-year-old was roasting himself on a sun lounger. This was Clark, a popular radio DJ and record remixer, who was out here ostensibly to work. He seemed incredibly friendly and relaxed. Crouched down beside him, trying to read a copy of *Viz* and brush the hovering flies away with a ridiculously wide-brimmed hat – which ensured no sun got near the enamel-coloured skin – was Tanya (or 'Ton-yerr', as Stevie pronounced it), who was Clark's girlfriend. She giggled a greeting and returned to her reading matter. On Clark's other side was Derrick – tall, dark hair, blue eyes and a body to die for. He was Clark's PR representative, who negotiated his deals and sorted out his daily agenda.

A tray of drinks was brought out by a guy apparently called Maffu, tall, muscular with a pair of tiny briefs that did little to hide an enormous cock scrunched up inside. The sun reflected off his smooth jet-black skin and, when he smiled and greeted Peter, he spoke with a broad Scouse accent, proclaiming his name to actually be Matthew. He also pointed out that he was Stevie's boyfriend. 'Not that you'd know it by the amount of innocent, pock-marked eighteen-year-olds he traipses back here with every night to fuck senseless!' he said with a smile in his voice.

Peter suspected Matthew probably did quite well himself, thank you.

Then Joe emerged. He was about twenty-one, very thin, and looked like he might fall over in a breeze. He had short, spiky hair, wet-gelled into place, and a tiny nose stud blemishing an otherwise beautifully unspoilt face. He was now wearing nothing but a baggy pair of shorts down to his knees, his shoulders and neck looking alarmingly red and peeling.

He grinned at Peter. 'Settled in? Have you eaten?'

Peter said he hadn't so Joe clapped his hands excitedly. 'OK, who's for lunch?'

There was a muted but enthusiastic round of acknowledgements from the others, so Joe wandered away again.

'We keep Joe around as our slave,' Matthew laughed. Peter thought Matthew probably laughed every time he spoke – he had that sort of demeanour. 'He cooks, cleans and does the laundry. Loves it.'

Peter shrugged. 'Seems a good idea to me.' He eased back towards Stevie. 'Thanks for this. I know it's a bit of an imposition.'

'Hell no,' Stevie said. 'I got the room spare. Andy explained that he thought you needed a break so it fitted in. Besides, Clarkie'll be happy. He's a card sharp and needs more people to screw money out of at poker. Matthew and I are dried up already.'

Peter grinned. 'I like poker. This could be fun.'

'Joe told you which room you're in?'

Peter shook his head, so Stevie pointed to a door at the end of the wall, overlooking the deep end of the pool. 'All yours, mate.' And as Peter's face clouded over – surely this must be the prized room – Stevie laughed. 'Not at all, if you're thinking what I think you're thinking. Clarkie and Her Highness go skinny-dipping at six every morning. It'll wake you up without fail. Sorry.'

Peter wandered over and tugged the double wooden doors open on-to a small but neat white-walled room. His bag had been placed beside the single bed, and a small lamp was lit. The smell of insect-repellent tablets wafted over and he noticed a small private shower and toilet to the right.

He went in, past the bed and out of the opposite door into the inside of the villa.

Strictly speaking, it was a one-level villa, although no two rooms were exactly on the same level. One step to the kitchen, eight to the back bedroom, four to another and so on.

To his left were some steps leading to a couple of double bedrooms plus a spare toilet. In front was the expansive, clay-paved living area with sofas, chairs and beanbags scattered around, plus a posh TV and stereo. A coffee table was on the middle of a huge sheepskin rug. At the far end was a slightly secluded dining area and, beyond that, the front door. To the right was another bedroom, although only a single, and next to that a vast kitchen area.

Peter crossed the room into the kitchen, where Joe was dancing around to the Spice Girls while he prepared a huge quantity of vegetarian food in the biggest wok Peter had ever seen.

He watched Joe bop while he cooked, waggling his cute little tush in time with 'Spice Up Your Life'. After a moment, some sixth sense must have told Joe he was being watched, because he turned suddenly, his adorable young face bright red. 'Well,' he said eventually, 'now you know what keeps this little queen happy.' He reached over and threw Peter a slice of green pepper. 'Nothing like your supermarket shite here, you know. Taste that.'

Peter did. It was cool, crisp and juicy. And indeed tasted better than any pepper he could remember eating before.

'So, beyond acting his house boy to all and sundry here, what d'you do, Joe?'

Joe jiggled the wok, turning the veggies as he stir-fried them. 'I work for a CD-packaging firm,' he said. 'We take out-of-copyright albums, rejacket them and sell them on to European stores that need English compilations to resell to English holiday-makers. I went into San An yesterday morning and spotted five CDs we did just a couple of months ago in a tourist shop, vastly overpriced. And selling well.' He smiled. 'Nice job, fun people, good money. Can't complain. You?'

Peter suddenly realised he hadn't got an answer. Before going to California, he had worked for a car showroom. He hadn't really thought what he was going to do next. He said so.

Joe shrugged. 'Good on you, though. Take your time. Stick around with Stevie or Clarkie at the clubs. They'll soon find you work. Selling drugs or something.'

The last sentence was said right under his breath but still Peter picked up on it. He was sensitive to that subject.

'Oh, ignore me,' said Joe when Peter asked him what he'd meant. 'They just take too much coke for my liking. Went into Ibiza last night, brought back these metal capsule things you stick into your nose – means you can take the right amount of coke in properly. Gets them high very easily and saves messing around with lines on tables and drinking straws. Twats.'

'You don't do drugs then?'

'Nope. Mr Boring, me, Peter. Don't drink, do drugs or smoke.'

'Sex?'

Joe stopped cooking and stared at Peter. 'Don't mess around, do you? No, I don't do sex much, either. Not out here. Sort of got a guy back home, but it's going wrong and I know he's fucking around, so that's why I came out here with Stevie.'

Peter nodded understandingly. 'So, we're all lame dogs together.'

Which was the wrong thing to say. Joe snapped, slamming his cooking utensils down hard. 'No. No, I am not a "lame dog", OK? I just don't happen to want to spend my life out of my head, with some strange Latino's cock up my arse, dying of fucking AIDS when I'm thirty and having done or seen nothing except the inside of Pachá or Space, all right?'

He glared at Peter, who took a deep breath.

'Man, I'm sorry, I didn't mean anything by that, OK?'

Joe shook his head slowly. 'Nor me. I'm really sorry. It's just the others . . . I can't stand peer pressure, you know, and it's all clubs and sex and drugs and clubs again for them. It's quite hard to stay in with everyone when you don't actually like what they do.'

'So, what do you do while they're out?'

'Sit by the pool, under a lamp, swatting insects and reading. I just want to relax. You clubbing or reading tonight?'

Peter shrugged. 'I intend doing a bit of both – minus the drugs. Had enough of that when I was in LA.' He paused. 'Fancy a bit of company this evening – I'm certainly too tired to go out tonight.'

Joe shrugged. 'Whatever. Don't stay home just for me, OK?'

Peter wanted to kick himself. He'd taken an instant liking to young Joe but had screwed that up royally, it seemed.

'OK, I'll take it as it comes,' he said and went back to his room, changed into shorts and ventured back into the blistering sun.

Matthew and Stevie were in the pool, trying to remove each other's kit. Clark was watching, Tanya was reading a copy of *MixMag* and Derrick was staring intently at the hills far away.

Peter sank his legs into the surprisingly warm water and sat on the edge of the pool nearest Clark. 'Going out tonight, then?' he asked.

Clark said he was. 'Doing a spot at Es Paradis tonight – foam party. Coming?'

Pete shrugged. 'Don't know – maybe tomorrow. I'm a bit tired.'

Clark understood this. 'Doing Space tomorrow – that's a great one. If you want, I'll sort you out a comp. See if you can drag Joe with you. I know he hates clubs, but mostly by reputation rather than experience. And I think Stevie and Matthew have been riding him a bit because he steers away from certain sceney substances, you know what I mean?'

Peter said he did and that he'd try twisting Joe's arm.

Tanya tugged on Clark's hand. 'I want to go for a walk. See the horses before lunch.' Tanya headed back to her and Clark's room.

Derrick was up a second later. 'I'll get the car.'

'She wants to walk, Dezza,' Clark said. 'For God's sake let her. The exercise will do her good. And me.'

'OK,' said Derrick. He took a mobile phone out of his pocket and punched a number. After a pause he spoke. 'Yo, André?

Clarkie's going out for a while, then it's lunch so, if you want anything, you'll have to wait an hour or so, yeah?'

Clark shot a look at Peter – it was clear he wanted to strangle Derrick and his overprotective business attitude. 'I feel like poor Diana must've. Can't do anything without this promoter or that club manager being told. Tell you, Peter, if someone wanted to assassinate me, they could. And it'd be Dezza's fault for telling them where I was every minute.' He paused and pursed his lips. 'I wonder if he tells them every time I have a crap. Oh well, let's find out.' He stood up and announced loudly, 'I'm off for a shit. Back soon.' With a friendly wink at Peter, he followed Tanya inside. Derrick looked flustered for a moment and scampered after them.

In the pool, Matthew had won the game to see who could be first to remove the other's kit, and to prove it flicked Stevie's trunks over the side of the pool surround into the orchards some way below.

'Bastard,' Stevie screamed and hauled himself out of the pool.

Peter had to admire his physique – really slender, but beautifully defined. He looked like one of those schoolbook pictures that showed you where every muscle in the human body was, but one that a thin layer of flesh had been stretched over. As he wandered to the railed edge of the paved surround, Peter could see a long, cut cock and shaved balls drooping between his legs.

Stevie turned back to Matthew who was standing behind him laughing, and then, quick as a flash, snagged Matthew's briefest of briefs, snapping the elastic and yanking them away, throwing them in roughly the same direction as his own had gone.

Peter watched as Matthew's dick flopped down, unsupported. It, too was circumcised, revealing a huge pink head at the end of a rich black length of thick, veined muscle. He winced at the thought of that entering Stevie's small arse and wondered if it actually could go all the way in without causing Stevie's guts some serious damage.

The couple scampered back inside the villa to change (or fuck, who knew?), leaving Peter alone.

He let himself drop into the pool and did six or seven lazy

lengths, getting right under the water, washing away the flight and the taxi journey.

When he stopped and started to climb out, he saw the disappearing figures of Clark, arm around Tanya, as they marched off to find her favourite horses, and Derrick, a few steps behind, his mobile still attached to his ear.

'Lunch in twenty minutes,' said a soft voice behind him.

Joe was dangling his feet in the pool, as Peter had done earlier. His long shorts were soaked at the bottoms, as Peter's strokes had sloshed the water up to his knees.

'Cool,' Peter said. 'Will they be back?'

'Oh yes,' said Joe. 'Tanya and her food are harder to prise apart than Tanya and her diaphragm, and that's saying a lot.'

Peter laughed. Then he swam over to Joe, and trod water in front of him, looking up at his sunburnt face. 'I am sorry about earlier.'

'So am I. I overreacted, as usual.'

Peter held up a hand awkwardly, trying not to sink. 'Mates?'

Joe took the hand. 'Mates,' he confirmed.

'Sure?'

'Uh-huh. Sure.'

'Good,' said Peter and promptly tugged him into the pool.

Joe screamed girlishly as he flopped face down, and flapped his arms around.

'You shit!' he cried, surfacing. 'You complete fucking, arsing, wanking, titheaded shit!'

And Peter dived under the water, swimming quickly to the other side to get away.

He got out of the pool rapidly and was almost at the door of his room by the time Joe, his soaked clothes holding him back momentarily, got out.

Peter slammed the doors shut, locking them from the inside, and caught his breath.

'Shit!'

The door to the rest of the villa was open and, before he could get to it, a wet and bedraggled Joe was there, dripping water into puddles on the floor, having come through Tanya and Clark's room.

Peter laughed. ' "Sorry"? "It was an accident"? How about "You look gorgeous when you're wet"?'

'No deal,' Joe said, eyes flashing dangerously. 'I'm going to spit in your lunch!'

Peter dropped to his knees in mock panic. 'Oh please, no, don't do that to me!'

Joe stood staring at him and then burst into laughter. Peter joined in, sitting on his bed, letting his wet trunks soak the sheets but not caring. At least, not until Joe sat beside him, making them far wetter.

'I have to sleep in that you know! Everyone else will think I've wet myself!'

Joe got up and went into the bathroom, tugging the door shut. He emerged moments later, wearing only a towel. Peter could see his soaking clothes in the shower pedestal. 'I'll swap this with mine later,' he said, waving at the towel.

He sat down again, and shivered slightly.

Without thinking, Peter threw an arm around him, hugging the younger man to him for warmth. 'You gotta admit, that was funny.'

'For you, gitface. I had paper cash in those pockets!'

'I'll pay you back then,' Peter said.

Joe said nothing, and then slowly turned to face his new friend and reached forward, pressing his lips against Peter's. Then he drew back a little. 'Sorry,' he said hoarsely. 'I don't know why I did that exactly.'

'I'm not complaining,' said Peter. 'It was nice. Unexpected. You can either do it again, or not. I'm not going to think badly of you whichever.'

'Then I'll do it again,' Joe said simply. 'Because you're nice.'

They eased themselves back on the bed, ignoring the damp they were creating. The lamp heating the anti-insect tablet flickered across from the other side of the room, creating the sort of romantic atmosphere no amount of drugs, music or money could hope to emulate.

Just the two of them, breathing in time. Joe was lying on Peter, his head pressing lightly on Peter's chest. With both of them facing upward, Peter couldn't see whether Joe's eyes were closed or whether he was staring at the same unremarkable mark on the ceiling. Perhaps Joe was trying to think of something to say as well.

Peter breathed deeply, inhaling the smell of Joe's damp hair. Of his freshly dried neck and shoulders. Slowly Peter brought his hands up, placing a finger on each of Joe's temples and slowly rotating them, massaging the tanned skin by his eyes. He tried to look down, but it made his neck hurt, so he made do with just lying there.

'That's nice,' Joe said quietly. Encouraged, Peter carried on, his heart beating that bit faster. Where was this going? Did it matter? Did he really care?

'Don't move,' he said back, and then shifted himself slightly upward, pushing himself towards the bed head, so that Joe's head was now resting on his stomach, enabling Peter to see Joe's face.

His eyes were closed, but he was smiling. While he massaged, Peter looked at Joe's body. OK, so it lacked the six-pack stomach or the powerful pecs. And it certainly didn't have the kind of sculptured hips Scott had possessed. But he revelled in its lack of perfection. Joe was veering towards love handles, his chest was a bit saggy and he had only a hint of calf muscle that might have been brought into existence by casual rather than regular cycling around the island.

But to Peter he was beautiful.

Joe sighed again, and Peter realised his towel had moved slightly, apparently of its own accord. Joe's cock was getting harder by the second, and Peter watched as under the towel it grew harder and harder, watching the outline solidify until it pushed the towel well away from Joe's groin. As if flicked by a switch, Peter felt his own cock swell up and stiffen, pressing against Joe's back. Despite Joe's obvious lack of embarrassment, Peter felt stupidly self-aware at this, and just managed to stop himself apologising.

'This is cool,' Joe said. 'I mean, this is what relaxation is all about.'

Peter was far from relaxed, and moved his fingers away from Joe's temples and began threading them through his hair, breathing in the coconut scent of whatever he had last washed it in.

Joe's eyes slowly opened and he looked up into Peter's face, grinning.

'Well, I guess this is slightly more than you expected,' he said.

Peter shrugged, trying to sound in control. 'Yeah. Yeah, I think it is.'

Joe lifted his head away from Peter's stomach, which at least gave Peter's cock some respite. Then he brought his lips up to Peter's and kissed softly. As he started to move away, Peter took the plunge. He slipped a hand under Joe's head and gently eased him back up and they kissed again. First, a casual brushing of lips, but, a few seconds later, he felt Joe's mouth open, and he did likewise, letting his tongue ease into Joe's mouth and discover his teeth, his cheeks, his tongue. Joe swivelled around without breaking the kiss too much, so that he was now kneeling astride Peter.

Peter felt Joe cup his head and press into his mouth harder. He was also aware that Joe's cock was pushing into his chest and he let his hand stray up to it, gently brushing the underneath with one finger. It quivered and Peter felt a slight dampness on his skin that hadn't come from the pool water. With another finger, he traced the outline of Joe's balls, then let them roll over the back of his hand.

Joe moved away from Peter's face, letting a tiny tightrope of saliva hang between them before it splashed on his chin. 'You're cute,' Joe said, then shook his head. 'No, make that "gorgeous". Dead gorgeous.'

Peter breathed out, before he realised he'd been holding his breath. 'You too.'

Joe ran his hands up Peter's chest, then drew a straight line from Peter's neck to his nipple with his tongue. Then he ran his tongue down to Peter's trunks, pushing down with his lips on his cock, which caused it to twitch even more within the confines of the wet briefs. 'Lose them,' Joe breathed. Peter didn't wait to be asked again, pulling at the button and flies, releasing them. Joe moved back, away from Peter, and clasped the top of Peter's trunks, pulling them down with a swift movement. Peter raised himself off the bed, just enough to let the trunks come off with ease, and then Joe fell back on to him. Both were naked now, both stabbing at each other with hard cocks.

They briefly kissed again before Joe arched up and then went down on Peter's cock, taking it right down to the base of the shaft in his mouth. Peter caught his breath as Joe began bringing his mouth up and down, sending waves of pleasure through his body. After a few movements, Joe released his prey, instead using his tongue across the head, around the foreskin and across the eye, before resuming his previous action.

Peter gripped the side of the bed – Joe's body was too far down for him to do anything useful with his hands, but they cried out for something to do. He eventually let his right hand stroke the top of Joe's head, without putting pressure on it. How much of this he could take, he wasn't sure, but the fear of coming early made him suddenly reach down and tap Joe's head.

Joe lifted his mouth away from the cock, letting his tongue lick across the swollen head one last time, before grinning. 'Yeah?'

'Not yet,' Peter said.

'Good,' Joe said, 'because I want you to fuck me.' He dashed across the room to his own pile of clothes in the shower, yanking a rubber from the back pocket of his shorts. 'Now!'

Without waiting for Peter to respond, he unwrapped the condom, placing it on Peter's twitching cock, sliding it down the shaft with his mouth. As soon as he'd done this, he knelt up so that his own cock tapped Peter's nose, then grabbed at Peter's shaft and sat back.

Peter felt the pressure as his cock began pushing its way into Joe's welcoming arse. He watched Joe's face as each grin or grimace matched an equivalent feeling in him as his cock pushed against Joe's inner flesh. A few seconds later, he was completely inside, trying to push further against the tight tunnel, while Joe began to raise and lower himself gently.

'Let me,' Joe said as he began to gently ride Peter, so Peter concentrated on letting his fingers stroke and massage Joe's cock, getting his finger under the foreskin and gently teasing it further back from the purple head. He played with his balls, feeling them swing and bounce in time with their owner's riding, and slowly started wanking the shaft, moving faster and faster as he felt himself preparing to come.

Joe had closed his eyes, wallowing in the sensations, and actually came first, shooting his wad on to Peter's chin and neck. Before he'd finished, Peter felt himself come, spurting his juice into the rubber's tip, slamming his left hand repeatedly into the side of the bed, while his right continued pumping Joe's spent cock, squeezing out a few last drops of come on to his chest.

Joe stopped riding, letting himself breathe hard for a moment until finally he let out a last deep gasp and opened his eyes. He smiled, sending an unexpected thrill through Peter. 'Great,' he said. 'Can we do that again?'

Peter grinned back. 'You're a bit of a monster really, aren't you? One minute it's all cute and sad and puppydog, when really you're a fuck-monster.'

Joe kissed him again, hard, and they pressed themselves against each other, letting the spent come spread over each other's skin. Joe reached down and eased the condom off Peter's prick, dropping it to the floor, then teasing the cock again, massaging the last few drops of seeping come into the cockhead.

'Listen,' said Joe quietly. 'As I said, I'm not into boyfriends right now, but if you'd like to do this again tonight that's great. But let's say right now: no commitment. You meet someone or I meet someone on this island we want to fuck rigid, we can, yeah?'

Peter nodded, amused by the change in Joe's personality where sex was concerned. 'On one condition.'

'What's that?'

'You go and find out what that burning smell wafting in from the kitchen is.'

Joe's eyes widened. 'Arse! The lunch . . .' And, stark-bollock-naked, cock rock-hard and stabbing forward, he scarpered across the villa and into the kitchen.

Peter replaced his shorts and followed him in, to watch him throw the windows open to get rid of the smell, and saw that whatever had been in a saucepan was now a boiled-to-death mass of green sludge.

Matthew and Stevie popped their heads round the door, alerted by Joe's shouts of annoyance at the inanimate and burnt saucepan. Peter noted that neither of them so much as blinked at Joe's nakedness (although his cock was shrunken down to normality now) and, indeed, both of them were naked, with hard-ons (and he had been right about Matthew's cock: no way was that going to go inside Stevie or indeed anyone comfortably).

'Lunch's ruined,' Joe said grumpily. 'Or at least one part is. Small rations I'm afraid.'

He looked up and saw Stevie's and Matthew's groins for the first time. 'Oh, hello – you too?'

Peter wanted to die – tell the world, why don't you?

But the other two laughed, Matthew slapping Peter's rump good-humouredly. 'Didn't waste much time, did you?'

'The hetties are back,' Joe announced, sending the couple scurrying away to get dressed. He winked at Peter. 'No, they're not, but it got them out of the way. Could you nip into my room and find me something to wear while I try to make the best of this, please?'

Shaking his head at the casualness of it all, Peter did as he was asked, and wondered if the rest of his week was going to be as adventurous as the first ninety minutes had been.

Seventeen

It was 11.30 p.m. Martyn was sitting in the upstairs balcony of Bang on Charing Cross Road, looking down at his fellow Londoners having a good time on the tiny dance floor.

Below, a group of attractive young men were gathered by the DJ booth, stuffing flyers into other people's hands.

The manager of the establishment and his boyfriend were on opposite sides of the upstairs bar, having a good laugh, while a couple of bar staff kept the drinks flowing for the handful of regulars joining in on the joke.

Already three people had offered him tablets or coke – and each time he had said no.

He'd had enough of drugs.

His contact was supposed to meet him by this pillar – the one with the Tom of Finland framed picture – at eleven. Maybe he wasn't going to show.

The whole place reminded him of La Diva in West Hollywood. And that made him feel remorse. Anger. Bitterness.

He was not in the best of moods when another punter tried to sell him some coke.

'Just fuck off, will you?' he shouted. Immediately, two bouncers appeared and Martyn thought he was in trouble – but no: it was the pusher. They grabbed him, pocketed the stuff and dragged him away.

Good security – shame it was necessary.

Why were London clubs full of drugs? OK, not full exactly, but he was sure it never used to be like this. Or was he just more aware of it now, conscious that one of these bastards was probably Peter Dooken, about to destroy someone else's life like he had Scott Taylor's.

'Are you Martyn Townsend?'

Martyn glanced up at the newcomer. He was tall and willowy with shaggy brown hair and wore a tracksuit that looked more than faintly out of place. He was carrying a freshly opened bottle of Pils, although Martyn hadn't seen him at the bar, despite his vantage point.

'Nick?'

'Nick Thomas, hi.' They shook. 'So, glad you could make it.'

'I'm glad you answered our e-mail.'

That morning, Ryan had dragged Martyn out of bed to go through the replies to their Queer London messages of the previous evening. One had been particularly interesting.

<NickSE> Hi. I think that's Peter Dooken. Do I win £10,000?

They had immediately e-mailed back, and Nick had suggested meeting that evening at Bang, just to chat.

'I didn't know what you wanted Peter for,' Nick explained, 'so I wasn't just going to tell you what I knew in the e-mail. Sorry.'

'No, no that's fine,' said Martyn. 'I'm glad, really. It implies he's a mate and not someone you want to get into trouble, which is fine by me,' lied Martyn.

Nick nodded, drinking. 'Why do you want to find him?'

'I just came back from the States and a friend wanted to get in touch, but only had his name and photo. He asked me to track him down and pass on a message. It's not that important really. I'm just doing Scott a favour.'

Nick nodded. 'Yeah, Scott. That was the guy he was seeing, right?'

Martyn nodded. 'Ah, I thought that might be it. Scott didn't even tell me that much – but that makes sense now.' Martyn

decided he was rather good at this lying-through-his-teeth lark.
'So, have you seen Peter?'

Nick nodded. 'Oh yeah, a couple of days ago. My friend Andy
had a big party at his place just down the road in Blackheath. I
met Peter there. He's really nice. He's gone to Ibiza. My old
flatmate Stevie has a villa there and he's gone to spend a week out
there with him.'

'Really?' Martyn feigned astonishment. 'Excellent.'

'Why?'

'Because I'm off there tomorrow – for the dance festival, with
my boyfriend Ryan. Oh, great. Maybe I'll bump into him.'

Nick smiled. 'Look, here's the address of the villa.' He passed
Martyn a small piece of paper. 'Sorry, I don't have the phone
number – I'm not sure it's even got a phone. But Stevie's got a
mobile, I could –'

'No.' Martyn held his hand up. 'No, I'd much rather turn up
unannounced. Be a nice surprise for Peter that way, don't you
think?'

Nick nodded. 'Oh yeah. He had a rough time out in America,
I think he said. That's why he went to Ibiza. To recover.'

Martyn shrugged and drained his drink. 'Another?'

Nick paused, then said he'd have a quick one.

Smiling, Martyn went back over to the bar.

Ryan swore as the telephone rang. He wanted to get to bed.

It was Martyn. From the noise and the shouting, he was still in
the club.

'Any luck?'

'Yeah,' came the bellowed reply. 'That Nick guy told me he's
in Ibiza, near San Antonio. I'm going to see if I can get a flight
for tomorrow.'

'At this time of night?'

'I called. Apparently the last flight is at just before one. I can
get to Heathrow by then easily.'

'You've not got any kit.'

'I'll buy some. Listen, I called my answerphone at home earlier
to check my messages. Nothing, but I recorded a new message,

giving your place as a contact for me for a couple of weeks. Sorry for that.'

'No, love,' Ryan said, groaning inwardly. 'That's fine and sensible. Where are you going to stay?'

'I'll find somewhere when I'm out there, OK?'

Ryan sighed. 'Well, I suppose so. Look, when you get to Ibiza, call me tomorrow, yeah? I'll be worried.'

'I'll try, but no promises. I want to find Peter.' There was a pause, then, 'Love you, Ryan. And thanks.'

And Martyn was gone.

Ryan was actually very worried. What the hell was Martyn going to do if he even found Peter? Hit him? Kill him? Burst into tears?

This wasn't a constructive way of dealing with his grief.

Nor was getting his arse fucked by Ryan last night – but, hey, at least that hadn't upset him.

Ryan threw off his boxers and clambered naked into bed. No Martyn tonight, no shag.

Shit, he was really horny now he thought about that.

The doorbell went.

Who the hell . . .? And at this time of night!

He crawled angrily out of bed, threw a silk dressing gown on and shoved his feet into a naff but amusing pair of Wily E. Coyote slippers he'd got from the Warner Brothers Store.

Mumbling, he went down the stairs and looked out of his peephole.

Two guys. No one he knew. Both cute.

'Hello?'

'Er . . . hi,' said the taller, older-looking one. 'We're real sorry to bother you, but is Martyn Townsend here? We may have the wrong address.'

Americans?

With a louder sigh, he slipped the chain on and then opened the door as far is it would go.

'Yes and no,' Ryan said deliberately unhelpfully.

'I'm sorry?' That was the younger one. Make that dead cute, actually.

'Who are you?'

'Friends from LA. I'm Mickey, he's Chad, and we want to talk to him about Scott –'

'Taylor,' Ryan ended the sentence, and slid the chain off, letting them in. 'Martyn mentioned you.'

'Good things, I hope,' Chad said, offering his hand.

'Surprisingly, considering his mood, yes, very much so. I'm Ryan.'

'We know,' said Mickey. 'We called his home as soon as we got into Heathrow, but it had a message saying to contact him here. No phone number, so we gambled you'd be here.'

Ryan showed them up the stairs and into his flat. He yawned unintentionally.

'Jeez, we're real sorry to call this late,' Chad said earnestly, 'but it's kind of important.'

Mickey sat heavily in a chair, undoing his coat.

Ryan couldn't help but notice how tight Mickey's jeans were.

He also couldn't help the way his own cock began to rise.

Not now, he wanted to scream. He turned his attention to Chad.

'What's the problem? Do the authorities want him back because of Scott's murder?'

'No,' Chad said. 'Although they're not best pleased that he's gone. But no, they seem satisfied he had nothing to do with it. Did Marty tell you that it was him who was meant to get shot, not Scott?'

Ryan nodded. Chad was quite adorable, too. He needed to get some clothes on.

'Do you two want a tea or coffee? If so, the kitchen's that way. I'm going to throw some more clothes on.'

He hurried into the bedroom, and shoved a pair of briefs and loose chinos on, plus a sweatshirt, and went back out.

Chad had made tea.

Both Americans had removed their jackets and jumpers and were sitting in just tight T-shirts, which showed off their bodies very nicely.

'Anyway, for starters, Martyn's not here. He's on his way to Ibiza.'

'Where?' Chad looked confused.

202

'A small Spanish island,' Mickey said. 'Lots of techno music.'

'It's also very old, very beautiful and has lots of good sights to see and restaurants to eat in.' Ryan sipped his tea. God, never trust Americans with tea. It was strong and too sweet, but Ryan was too polite to complain out loud. 'But yeah, right now the dance festival is going on.'

'Peter's there?'

'Uh-huh.'

Mickey swore. 'We're always one step behind him.'

Chad agreed. 'OK, let's get back to Heathrow and get a plane there tonight.'

'No way,' Ryan said. He smiled at the newcomers. 'I mean, I don't know that Marty's going to make the last flight, but you two haven't a hope in hell. Stay here tonight. If he doesn't come back in the morning, go off then.'

'Hope my credit card can take this,' Chad grunted.

Mickey shrugged. 'It'd better. It's too important.'

Chad smiled at Ryan. 'Thanks. That's a very kind offer considering you don't know us.'

Ryan drained his tea, trying not to grimace. 'Listen, Marty seemed to think you two looked after him, so I can do nothing more than that in return. But why are you here? What is so important that Martyn has to know that couldn't be phoned or written?'

Chad stood up. 'Because Marty's made a huge error and if we don't stop him, he's going to make a bigger one. What do you think he's going to do when he finally meets this Peter Dooken?'

Ryan shrugged. 'That's been going through my mind. I hope they talk. But Marty's a bit wild right now. I think he'll probably say or do something he might regret. Had he come back this evening, I might have been able to talk some sense to him, but not now . . .'

Chad nodded. 'Exactly. That's why we're here to stop him.'

And they told him what they had told Lieutenant O'Malley of the LAPD that had won him over.

And Ryan sat there, nodding. 'You know, I sort of wondered about that. But Marty was in no mood to listen to me.' He slapped the arm of his chair. 'Damn, but I should have tried.'

Mickey reached over and touched Ryan's knee. 'Hey, it's not your fault. It's no one's, certainly not Marty's. But you see why we've got to catch up with him.'

Ryan looked at the small hand on his knee.

He wanted to fuck this boy senseless – a thought completely unbidden, one that just shot through his mind.

Instead, he got up and crossed to the phone, flicking through his address book. 'Bear with me, guys.'

Ryan found the number he wanted and punched it into the phone. After a couple of rings, it was answered.

'Hi, Roger? Sorry to ring so bloody late, mate, but it's an emergency. Yeah, and you start at what time? Oh well, you'd need to get up soon anyway.' There was obviously a very tart and sarcastic response to that. 'No, listen,' Ryan continued, 'I really need a big favour. I can pay you back in a day or two but can you sort me three first-class to Ibiza on the first out? Oh, all right, the next one. No, nine ten. that's great.' Another response of some length. Ryan sniggered. 'Cash, cheque or a blow job, which? Oh cheers, matey – it'll be a bloody cheque, then. No, you're lovely. In your name? Cool. Sorry to wake you. No, really!'

He replaced the phone, then turned back to the others. 'My friend Roger, works for BA's bucketshop trips to Europe. We're going to Ibiza first thing – need to get a cab from here. Be there at eight, leave here six thirty.' He looked at his watch. 'Five hours' sleep. Great. No, less actually.'

'Why?'

'Because we don't know where we're going, do we? Oh, let's hope this works.'

He turned his computer on, and after a few moments opened his e-mail account. 'C'mon, must be here . . . Ah, good. One Nick Thomas. I'm just going to e-mail him and see if he'll give me the same info he gave Martyn, saying we need to find Martyn urgently. Oh, I dunno . . . I'll say his mum's died!' He finished the e-mail with a flourish and sent it. 'Hopefully, if he's out clubbing, he'll look at it when he goes home.'

'And if he doesn't look at it until midday tomorrow?' Chad

frowned, realising that finding Martyn on Ibiza wasn't going to be very easy.

Ryan pointed to an oblong in the far corner of the room. 'I'll take my laptop. It's got a modem and I can patch myself through to my e-mail account from the island. Simple, really.'

He shut his computer down, and turned back to his fellow conspirators. 'OK, bedtime. We have a long day or two ahead of us. Now, you two are a couple, right?'

They nodded. 'OK, spare room only has a single bed, so you can get really close, or you can crash here on the floor or . . .'

'Or what?'

'Nothing. Well . . .' Ryan took a deep breath. 'Or you can crash in with me because firstly it's a huge bed, certainly big enough for three and secondly . . .'

Chad started to take his T-shirt off. 'Secondly,' he finished on Ryan's behalf, 'because all three of us are in the mood for sex, yeah?'

Ryan nodded. 'Yeah, I guess so.'

Chad's and Mickey's clothes almost fell off – they certainly dropped quickly with practised ease.

Ryan stared at the two naked, gorgeous American guys, his hard-on appearing like magic. He turned and pushed open the door of his room, stripping himself off and flopping on to the bed, then turning and facing them.

They were on him like piranhas on a dead antelope – Mickey taking Ryan's cock in his mouth, Chad kissing him hard.

Ryan just lay back and took the attention, realising from the signals he was getting that not only did this couple make a habit of this, they knew just what they were doing. It was selfless sex from their point of view: they sucked at him, they kissed him, they licked him, they rimmed him, and apart from a couple of brief mouth fucks, he had to do very little in return.

Mickey was the really energetic one, one minute at his groin, the next, rolling him on his side, eating at his arse, his hands stroking and rubbing everything they could touch. Chad was far more sensual, with deep but pleasurable kissing, while gently wiping his cock over Ryan's chest, leaving trails of pre-come in his chest hair and around his nipples.

'Do you fuck or get fucked?' Chad whispered in his ear.

'Either,' said Ryan, 'but right now, you can do what you like with me.'

Chad rolled Ryan on to his front, easing him down the bed so his legs were off the end, and then spread them. While Mickey continued using his tongue to relax Ryan's arse, Chad found some rubbers and put one on himself and one on Mickey.

Ryan lay there, Mickey's tongue sending shivers up his back, making him sweat very slightly, and then he felt the tongue replaced by a finger or two. He moaned gently, letting the American guys know this was OK. He wasn't sure whose fingers they were, but they manipulated his hole with actions clearly borne out of experience, raising Ryan's temperature and making his balls fill with turbulent come, ready to make its escape when the time was right.

He felt one of them enter him – it had to be Mickey because his dick was definitely a lot smaller than Chad's and he felt the touch of balls against his own quickly. Mickey started going in and out in slow but powerful strokes, hitting Ryan's prostate, making him quiver every so often.

Suddenly there was another sensation, one Ryan had never experienced before, and one that brought a terrible ache in his arse and he cried out suddenly.

'Sorry.' That was Chad's voice.

And then his arse began to adjust to this new pain, and Ryan realised what it was – Chad had slipped his own thicker and longer cock in beside Mickey's, tugging Ryan's arsehole wider than it had ever been before. The two cocks were penetrating him deeper now, making identical movements, spreading his insides and making him feel as if his guts were on fire.

'Fuck – this hurts,' he yelled, 'but don't stop. If anything . . . go . . . faster . . .'

As bidden, Mickey and Chad speeded up their dual actions, getting more and more powerful with their jabs, taking Ryan into places of pain and hurt he'd never experienced, never imagined. Yet, at the same time, it was a powerful feeling, a tremendous longing inside him – he did not want them to stop. With each stab into his guts, it got better as the wrenched flesh became adjusted to the extra objects buried deep inside.

'Make it hurt more,' Ryan said, and, in response, Chad slapped his arse cheek hard.

'More,' Ryan begged. 'Keep hurting me . . .'

Both Americans smacked Ryan, the pain going to his butt rather than his insides, making him feel more comfortable with these two fantastic man-tools drilling into him.

'Faster,' he shouted, feeling one of the guys push his legs further apart so they could get a faster rhythm.

One of them came, Ryan guessed, because the rhythm momentarily became uneven but then started again. It must have been Mickey, because Ryan was sure Chad was on his left, and that cock didn't alter.

He was right – Chad came, and let out a slow moan. Ryan could feel the cock bucking and pulsating inside as it pumped out its seed.

'Pull out,' Ryan said suddenly, and as one they did.

Ryan rolled over really quickly and Mickey was first to shove his mouth on to Ryan's huge cock, taking it right into his throat, almost opening his mouth wide enough to take both Ryan's balls in as well.

Ryan came with a yell of triumph, pumping wad after wad of warm, white juice into Mickey's throat, twitching slightly as he did so.

Mickey didn't stop there, but kept sucking until it hurt, determined to drain every last morsel of come from the depths of Ryan's sac. Eventually he eased his mouth off and Ryan started breathing more evenly.

'Rubbers off,' he murmured – Chad had already removed his, and Mickey let him take his away too. 'OK, lads,' Ryan said, and grabbed their cocks, one in each hand and dragged them towards him, taking both cocks through his lips at once, and they started fucking his mouth, kneeling either side of him, Chad casually flicking his right nipple while Mickey stroked his still erect cock.

Mickey was pumping Ryan's mouth really hard, coming again, but Chad didn't. Instead he slowly eased off after Mickey had withdrawn, letting Ryan calm down as well.

'Fucking hell, that was good,' Ryan said. 'Don't ever, ever go back to America. I could pay you to stay and do that every night.'

Chad and Mickey smiled at each other and then curled up, one either side of him. Mickey's hand stayed on Ryan's cock, even when they all finally fell asleep, and it was still resting on his groin when they awoke in the early morning, ready to go and find Martyn and Peter.

And hopefully avert a tragedy.

The sun was up – Peter could feel it even through the heavy wooden doors of his room. Beside him, Joe stirred.

'Good morning.'

Joe opened an eye. 'Already?'

'Uh-huh. The troops will be wanting breakfast.'

'Not today – they didn't get back from Clarkie's gig until about five. No one on this island bar you and me is awake yet.'

Peter laughed. 'I beg to differ, young man. Listen.'

He held up his hand and Joe frowned. Then there was an almighty splash and a shriek of pleasure.

'Nonononono . . .' Joe buried his face in Peter's already sweating chest. 'They can't be swimming – it's not fair.'

Peter eased him off and crawled out of bed, grateful for the closed doors. If he was this hot already, what was it like outside? He stood in front of the mirror on the dresser, looking at Joe's reflection, curled up like a little boy again, transformed back into cutie Joe rather than sexual prowler Joe.

He looked at his own body – a couple of fading love bites around his nipples and one right down by his balls, on the inner thigh. Joe was no slouch when it came to aggressive sex, that was for sure.

But it wouldn't last – he knew that instinctively. Last night's sex had been more for the hell of it than passionate – neither of them really had his heart in it. Peter knew he was unlikely to sleep with Joe again – that particular fling had already run its course.

Which was fine. He liked Joe, indeed thought it likely they'd stay in touch once back in Britain, but, if they ever had sex again, it would be one of those two-or-three-times-a-year jobs.

He showered and brushed his teeth. On going back into the

bedroom, he noticed Joe was gone and the clatter from the kitchen told him that was where he was.

He pulled open his double wooden doors. The wave of heat that hit him dried off the last few drops of moisture from the shower, replacing it with more moisture from sweat. Clark and Tanya were fooling around in the pool, while Matthew was asleep on a lounger.

'Stevie's gone for some milk and juice,' Tanya explained. 'We didn't want to wake you two lovebirds.'

Clark resurfaced amid a spray of water and foam. 'Morning, Peter. You missed a good night. Come on tonight. Bring Joe if you can.'

'No, thanks,' came a shout from the kitchen, followed by Joe popping his head out of the window. 'I'm out tonight, seeing the Diesel gang.'

Peter frowned, so Clark mouthed 'Lesbians'. 'In that case,' Peter added, 'I'm coming. El Paradis, yeah?'

Clark clapped his hands together. 'Good, nearly the whole gang.'

Matthew woke up and was about to say something when both Tanya and Clark reached up and yanked him into the pool.

Peter smiled at the happy antics. Andy had been right: this was what he needed.

He went back into the kitchen, where Joe was again dancing while he cooked, this time to Aqua. 'You don't mind if I go out, then?'

'No strings, Peter. We agreed.' Joe planted a kiss on his cheek. 'But thanks for asking. Very sweet.'

He told Peter to go and find Stevie, as breakfast was nearly ready. 'He's probably stopped off to talk to the Polish guys in the next villa down.'

Nodding, Peter went off to complete his mission. He left by the front door and wandered down the gravel path, wincing slightly as odd pebbles dug into his bare feet.

Finally he came to the slightly less savage path leading down to the other villa, but something caught his eye.

A man was standing about half a mile away, on the road that

led from the main road that the taxi had brought him up, when he'd thought he was going to be robbed.

The man was just standing there, staring up at the villas. Perhaps he was a local, but there was something about his stance that indicated otherwise. He was watching something. Peter felt he was watching him.

'Stevie,' he called, without actually looking to the Polish guys' villa. A moment later, Stevie wandered over. 'Sorry, don't tell me – Joe's pissed off because I've missed breakfast, yeah?'

Peter didn't reply. Instead he pointed at the mysterious man on the road.

'Yeah, saw him this morning,' Stevie said. 'He's just been standing there for at least an hour and a half.'

'Should we find out what he wants?'

'Why?'

Peter shrugged. 'Maybe he's "casing the joint" or whatever it is you East End criminal types say.'

Stevie thumped Peter's shoulder in mock outrage. 'I'll have you know man-from-the-flatlands, that in the East End we are a refined, cultured breed of human beings and leave petty crime to our European neighbours.'

Peter laughed and wrapped his arm around Stevie's. 'C'mon then, let's go and eat.'

Together they gave the strange observer one last glance, but he had gone.

About three hours later, Peter, Joe and Clark were in Ibiza Old Town itself, on the southern coast. It was very different from the concrete jungle that was San Antonio – most of it was encased within a walled city from the Middle Ages, packed with a market square, shops and lots of temporary trestle tables selling a variety of overpriced knick-knacks to gullible tourists. Peter was happy to be one of these, having just bought an olive-green T-shirt with IBIZA '98 down one side. Clark had a handful of local twelve-inch vinyl singles and Joe was selecting fresh fruit and veggies for tonight's meal.

They wandered across the drawbridge that separated the shopping quarter from the more residential end.

'These are the ramparts,' Joe was explaining to Peter – Ibiza's answer to the bushes of Hampstead Heath or Kemptown. Pop up here at around 2 in the morning and you can either pick up or see some action. No one is very discreet.'

'And the view is lovely,' Clark added, meaning the sights over the bay and out to the sea. 'Not that anyone notices that.'

They turned away from the ramparts, down a gentle hill and under an arch, finding themselves amid a plethora of local restaurants, each one doing a roaring trade. Clark pointed to one with yellow tables.

'I recommend this for a light lunch, OK?'

They sat down and, within minutes, had ordered seafood and salads. They chatted about each other's life and job and stuff (Peter soon realised that Joe had never met Clark or Tanya before the holiday and none of them had ever met Matthew, although Stevie was their common link). Banal but not uninteresting.

Halfway through their ice creams, Peter got the feeling he was being watched. He glanced around and spotted the likely suspect.

A young man, about twenty-fourish, sitting alone at a bar a couple of doors up. Dark hair, slimmish build, nice eyes. Peter was sure that he had been staring at him, shifting his gaze just as Peter had turned.

It looked like the man from the road that morning.

'Excuse me, guys.' Peter pushed his seat back and started to get up, but the guy at the bar was quicker and was gone, hurrying further up the slope, back towards the ramparts or the drawbridge to the town.

'Problem?' asked Clark.

'Don't know.' He nudged Joe. 'Attractive guy, just went up there. You see him?'

Joe shrugged. 'Sort of. Looked European, yeah?'

Peter nodded. 'He was looking at us. At me, I think.'

Clark smiled. 'Been here twenty-four hours and struck gold, Peter. Lucky you.'

'I'm not sure. Stevie and I saw a guy this morning, watching the villa. I'm sure it was him.'

Joe was immediately interested. 'Hey, James Bond is on our

tail. Which of us is smuggling guns to the Contras or drugs to the Chinese?'

But Peter wasn't listening. He needed to find out more. However, the mystery man was long gone by now, so he finished his ice cream silently, letting Joe and Clark swap stories about the music industry, the pitfalls of deejaying and how many times R. Dean Taylor's Tamla Motown output had been repackaged without the consent of his estate.

They left, Clark generously putting the tab on his credit card ('Well, actually, it'll be paid for by Kiss or Radio 1 or whoever I put it through to') and headed back to the shops.

As they crossed the drawbridge into the market area, Peter was jostled by a group of three men, arguing furiously. At least one of them was an American queen, making up for his lack of height by being loud and vaguely obnoxious. Peter's new T-shirt fell to the ground.

'Sorry,' one of the other two yelled back at Peter in a very English accent. 'He's from California.'

'I might have guessed,' Peter muttered under his breath, and was about to catch up with Clark and Joe when the Englishman called out again.

'Excuse me . . .'

Sighing, Peter turned back about to say, rather testily, 'What?' when he saw the expressions on their faces.

He wondered if he had spilt ice cream on his chin or something.

The Englishman moved closer. 'Look,' he said, 'this is going to sound really stupid, but . . . ah . . . are you Dutch?'

This was too weird. He was being spied on by one guy, and now three others guessed his nationality just from walking into him.

'Why?'

The other one spoke, the tall (frankly good-looking) one. Another American.

'Are you Peter Dooken?'

And Peter went cold.

They'd found him, even here. Escaping Los Angeles, escaping Scott, still they'd sent people after him.

Fuck!

He waited a second, and then turned and ran straight into the crowded market, the other three close on his heels.

Vaguely he could see Joe and Clark, alerted by the commotion but clearly ignorant of his part in it.

Good, he'd go in the opposite direction. The last thing he needed was to cause trouble for his newest friends.

Peter pelted down a cobbled street that brought him out on to the main Ibiza Town road, which curved around the upper bay, where lots of traditional fishing boats were moored.

The slightly upper-class shops, boutiques and hotels were ahead – he'd head for those and dive down a side street, perhaps losing his pursuers. And hopefully not getting too lost himself.

Damn, that other guy had been watching him. He must have been keeping an eye out, then alerted these three. Good disguises, sure, but, now they'd been rumbled, they'd have to find him or get off the island. If he could hide . . .

He saw a flight of steps up the side of a bar and took to those, not caring where they went. Two or three flights later, he was on a roof overlooking the bay. Below him, people looked like ants, four or five storeys down. No one saw him go up there, at least.

'Jesus . . .' he breathed.

And realised he was not alone. Someone had followed him up.

He turned and saw the man from the road, the one from the bar.

'Peter Dooken?' he asked in a nice English accent. He was wearing a dark T-shirt and cut-off jeans – pale but nice legs, and a slim body, as he'd thought earlier. But his eyes were something else. They were cold. Colder and more empty than anyone's eyes Peter had ever seen.

Attractive in any other circumstances perhaps – the sort of eyes you looked at on a model in a magazine and thought, Fwoar! I'd have him, given half a chance. But here, on top of a strange building in a strange town, this bewildering young man just gazed at him.

'Peter?' he asked again.

'Who . . . are . . . you?' Peter was appalled at how out of breath he was, the words coming out in short gasps.

The young man came closer. And punched Peter straight on the jaw.

Peter went down instantly, completely fazed by the blow – it had been the last thing he had expected. He tried to get up, but the man pushed him as he did so, and Peter realised he was falling closer to the front of the building.

Oh God, he was trying to kill him. Make it look like an accident. Dutch tourist drunkenly runs up steps, on to roof, falls on to road. Dead.

They had finally caught up with him.

He looked up into the face of his would-be killer, wondering if this was the last thing he'd see – dark hair, those compassionless eyes, nice cheekbones, red lips . . .

Christ, this assassin was attractive. He was going to die with a hard-on!

'You betrayed him,' the English boy said. 'You left him behind to die. They tried to kill me because of you!'

Peter went cold. Really cold. This was no ordinary attack, like he'd expected. This was something else, something he didn't understand.

'You fucked-up, drug-crazed bastard – you let him die!' The Englishman raised his fist again, but stopped.

'Martyn!' An American voice, sharp. Harsh. Warning. Then softer. 'Martyn, you've got it all wrong.'

Peter was able to move back slightly, see the speaker. It was the small guy who had jostled him earlier.

What the hell was going on here? Who was this Martyn? Who were they if they weren't here to kill him? Unless they wanted to kill him and not let Martyn kill him. Great, the things that go through your mind as you are about to die!

Why didn't he stay at home with Joe? Maybe that was it. This was a dream and he'd wake up, Joe snuggling him, hand stroking his cock and . . .

Nope, still here.

Arse!

'What's going on?' he managed to ask, and realised his jaw hurt. Martyn had hit him very hard. If he didn't get turned into red jelly in a few moments as one of the four chucked him off the top of this building, he was going to have a rather unsightly bruise on his chin.

Martyn had stepped back, and Peter was free to crawl away from the edge, slowly pushing himself up.

The English guy was looking at him, his fingers to his lips.

Fair enough, he'd stay shut up for now.

'Mickey? Chad? Ryan . . . What are you doing here?' Martyn dropped to his knees suddenly, as if all the fight had gone out of him. He looked instantly lost, confused and very frightened. He glanced at Peter, then back to his . . . friends?

The tallest guy (Chad?) moved closer to Martyn and took his hands.

Jesus, the Martyn guy was a fruitcake, escaped from somewhere – that had to be it.

So how come everyone knew who Peter was and yet he didn't know any of them?

'Listen to me, Marty,' Chad was saying. 'Listen good. You're not going to want to hear this but you have to, or you're going to do something you'll regret. And so will we.'

'Yeah, and it's cost us a fortune flying in from LA, then Heathrow, then here –' Mickey was kicked by the English guy.

Chad was sitting with Martyn now, hugging him. Martyn was shaking. Christ, poor bastard looked so . . . so vulnerable.

'It's about Scott . . .' Chad said, and suddenly Peter cried out. Involuntarily, but he did. Because it then hit him exactly what Martyn had said.

'Oh fuck. . . . Oh no . . .' Peter could feel he was going to cry and he found himself alone.

On top of this building.

Scott was dead – this guy thought he was somehow responsible, and he felt very cold.

Very alone.

He crawled towards this Martyn guy, ignoring a warning look from Chad. No, he had to take the risk. He had to know.

'Is . . . is he dead?'

Martyn nodded, and Peter felt his eyes filling up and then he let the tears go, silently running down his face.

Martyn was crying as well.

Chad breathed deeply, throwing Peter a 'Here goes' look.

'It wasn't Peter here, Martyn. It was Scott all the time. You asked Mickey and me to find out whatever we could, and we did, but we couldn't find you. Scott's been dealing in drugs for years, really heavy stuff from what we gathered. Lieutenant O'Malley . . . remember him? Well, he investigated Scott and found out it's all true. It was him all along. They weren't using him, or you, to get at Peter. They wanted him all along.'

Peter swallowed hard. Would Martyn listen to reason? He had to try.

He felt his own voice waver as he started to talk, everything he'd tried to forget rushing back over him.

The sound of Scott's soft voice.

The smell of his gorgeous hair.

The touch of his soft skin as he cried about his family, his pa.

Crocodile tears, nothing more.

Scott had been the ultimate actor.

Falteringly, he heard himself tell Martyn how he'd discovered Scott's addiction, his secret deals. The late-night calls, the early-morning runs. And, when Scott ripped some very dangerous people off in his unending quest for danger and excitement, the almost sexual thrill of getting away with it, everything had gone pear-shaped.

And, instead of leaning on Scott, they had begun to threaten him, Peter. Begun to track him down in clubs and toilets, in shops and libraries.

Telling him that, if he didn't get Scott to pay what he owed, they'd kill him long before they got to Scott.

'And Scott didn't give a damn,' Peter was saying. 'He thought it was all one huge game. I was completely irrelevant to him. I thought he loved me, but eventually I realised that he needed me not as a lover but as a wall between him and them. So long as he had someone else around, he was physically safe.'

He swallowed, letting himself cry now, facing the truth himself properly for the first time.

'I would have been killed eventually. They beat up a friend of mine, someone Scotty didn't even know, just to get the message across. So I ran.'

'You . . . ran away from him . . . left him to die . . .'

'No! No, Martyn, I left him so that I could live. I loved him, I loved him so much, like you did. But it wasn't real – not from him. It was just another way of playing dare, if you like. And then I realised I meant nothing. All the days and nights, the places and the laughs and the fun were totally insignificant to him, so I went. I had to keep my self-respect. And above all, I was terrified, of them and of him.'

Martyn was gone completely now, finally letting out everything he had obviously kept bottled up since the moment Scott had died.

'The last . . . last thing he said was that he loved me . . .'

Peter tried to calm himself. 'Then he did love you. He must have, because you know what? I don't think he ever said it to me. Not meaning it. You were very lucky, then.'

Martyn just sobbed. 'He was so beautiful . . .'

'Yes. Yes, he was.' And Peter took Martyn in his arms and held him tight, letting his own grief and torment merge with Martyn's.

Both of them were finding a final release from Scott Taylor.

Eighteen

Martyn Townsend was woken by a combination of bright light, heat and the impossibly close sound of a lorry passing – a sound that shouldn't have been there.

OK, so Port Douglas in October was usually hot. And the sunlight had been exceptionally bright recently. But if a lorry was passing it was either an emergency or he had slept far later than he had intended.

He tiptoed across the room, peeking between the blinds. Yup, the sun was up high – it had to be nearly midday. Typical.

The lorry was a supply truck, delivering fresh food and vegetables to the resort they were in – the delightfully named Turtle Cove, a wonderfully relaxing gay place, with a mile or two of private beach, and fantastic rooms in which to relax, sleep or do anything else. It wasn't like one of those seedy gay hotels in some bad seaside resort in England or France. No, this place was a touch of class, staffed by warm and friendly people who knew when to be attentive and when to be discreet.

He would recommend this to Andy and Jon next time he called them.

From beside him came a familiar moan and someone rolled away from where Martyn had been lying and turned on to his back.

Martyn looked down at the most beautiful person he had ever

218

known, not just physically perfect but perfect inside, too – a shining star.

He crossed back to the bed and crawled back under the single sheet, his cock getting harder with each breath he took until it stabbed his partner violently in the side.

A hand flapped around aimlessly, as if swatting a fly, and Martyn grabbed it, placing it around his cock, adding his own hand to his partner's, and feeling his cock swell and stiffen at the combined touch.

Martyn leant over and kissed those beautiful lips, feeling the mouth open expectantly at the touch, and, despite the early-morning breath, to Martyn, it was the sweetest kiss in the world.

Two arms reached around and hugged Martyn tightly, pulling him on top, so that their cocks ground against one another slowly.

Martyn kissed again, this time letting his partner's tongue feel its way into his mouth, and they stayed together for a few minutes, enjoying each other's scent as their hormones raced and the two men began working as a well-oiled but never bored machine.

They kissed, they groped, and finally Martyn went down on the beautiful meat twitching between the other guy's legs, taking it in with a long, practised swallow, moving his lips up and down the shaft expertly, knowing which ridge of skin, which millimetre of vein and which point of contact would send the cock's owner into ecstasy.

Up and down he went, really slowly, the cock somehow finding the strength to become even harder with each movement.

His own cock was suddenly engulfed in the other's mouth and they lay next to each other, teasing and stimulating each other for ages, Martyn immeasurably happy at the synchronicity of their actions, both coming simulantaneously, satisfying each other completely. And he knew everything was going to be all right.

Three months ago to the day, he and this beautiful man had sat together on a rooftop in Ibiza, holding each other in shocked comfort as they had accepted the death of someone they both loved but never really knew or understood.

Together, Martyn and Peter had learnt more about Scott and his influence on their lives as the days passed. Stevie had let them take the villa for as long as they wanted. He, Matthew, Clark and

Tanya had gone home at the end of the week, followed a day later by the ever-present Derrick, his mobile still glued to his ear. Joe had stayed on to look after both guys, knowing that they were badly shaken and needed a bit of company, but also knowing when they didn't.

Ryan had headed straight home, but Stevie had given Chad and Mickey one of the other rooms in the villa, to make their trip worthwhile.

The five of them had spent a couple of evenings discussing Scott, Chad and Mickey caring for both him and Peter as the truth came out, while Joe did what he enjoyed, camping it up as token houseboy. He found a young German down at the Water World near Space one afternoon, whom he insisted on introducing to everyone as 'Fritz' despite the fact that it wasn't his name. Joe seemed anxious to spend the rest of his life (or at least the next few days) shagging him senseless, and 'Fritz' seemed equally keen on the idea.

Talking had been therapeutic for both Martyn and Peter. If it were at all possible, Martyn fell even deeper in love with his two American friends as a result of their time in the villa, learning to appreciate just how much they cared. Chad was the serious, well-meaning one, Mickey the one to defuse a tense moment or potentially tricky situation with a naff, childish quip, but, beneath that, Martyn knew that a lot of it was an act. It was his way of dealing with things.

They had gone back to California shortly after Joe had returned to England (sans 'Fritz'), leaving Peter and Martyn alone for the last night.

Chad had been dubious, but Mickey, sweetheart that he was, knew that, if they didn't get some time alone to talk, without any interruptions, the wounds weren't going to heal completely.

'And if one of them turns around and kills the other?' Martyn had overheard Chad say, to which Mickey had said, 'If you still think that's likely, you're even dumber than I thought.'

After driving them to the airport, Martyn had returned to find a candle-lit dinner ready beside the pool.

Peter had held up a glass of wine halfway through the meal, offering up a toast.

'Forgive me for this, Marty. But here's to Scott. We loved. We lost. But it was fun.'

Martyn surprised himself by not hesitating in returning the toast.

After dinner they had gone into San Antonio, to a small bar Clark raved about called Café del Mar. There they had watched one of the most beautiful things happen either of them could remember – the huge orange orb that was the sun had moved across the sky and seemed to be sinking into the water, casting orange ripples across the sea as it went down.

People videoed it, photographed it and, when the last orange glow had gone and the darkness arrived just as suddenly, they cheered.

Peter and Martyn had cheered as well and Peter had knocked someone's camera aside.

Apologising, he turned back to Martyn with an expression on his face that said, 'God, I'm a twat' – and Martyn had leant forward and kissed him on the lips.

That moment of self-depreciation, of wit and of charm was etched into Martyn's memory for ever.

Astonished, Peter pulled back, but as he did so, he checked himself.

'No, sorry,' he said. 'Let's do that again.'

And this time they really kissed, deeply and passionately, a friendship created out of the most appalling adversity.

And, when they drove back to the villa that night, they found that, without saying a word to each other, they knew.

They used Martyn's room, the one that had been Clark's and Tanya's. As they loosened each other's clothes, there was a real sexual tension in the air – they both wanted this. They both needed it. But was it right?

Before they actually touched the bed, as they both stood naked, cocks hard and ready, they looked into each other's eyes, searching for the truth. Was this right? Was this really what they wanted? Or should they feel ashamed?

Peter had cried first, but Martyn followed, both realising that what they were doing was so right, but so powerful, so much more than any other sex had been or was ever going to be.

As they entered each other that night, they both knew that this wasn't happening out of guilt, or shame, or even lust.

Some bizarre twist of fate had brought together two people who were meant to be together for ever.

'Five days ago, you tried to kill me,' Peter had said, grinning, the next morning.

'Five days ago, I was a different person,' Martyn had replied.

'Can we make this work?' Peter had asked. 'Can we put our connected past aside and build on *us*?'

Martyn wasn't able to answer that, so he asked another question. 'Do you want to?'

Peter's answer had been delivered without hesitation, without anything other than instinct. 'Yes. I think I've fallen in love with you and I want to take this as it comes and find out whether I have.'

Martyn knew he had fallen in love with Peter, but thought it was wrong to say so. He just agreed to go with the plan, and see where they ended up.

So here they were now, taking their first holiday together, in Northern Australia, an early Christmas gift from Andy and Jon (although Martyn suspected there was a bit of a tax dodge going on as well, but who cared?).

They parted from their blow jobs, and hugged each other again.

Peter took a deep breath. 'D'you remember what you asked me after our first night together in Ibiza?'

Martyn nodded. 'I asked if this was going to work.' Shit, what was Peter going to say now?

'And I said I thought I'd fallen in love with you and wanted to see how it panned out.'

Martyn nodded. Was this the time to say he was in love with Peter more deeply, more perfectly, than anyone ever before?

But, if Peter was about to end it, best not to speak.

'I think . . . I think everything has worked out fine, but I need to know this. Martyn Townsend, do you love me as much as I love you?'

And Martyn just spoke the one word they both wanted to hear, and then made love, really made love, for the first time in what was going to be a partnership for the rest of their lives.

IDOL NEW BOOKS

Also published:

THE KING'S MEN
Christian Fall

Ned Medcombe, spoilt son of an Oxfordshire landowner, has always remembered his first love: the beautiful, golden-haired Lewis. But seventeenth-century England forbids such a love and Ned is content to indulge his domineering passions with the willing members of the local community, including the submissive parish cleric. Until the Civil War changes his world, and he is forced to pursue his desires as a soldier in Cromwell's army – while his long-lost lover fights as one of the King's men.

ISBN 0 352 33207 7

THE VELVET WEB
Christopher Summerisle

The year is 1889. Daniel McGaw arrives at Calverdale, a centre of academic excellence buried deep in the English countryside. But this is like no other college. As Daniel explores, he discovers secret passages in the grounds and forbidden texts in the library. The young male students, isolated from the outside world, share a darkly bizarre brotherhood based on the most extreme forms of erotic expression. It isn't long before Daniel is initiated into the rites that bind together the youths of Calverdale in a web of desire.

ISBN 0 352 33208 5

CHAINS OF DECEIT
Paul C. Alexander

Journalist Nathan Dexter's life is turned around when he meets a young student called Scott – someone who offers him the relationship for which he's been searching. Then Nathan's best friend goes missing, and Nathan uncovers evidence that he has become the victim of a slavery ring which is rumoured to be operating out of London's leather scene. To rescue their friend and expose the perverted slave trade, Nathan and Scott must go undercover, risking detection and betrayal at every turn.

ISBN 0 352 33206 9

HALL OF MIRRORS
Robert Black

Tom Jarrett operates the Big Wheel at Gamlin's Fair. When young runaway Jason Bradley tries to rob him, events are set in motion which draw the two together in a tangled web of mutual mistrust and growing fascination. Each carries a burden of old guilt and tragic unspoken history; each is running from something. But the fair is a place of magic and mystery where normal rules don't apply, and Jason is soon on a journey of self-discovery, unbridled sexuality and growing love.

ISBN 0 352 33209 3

THE SLAVE TRADE
James Masters

Barely eighteen and innocent of the desires of men, Marc is the sole survivor of a noble British family. When his home village falls to the invading Romans, he is forced to flee for his life. He first finds sanctuary with Karl, a barbarian from far-off Germanica, whose words seem kind but whose eyes conceal a dark and brooding menace. And then they are captured by Gaius, a general in Caesar's all-conquering army, in whose camp they learn the true meaning – and pleasures – of slavery.

ISBN 0 352 33228 X

DARK RIDER
Jack Gordon

While the rulers of a remote Scottish island play bizarre games of sexual dominance with the Argentinian Angelo, his friend Robert – consumed with jealous longing for his coffee-skinned companion – assuages his desires with the willing locals.

ISBN 0 352 33243 3

CONQUISTADOR
Jeff Hunter

It is the dying days of the Aztec empire. Axaten and Quetzel are members of the Stable, servants of the Sun Prince chosen for their bravery and beauty. But it is not just an honour and a duty to join this society, it is also the ultimate sexual achievement. Until the arrival of Juan, a young Spanish conquistador, sets the men of the Stable on an adventure of bondage, lust and deception.

ISBN 0 352 33244 1

TO SERVE TWO MASTERS
Gordon Neale

In the isolated land of Ilyria men are bought and sold as slaves. Rock, brought up to expect to be treated as mere 'livestock', yearns to be sold to the beautiful youth Dorian. But Dorian's brother is as cruel as he is handsome, and if Rock is bought by one brother he will be owned by both.

ISBN 0 352 33245 X

CUSTOMS OF THE COUNTRY
Rupert Thomas

James Cardell has left school and is looking forward to going to Oxford. That summer of 1924, however, he will spend with his cousins in a tiny village in rural Kent. There he finds he can pursue his love of painting – and begin to explore his obsession with the male physique.

ISBN 0 352 33246 8

DOCTOR REYNARD'S EXPERIMENT
Robert Black

A dark world of secret brothels, dungeons and sexual cabarets exists behind the respectable facade of Victorian London. The degenerate Lord Spearman introduces Dr Richard Reynard, dashing bachelor, to this hidden world. And Walter Starling, the doctor's new footman, finds himself torn between affection for his master and the attractions of London's underworld.

ISBN 0 352 33252 2

CODE OF SUBMISSION
Paul C. Alexander

Having uncovered and defeated a slave ring operating in London's leather scene, journalist Nathan Dexter had hoped to enjoy a peaceful life with his boyfriend Scott. But when it becomes clear that the perverted slave trade has started again, Nathan has no choice but to travel across Europe and America in his bid to stop it.

ISBN 0 352 33272 7

SLAVES OF TARNE
Gordon Neale

Pascal willingly follows the mysterious and alluring Casper to Tarne, a community of men enslaved to men. Tarne is everything that Pascal has ever fantasised about, but he he begins to sense a sinister aspect to Casper's magnetism. Pascal has to choose between the pleasures of submission and acting to save the people he loves.

ISBN 0 352 33273 5

ROUGH WITH THE SMOOTH
Dominic Arrow

Amid the crime, violence and unemployment of North London, the young men who attend Jonathan Carey's drop-in centre have few choices. One of the young men, Stewart, finds himself torn between the increasingly intimate horseplay of his fellows and the perverse allure of the criminal underworld. Can Jonathan save Stewart from the bullies on the streets and behind bars?

ISBN 0 352 33292 1

CONVICT CHAINS
Philip Markam

Peter Warren, printer's apprentice in the London of the 1830s, discovers his sexuality and taste for submission at the hands of Richard Barkworth. Thus begins a downward spiral of degradation, of which transportation to the Australian colonies is only the beginning.

ISBN 0 352 33300 6

WE NEED YOUR HELP . . .

to plan the future of Idol books –

Yours are the only opinions that matter. Idol is a new and exciting venture: the first British series of books devoted to homoerotic fiction for men.

We're going to do our best to provide the sexiest, best-written books you can buy. And we'd like you to help in these early stages. Tell us what you want to read. There's a freepost address for your filled-in questionnaires, so you won't even need to buy a stamp.

THE IDOL QUESTIONNAIRE

SECTION ONE: ABOUT YOU

1.1 Sex (*we presume you are male, but just in case*)
Are you?
Male ☐
Female ☐

1.2 Age
under 21 ☐ 21–30 ☐
31–40 ☐ 41–50 ☐
51–60 ☐ over 60 ☐

1.3 At what age did you leave full-time education?
still in education ☐ 16 or younger ☐
17–19 ☐ 20 or older ☐

1.4 Occupation _____

1.5 Annual household income _____

1.6 We are perfectly happy for you to remain anonymous; but if you would like us to send you a free booklist of Idol books, please insert your name and address

_____

_____

_____

_____

SECTION TWO: ABOUT BUYING IDOL BOOKS

2.1 Where did you get this copy of *Shame*?
    Bought at chain book shop ☐
    Bought at independent book shop ☐
    Bought at supermarket ☐
    Bought at book exchange or used book shop ☐
    I borrowed it/found it ☐
    My partner bought it ☐

2.2 How did you find out about Idol books?
    I saw them in a shop ☐
    I saw them advertised in a magazine ☐
    I read about them in _____
    Other _____

2.3 Please tick the following statements you agree with:
    I would be less embarrassed about buying Idol
    books if the cover pictures were less explicit ☐
    I think that in general the pictures on Idol
    books are about right ☐
    I think Idol cover pictures should be as
    explicit as possible ☐

2.4 Would you read an Idol book in a public place – on a train for instance?
    Yes ☐   No ☐

SECTION THREE: ABOUT THIS IDOL BOOK

3.1 Do you think the sex content in this book is:
    Too much ☐   About right ☐
    Not enough ☐

3.2 Do you think the writing style in this book is:

      Too unreal/escapist ☐   About right ☐

      Too down to earth ☐

3.3 Do you think the story in this book is:

      Too complicated ☐   About right ☐

      Too boring/simple ☐

3.4 Do you think the cover of this book is:

      Too explicit ☐   About right ☐

      Not explicit enough ☐

Here's a space for any other comments:

SECTION FOUR: ABOUT OTHER IDOL BOOKS

4.1 How many Idol books have you read?

4.2 If more than one, which one did you prefer?

4.3 Why?

SECTION FIVE: ABOUT YOUR IDEAL EROTIC NOVEL

We want to publish the books you want to read – so this is your chance to tell us exactly what your ideal erotic novel would be like.

5.1 Using a scale of 1 to 5 (1 = no interest at all, 5 = your ideal), please rate the following possible settings for an erotic novel:

      Roman / Ancient World ☐

      Medieval / barbarian / sword 'n' sorcery ☐

      Renaissance / Elizabethan / Restoration ☐

      Victorian / Edwardian ☐

      1920s & 1930s ☐

      Present day ☐

      Future / Science Fiction ☐

5.2 Using the same scale of 1 to 5, please rate the following themes you may find in an erotic novel:

Bondage / fetishism ☐
Romantic love ☐
SM / corporal punishment ☐
Bisexuality ☐
Group sex ☐
Watersports ☐
Rent / sex for money ☐

5.3 Using the same scale of 1 to 5, please rate the following styles in which an erotic novel could be written:

Gritty realism, down to earth ☐
Set in real life but ignoring its more unpleasant aspects ☐
Escapist fantasy, but just about believable ☐
Complete escapism, totally unrealistic ☐

5.4 In a book that features power differentials or sexual initiation, would you prefer the writing to be from the viewpoint of the dominant / experienced or submissive / inexperienced characters:

Dominant / Experienced ☐
Submissive / Inexperienced ☐
Both ☐

5.5 We'd like to include characters close to your ideal lover. What characteristics would your ideal lover have? Tick as many as you want:

Dominant	☐	Caring	☐
Slim	☐	Rugged	☐
Extroverted	☐	Romantic	☐
Bisexual	☐	Old	☐
Working Class	☐	Intellectual	☐
Introverted	☐	Professional	☐
Submissive	☐	Pervy	☐
Cruel	☐	Ordinary	☐
Young	☐	Muscular	☐
Naïve	☐		

Anything else? _____

5.6 Is there one particular setting or subject matter that your ideal erotic novel would contain:

_____

5.7 As you'll have seen, we include safe-sex guidelines in every book. However, while our policy is always to show safe sex in stories with contemporary settings, we don't insist on safe-sex practices in stories with historical settings because it would be anachronistic. What, if anything, would you change about this policy?

_____

_____

SECTION SIX: LAST WORDS

6.1 What do you like best about Idol books?

_____

6.2 What do you most dislike about Idol books?

_____

6.3 In what way, if any, would you like to change Idol covers?

_____

6.4 Here's a space for any other comments:

_____

_____

_____

_____

Thanks for completing this questionnaire. Now either tear it out, or photocopy it, then put it in an envelope and send it to:

> **Idol**
> **FREEPOST**
> **London**
> **W10 5BR**

You don't need a stamp if you're in the UK, but you'll need one if you're posting from overseas.